THE LAST DRAW

THE LAST DRAW

ELISABET PETERZEN

TRANSLATED BY

LAURA DESERTRAIN

† † †

THE SEAL PRESS

Originally published in Swedish as *Sista Sticket.*

Publication of this book was made possible in part with support from the
National Endowment for the Arts.

Library of Congress Cataloging-in-Publication Data
Peterzen, Elisabet, 1938-
    [Sista sticket. English]
    The last draw / Elisabet Peterzen : translated by Laura Desertrain.
      p. cm.
    Translation of: Sista sticket.
    ISBN 0-931188-67-9 : $8.95
    I. Title.
    PT9876.26.E74S5713 1988
    839.7'374--dc19   88-19862
                                                           CIP

Cover illustration and design: Deborah Brown

Printed in the United States of America
10 9 8 7 6 5 4 3 2 1
First edition, October 1988

Seal Press
P.O. Box 13
Seattle, Washington 98111

THE LAST DRAW

TIME	Spring and summer in the beginning of the 80s
SETTING	Stockholm and environs
NARRATORS	KATRIN and ERIK SKAFTE, journalists
VICTIMS	HASSAN ABDEL KARIM, student, immigrant
	STHEN CARLSSON, member of parliament (socialist)
	MARTIN BJÖRKBOM, playwright/journalist
	CURT SAMUELSSON, computer salesman
	TORSTEN GRAHN, retail stocker
	PER GUSTAVSSON, psychologist
	YNGVE YXBERG, TV producer
	Along with a number of others involved, including
	THE MURDERER

My name is Erik Skafte, my wife is Katrin. We're both freelance journalists. Every month we say to each other, "No, dammit, now it's your turn to find a job; this isn't working anymore." It's hard to make it as a freelancer, in case you ladies and gentlemen were wondering. Of course we sell quite a bit just on the strength of our names, which are familiar to people in the field after our many years with the evening press. But there's a hell of a difference between having a salary and an expense account—living the good life with overtime pay and the same wages no matter what you happen to accomplish—and having to be responsible for everything yourself.

Luckily, we're in good standing with the Author's Foundation and managed to get a grant after our book came out about the male fear of orgasm. We're hoping for a long-term stipend next time. Of course many applicants don't get a thing and they're struggling now that the Foundation has begun to apply the same marketing rules as the publishers, but what can you do?

In spite of it all, we're thriving and working better than ever. What we find unfortunate is the way the position in and of itself is compensated with money, rather than the actual work. When we were employed, Katrin and I, we didn't produce nearly as much good material as we do now. We sat around, talked a little on the phone, drank some coffee, wrote a few lines and earned good money.

But we wanted to write about the real stuff and no newspaper felt like hiring us to do that. We were fed up with "Little Kitty comes home" and "Agnes, 72, is disappointed in society."

Who the hell isn't disappointed in society?

First I quit, and Katrin stayed on at the paper for a while.

She was moved from "What did I do wrong, wonders Peter, 17" (suffering a 50,000 kronor loss in damages by vandals at a graduation party), to "TV personality's live-in partner is cheating on taxes."

Now we have a varied life, though uncertain. We live on different commissions—short stories for the weekly press, interviews with famous people (for which we can thank our earlier contacts) and sex letters to the men's magazines.

But when this case came up, the one we're about to describe here, we couldn't tear ourselves away from it. Gradually it began occupying all of our time.

Considered as a case, it never really was just one case. It was divided up into sections and some of it was kept quiet. Parts were published here and there, but since it was separate and disconnected, and no particular murderer could ever be caught, it ended up being filed away with the general statistics about unsolved crimes. There were so many well known people directly involved that it was quite simply seen to it that nothing came out. Important interests could be jeopardized, as they say. Certainly police reports have been written—miles and miles of columns—and there are probably two or three other journalists who know as much as we do through their jobs and unofficial contacts.

But we hope to be the first ones out with the book.

Katrin and I didn't really become aware of the matter until murder number three. Partly because the victim was someone we were acquainted with and partly because it was then that we began seeing a certain defined pattern. I'll be honest: Katrin saw it first. She didn't know yet what kind of pattern she was seeing, but my wife has intuition; she felt something in the air. We'd already taken an interest in the earlier crimes in a routine manner, even though we didn't think they were especially fruitful material for authors. It has to be sex murders to get people interested. A bunch of fully clothed men who go and get a knife in themselves, so what?

We trotted around with our stories from one newspaper to the next but they weren't very enthusiastic. "Forget about it," or, "Well listen, we have so much going on right now, you know, people are tired of murders, they want to hear some good news." Or else they bought it and didn't publish a single line.

Naturally we had copies.

Here's our description of the case, how it came about, what occurred, and why. Katrin and I have reconstructed the characters' actions from what we know. Of course we can't guarantee that this is exactly the way everything really happened.

We decided to do the interview with the murderer together, even though our perspectives by that time were completely different. But neither one of us dared do it all alone.

Erik Skafte

HASSAN ABDEL KARIM, 28
Immigrant, student

Hassan Abdel Karim studied Swedish and economics while awaiting notification from the Immigration Department about his permanent residency in Sweden. He rented a room from a Swedish woman with whom a personal relationship had been established.

On the night in question, Hassan Karim had left home after an argument. The landlady/girlfriend hadn't seen where he went. She figured he'd look up some countrymen he often spent time with. She wasn't worried when she didn't hear from him, because on previous occasions he'd spent several nights with these friends.

The man was found lying in a park known as Bergsgruvan near the South Station. His life had been taken by several stabs with a sharp instrument in the stomach and intestines.

Suspects:

Girlfriend/landlady?

Some countryman, maybe an internal affair?

† † †

Drugs?

He'd decided not to let them get to him.

They would never get to him.

He'd seen it happen to his friends. One after the other. He wanted to warn them, stop them in the door—don't come here, brother! You only see the glitter, don't know what's behind it, don't suspect there are sharp teeth behind such soft lips.

Naturally he didn't tell them that so as not to lose face himself. He was one of the guys who stood around in the group, thumping the new fellows on the back, laughing and promising, teasing, enticing.

More and more were coming. Smart, tough, lean boys who didn't know anything about life, nothing. Boys who'd obeyed their mothers and respected their sisters learned to steal money from women and hit them. Then people said they'd been like that all along—just look at their attitude towards women.

He could cry over it. She never got to see him cry, but his hatred rose with the blood to his head when she started nagging and whining.

She would want something in return for her remarks. Her feelings, her money—she wouldn't invest them for nothing.

These women, nibbling their way under your skin!

He couldn't help it that he couldn't get a job. He was strong and willing to work. He had an education. It hurt him, it tormented him to be viewed here solely as a manual laborer, as a servant. As a "you there, come here, do this." And lower than that—he didn't get a chance to work at all, he had to live on charity. Like a beggar, like the old man at the wall outside of the bank. But even that old man wasn't so despised; he was a servant of God, in whose cup it was a holy duty to drop coins.

He wasn't examined, scrutinized, forced to show his papers. And yet he was a beggar!

The rage mounted daily, little by little, receiving no outlet. Margareta's little pinpricks, the lack of a job and money, the uneasiness in his body from sitting too much and too quietly, from not getting going and using his powers; the rage always had to be suppressed and forced inwards. Everything contributed to his oppression: Margareta's actual physical size in relation to his and the fact that everything was hers—the apartment, the money, the furniture, the food, everything—while he lived by her grace and nothing in his life was his own.

The quarrel had begun already in the morning. Margareta was up getting ready for work. He was still lying in bed. He'd gotten home a little late the night before and there was a headache hovering around his temples. While she showered,

Margareta let the water in the bathroom roar pointedly. She watched him as she got dressed—he could feel her eyes through the pillow, covers and all. She banged the drawers loudly and when he didn't move, she went into the bathroom again and started slamming the door to the medicine chest. He kept still, closing his eyes.

"You sure can sleep through anything!" she yelled.

It was just a matter of time. She hadn't managed to provoke him with her noise and it'd annoyed her even more that he continued sleeping, seemingly unconcerned, while she was well underway with her activities.

He still pretended not to hear and she tore the covers off him.

"What?" he said. "What do you want?"

"You're lying there snoring like a pig!" she screamed. "Can't you at least get up and put the tea water on for me?"

He mumbled, faked a yawn.

"Why don't you ever help out?" asked Margareta. "Why do I always have to do everything?"

He swallowed, rubbing his eyes while he tried to think of something appropriate to say. If he asked her to put on the tea water herself, it'd start a new argument. Therefore, he continued to mumble and act like he wasn't really awake. Margareta looked down at him for a minute and then flung the covers back on top of him. Otherwise the only choice would have been to reach his arms out to her, pretending to want love. She would have been angry about that too, saying he didn't think about anything except sex, but it might have worked and then he would have gotten a respite.

However, it was best not to stay in bed now that she'd seen he was awake. He went into the bathroom, splashing around as she prepared breakfast.

"So what are you planning to do today?" she asked when he came into the kitchen.

He shrugged his shoulders.

"I should've told you before, there's a note down at the store. Someone needs help with their yard. You could go check it out."

"Yard?"

"Yeah, you know. Retired people, they probably live in a house and can't take care of the yard by themselves. There are lots of them down there by the railroad, maybe you've noticed. Don't you want to go find out about it?"

"I don't know," he said. "I don't know anything about yards."

"You don't have to. It just involves a little digging and raking. Surely you can handle that?"

Dig like a farmer? He'd never had to do that at home.

"I don't know. It'd be better if I could find something in economics, don't you think? That's what I really know, that's what I have work experience with."

"Of course people don't just get exactly what they want right away," she said sharply. "I know a Pole who used to be a professor, but he had to take a job washing dishes. If he could do it, then so can you."

"Of course I can, I'll go there like you said. I'll check into it, Margareta."

He knew he didn't plan on doing it but it was enough to get her to soften.

"You really won't have to keep it for very long," she said. "But it'll be something to do, and you can earn some money. OK?"

She reached her hand across the table, smiling at him. He forced himself to take her hand and look her in the eyes.

"It'll just be for a little while," she said. "Until you get your work permit. When that comes through, everything will be so much easier. But you have to understand we can't just let a bunch of people come and work willy-nilly without permission. No country can allow that. And naturally you need to know the language."

He nodded and kept holding her gaze and her hand.

"There's got to be a limit," she continued appeasingly. "Otherwise the country would be overrun."

"Do you think the entire population of the world is just dying to come here?"

He hadn't meant to say it, but the words popped out of his mouth anyway. She immediately pulled back her hand, sticking her chin out. The fight was off on a new tangent.

"Well, it seems like it anyway!"

"You people think everyone wants to be like you! Have it your way!"

"Then what are you doing here yourself?" she asked as a tear ran down her cheek. "You're here yourself, you know! Who asked you to come?"

"If you don't like it, I can just go!"

"You do that! See how well you get along without me!" Superwoman, great and fair in her own home, possessor of everything: work, apartment, furniture, bank account and a kept lover. A man-owning woman, enormous. She had everything and she was everything and she was going to devour him!

After she left, he took the commuter train into town where he knew he'd meet friends, on Svea Street at Sergel's Square. Many of his countrymen were idle during the day, getting together and bragging. Jamal boasted that he had two women chasing him, a Swede and a Finn. They were both after him. The first, Sinikka, had a two-room apartment in Hagalund. She'd had a child before with another guy from home. It was a boy for whom she wanted to find a daddy. Jamal got to come and go as he pleased, just so long as he came. He didn't have to work—she even got hash for him if he stayed with her— anything he wanted. The other girl had wealthy parents. She went to the university and was studying social anthropology. She wanted to teach him how to be a good Swedish man and respect women. She wanted them to travel to his homeland together so she could talk with the women there, help and teach them. He would serve as the interpreter.

They roared with laughter.

Hassan listened for quite a while and then told them how Margareta had been hassling him about not having a job.

"What does she expect? You know I don't have a work permit. Now she wants me to start digging in the ground. Does she want me to get in trouble for such a little shit-job? Hell, you can get kicked out of the country for that."

He got some tips about other types of work under the table. But the whole time, his resistance was growing. It was like a

10

pressure in his diaphragm, as if a fist had shot up through his stomach and when it got to his throat, it'd strangle his speech and then he didn't know anymore. It might shoot up through his head in a violent blow that could kill someone, man or woman. Sometimes he just wanted to fight. Like the boozers, the beer drinkers, the brawlers. Wasn't that how Swedish men behaved?

He hated Swedish men for their noisiness, the odors of their bodies, their bottles and flasks that they used to lengthen their manhood. He himself had read the Holy Book and learned the answers to questions they'd never even bothered to ask. He'd gone to school for thirteen years, mastered two languages completely and fluently—of which unfortunately neither was Swedish. He was educated in economics and could conduct himself in company where the Swedes' yelling and drunkenness would be disdained as primitive, barbarian. He honored his mother, had respect for women who demanded that respect.

In spite of this he was viewed begrudgingly by Swedish men. They avoided him, looked down at him. The women's world became his, and he didn't feel comfortable in it.

His buddies were heading downtown. They invited him to come along but he didn't want to. Hearing his friends' empty bragging was just as torturous as the red-hot anger that rose within him when he sat on Margareta's couch, forbidden even to play his own music. ("I've been working all day long for your sake. At least I should get to have a little peace and quiet in my own home? Please, Hassan?")

What they said was certainly true. It was true that Jamal had a Finnish girlfriend in Hagalund who did everything for him, and a rich Swedish girlfriend who went to the university and wanted to preach women's salvation in his homeland. It was true, but it was also pathetic for a man's worth be determined by whether or not women wanted to buy him. His value diminished in every respect if he let women bargain over his flesh.

It didn't involve anything but flesh—his powerful, taut phallus. His soul was withering away. Everything that comprised his real self, his beliefs and his life had to be changed. Had to be corrected. Had to be Swedified. He had to learn to see women the way Swedish men did. He must Swedify himself, act like a Swede. He got daily lectures about how a Swedish man should be. If you've chosen to live in Sweden, then you can certainly learn about this, Margareta maintained.

The worst was when she asked why he didn't go home.

"Go home then, if it's so awful here! Go home if it doesn't suit you, I never asked you to come!"

No one had asked him to come. He was uninvited, undesired, and no one really wanted him to be here except Margareta, who actually just wanted his manhood.

This was what he'd been reduced to—a wandering sex organ. A man who sold himself to a woman for food and shelter.

He couldn't go home like this. He couldn't show himself as such a man on his hometown streets or to his mother, his sisters, his father and his friends. If people found out that their Hassan was a man who lived on a woman's favor and gave her his manhood in return, there would be laughter and more laughter, forever. The customers at the bank would laugh till their pants split. His colleagues would laugh till they cried. His sisters would be ashamed and not want to go out because everybody would be giggling behind their backs; his mother would be too embarrassed to look her friends in the eye. Going home was his only hope, the only way he could keep everything from getting worse.

But he couldn't go home, that was absolutely the last thing, the most impossible. Even if they never found out what had happened and how he'd lived, they'd expect presents. They'd all want wonderful presents from the wonderful country and fantastic stories about his wealth and success. Just the way he himself had once lapped up Hamid's stories. They'd turned out to be just as empty as his own.

Nowadays he stayed away when Margareta was due home from work. He'd gotten in the habit of running away. She wanted him to have dinner ready when she got there. At first, he'd fixed a meal for her every day, splendid dishes with all of his fantasies and gratitude and love in them. She'd adored his cooking and cuddled on the sofa with him after they'd finished eating and said at least he wasn't like Swedish guys—he cared, he had sensitivity and warmth. She'd burrowed her head into

12

his throat, sighing with contentment. He'd sat with his arms around her feeling like he could do anything—that this was a real future for him.

Then she started taking it for granted that there would be delicious food every day. Now and then, maybe he wasn't in the mood to cook. Or just didn't have time. Or happened to go out and meet someone, ending up in town. Then she was irritated when he came back. She thought that after working all day long to support them both, it wasn't asking too much for him to fix a little dinner. He had to realize that here in Sweden, women and men share the chores. It was as if she grew and he shrank. It was as though her body got bigger and his got smaller.

Nowadays, he went out more and more often. He said, if she asked, that he was looking for a job.

The residence permit hadn't come through, but he'd filed a new application based on the fact that he lived with her and they were planning to get married. In the meantime, he studied Swedish and, on the side, economics.

But their quarrels became more frequent and more bitter.

He got home late, hoping Margareta would be in bed asleep. She, who worked, always got up early.

From the parking lot, he saw a light in the kitchen window and the fist inside him drew up sharply. But he didn't have the energy to ride back to his friends and go through the whole routine with them:

"Did you get locked out? What kind of a man are you? Doesn't your woman have any respect for you?"

The long trip into town and then that on top of it. He just couldn't.

She might have forgotten to turn out the kitchen light. Or left the light on for his sake. It wasn't pleasant to come home to a dark apartment.

But already in the doorway, he knew from the cigarette smoke that she was up. She knew he didn't like her smoking—her mouth smelled bad and she breathed smoke on him. She accomodated and lit up while he was away.

He opened the door as gently as he could. She didn't say

13

anything, but the smoke trickled out of the living room through the crack in the door. Quietly, he took off his shoes, and just as quietly, without turning on the hall lamp, he snuck towards the bathroom.

"Hassan."

He stood completely still and didn't answer.

"Hassan, stop making a fool of yourself, I know you're there."

He still didn't answer. First he had to work down the rage, grind it apart, flatten it out, straighten its edges, fold it under and roll the fringes together. When it was even and calm and smooth, he could lift his head and answer:

"Yes."

"Why are you sneaking around like that? Of course I know it's you."

He didn't answer that either.

"I have to talk to you."

"It's late, Margareta."

"Hell, I know that! How long do you suppose I've been sitting here waiting?"

Once again, he refused to answer, making himself inscrutable.

"Do you know how long I've been sitting here waiting?" she repeated.

"No."

"You know when I got off work?"

"Yes."

"Then you can figure it out for yourself. That's how long I've been waiting."

"I'm sorry, Margareta. I was delayed."

"What do you mean, delayed?"

"I met some friends."

"Your buddies, of course!" she exploded.

"Come here!" she shouted, beginning to sob loudly. "Hassan, come here, I've got to talk to you, I just don't know what the matter is. You've got to talk to me, why don't you ever talk to me? You just go around keeping to yourself and I don't know what to do, what is it, Hassan, what have I done wrong?"

She was still crying, sitting under the switched-off lamp in the living room. He stood uneasily in the hallway. The kitchen light was on, but nobody was there.

"We might as well talk about it in the morning, don't you think?"

"I've got to talk *now*!"

"I'm tired, Margareta."

"He's tired, he says! And what have you gotten so tired from? You haven't worked a day since you came here!"

He was still standing in the darkness of the hall. She couldn't see him. She didn't see how his jaw was strained, how he made fists and opened them, closing and opening his hands.

"Hassan, where are you? Come here!"

While she called, he took in several deep breaths, opening and closing his eyes. His arm felt ready to be raised and driven right into the mirror or through a window.

"Are you there?"

He forced the fire down again, breathing slowly and deeply. He shook out his hands.

"I don't want to talk right now, Margareta. You're tired too. Let's go to bed."

"But we've got to talk about this, about us, about our relationship! You can't just solve everything in bed! You've got to be able to talk!"

As if it changes anything, talking! he laughed scornfully to himself and would have spat on the floor if he hadn't realized what he was doing and caught himself in time.

He went in and stood in front of her. She reached her arms out to him. He turned away.

"Hassan, what is it? Say it! Is it something I did?" He shook his head.

"Why don't you ever talk to me anymore? Are you tired of me? Is that it? Did you meet somebody else?"

"No."

"But what is it then? What is it?"

She wept, wanting him to comfort and caress her, say that everything would be OK, that he loved her, that he'd get a job, that soon everything would work itself out.

He opened his mouth to say it, but couldn't manage to bring out the words.

15

If only he could go home.

If only he could get away from her, her whining, her tears, her complaints—so much more painful because they were true.

No, he couldn't go home. Without a car, without money, without a beautiful woman—come home like a dirty little boy and get rapped on his fingers and laughed at by his sisters!

He sat down at her feet, laying his head in her lap. She stroked his hair.

"Hassan?"

"Yes."

"Please, let's talk about it."

She never knew when to quit! She always scratched one time too many. He felt, and she felt, how his body stiffened, becoming like a tightly woven rope with taut muscles and stretched tendons.He couldn't take it anymore. This time it would press through, hurling itself out—the rage, the fire, maybe madness. If he succeeded in resisting now, the explosion would have to come soon. It lay so very close, bubbling under the surface.

He got up in a single movement and went into the kitchen. She ran after him.

"Hassan! Please! It can't go on like this, you've got to understand! I've got to know how it'll be between us, what's going to happen in the future!"

His arm shot out, meeting the edge of the door beside her. She ducked, screaming.

"Hassan, are you out of your mind? Are you going to hit me?"

She stood there crouched, ready to jump, the tears streaming down her face, her mouth distorted by grief. He had frozen to a statue of ice with uplifted arms.

"You're trying to hit me, you asshole! Is this the thanks I get?"

She straightened up, lunging at him with raised hands and outspread fingers. He caught her hands in his, holding them firmly. She kicked, turned sideways, tried to bite, but couldn't free the hands that he still held between stone-hard fingers. He laughed.

"Have you learned to be quiet when I say so?"

"Let go of me, I said!"

He laughed loudly and bitterly.

"So this is what you're really like! Now I see! Now I know! Now you're showing your true self!"

He didn't answer but he thought, maybe so! Maybe here, at last, was a man who didn't let himself be browbeaten anymore, a man who didn't beg your pardon anymore, a man who finally spoke up!

He released her suddenly, pushing her down on the floor. He was on his way out of the kitchen but she threw herself forward, grabbing his leg.

"Stop, Hassan! Wait!"

He didn't want to kick her, but he had to in order to get free. It was awful to hear the sound.

"You shouldn't have done that!"

He managed to close the kitchen door, but it would only stay shut as long as he stood there holding it. As soon as he let go, she'd come plowing through. Lord, how had he ended up like this? How had he run across this crazy woman? He had to get away. Wouldn't have time to gather his things, he'd have to come back for them some other day. He knew that if he started packing now, he'd have her around him the whole time, crying, howling, begging, threatening, appealing. And just thinking about it, the anger was back and he longed to strike out.

He had to get away before he hit her too hard, he must go, he didn't want to fight with her, but he had to if she kept on eating her way in, gnawing and burrowing herself into him.

She was still hammering on the kitchen door, crying.

In God the compassionate, the merciful's name, how had he ended up like this? In one sharp glimpse, he saw his town, his street, his home, his mother. A baby goat who used to follow him around; it'd bothered him then, but now he laughed about it. He'd been afraid of the teachers at school. And his job in the bank had been tedious. Hamid had come and told him about Sweden, about the girls, the money, the wonderful life.

Hell!

"Margareta!" he called through the closed door.

"Let me out, Hassan! Please. I can't sit in the kitchen all night long!"

17

"I'll open it. Can you just wait a little bit?"

"Why?"

"I beg you. Just two minutes."

"What are you going to do?"

"Wait, you'll see."

She sat on the kitchen chair with her hands folded and waited for two minutes.

When she opened the kitchen door, he had already gone.

† † †

A man's corpse was discovered early one Wednesday morning by a newspaper carrier in Södermalm. Elin Axelsson was pulling her cart down Timmermans Street when she saw a man's legs sticking out from under a bush in Bergsgruvan Park, where it borders on the street.

She sighed, setting the cart aside. It wasn't unusual to find drunken men sleeping under the bushes, especially in the summer. But now it was March and it'd snowed during the night, wet snow that had fallen on top of the soft melting mark. The grass was still powdered, but as soon as the sun came up, the moisture would flow right down into the earth.

She ought to wake the man up and tell him to move. In general, they were grateful.

She left her cart on the sidewalk, walking across the damp lawn. Her steps splashed and she left black footprints behind her in the whiteness.

It was a small, dark-complected man lying there. Thin jacket, low-heeled shoes. No real outdoor clothing.

An immigrant, poor thing. They were seldom found drunk. Say what you will, thought Elin Axelsson. But I, at least, have never seen a drunken Turk.

It almost didn't feel right to poke him with her foot, as she usually did with Gunnarsson, Holm and the other clientele whom she had gradually gotten to know. They were coarse old men, big and robust in spite of their habits. But this one here was such a sorry little skinny thing.

She bent down, shaking his shoulders carefully. She felt like a mother. Poor little guy, what have they done to you? How did

18

you end up like this?

His joints were so strangely limp, he didn't resist the way they normally did, no matter how drunk they were. It was as though he were completely relaxed. Completely—

She took a step back, putting her hand over her mouth.

If only the newsstand were open. Then she could've asked Hjördis.

Or she could race down to the South Station—it must be open for the five o'clock train.

She bent down again, gently shaking his shoulders.

No response. She lifted a dark lock of hair that was lying on his face covering one eye.

The eye stared back at her coldly and vacantly.

She didn't scream, because no one would have heard her anyway. She held her hand over her throat and felt her stomach heave several times, but nothing came up. She was still crouching beside the dead boy, and only gradually became aware that tears were running down her cheeks.

It was soon established that the man had been dead for a couple of hours when Elin Axelsson found him. His life had been taken by repeated stabs in the stomach and waist with a sharp object. The autopsy determined that the number of blows must have been at least eight, with several overlapping wounds. Death had followed almost immediately. Tracks left by the perpetrator couldn't be substantiated because of the continual light snowfall during the night. The snow visible now had fallen since the deed was committed. The clay under the snow was examined closely in search of imprints. It would be a tedious process to sort them out and classify them—some of the heavier tracks in the mud could be several days old.

A walkway led into the park from Timmermans Street, past a youth center, up to Bergsgruvan itself. On this path, Hassan Abdel Karim had met his destiny. He had lain prostrate with his feet still on the path and his head almost concealed by a bush. The earth beneath him had been mixed with blood.

Undoubtedly, the location of the body was identical to the location of the murder. A man in the victim's condition would not have been able to move without leaving a trail of blood. He'd had some final transaction with one or more assailants at this shrub by the path near Timmermans Street.

No other witnesses besides Elin Axelsson reported themselves. She couldn't remember whether she'd seen anyone before she found the dead man. Later, she thought she might have met a cyclist at the corner of Högberg Street, an older man, but she wasn't completely sure.

An older woman living in the house at 41 Timmerman Street had had insomnia and been disturbed by noise in the park about three o'clock. She was so used to it, she said, that she hadn't even bothered to look. She'd had the shades pulled down anyway.

The man had his ID papers on him: He was Hassan Abdel Karim, North African, twenty-eight years. A c/o address in Huddinge was given.

The fiancée's name was Margareta Åström.

† † †

As soon as the police had gone, we were there. We crowded in the stairway with quite a number of other journalists. *The Express* would surely come out with a new, indignant article about Arabic barbarism and the oppression of women, *The Evening News* with one about the immigrant's lot in the cold Swedish society. We went back a couple of days later when Margareta had gotten a chance to recover a little and had actually begun feeling the need to talk to someone. Now the empty days would come, with questions and regrets. Now she could want our support, and we might find something out from her.

She'd pulled herself together quite quickly after the initial shock. She was lying on her sofa covered by a blanket, pressing a handkerchief in her hand and occasionally blowing her nose. Katrin smiled encouragingly at her and Margareta smiled back. We explained who we were, and why—freelance journalists wanting to investigate the case in depth for a series of articles we were planning.

"Do you think you can talk about it?"

"Oh yes."

"How long had you and Hassan known each other?"

"Almost a year."

"How did you meet?"

"A girlfriend of mine went out with one of Hassan's friends. So he came over, and he needed a room. They thought I could rent the room out and besides, I needed the money. Then everything just happened."

"And so that night he left home and didn't come back."

"I never saw him again. We had, you know, had a fight that night, and I took some pills and went to sleep. He'd been away before so I wasn't really worried. But then when the police came and told me, I couldn't go to work for a few days...."

Tears ran down her cheeks. She dried her eyes with the handkerchief. Katrin bent forwards, touching her arm.

"You've been through a lot. We could come back another day if you'd rather."

She shook her head vigorously and drew her sob in through her nose.

"Oh, no. I want to find out about this too. I want to get hold of the bastard who did it. Hassan was a shithead in a lot of ways, but he didn't deserve to be murdered. He was a nice guy, really. Just ask around."

Katrin gave her a pat and we continued:

"Can you say exactly what happened that night?"

Margareta told the story while I took notes.

"So he abused you?"

"Yeah, but not that bad."

"Do you have any bruises from it?"

"I don't think so. He never really hit me. The only thing was he kicked me when I was lying on the floor. I did get a bruise on my hip."

"But hardly a case of intentional abuse? More like an argument?"

"That's probably what you'd say."

"Did you have quarrels like this very often?"

"Yes, often, but he'd never hit me before. He was hard to live with, but never violent. It was the opposite, really. He just slid away from me, I couldn't ever reach him."

The tears were streaming down Margareta's cheeks again as she told about the troubles she'd had living with Hassan. How

21

he was never on time. How she hadn't been able to depend on him, how he sometimes stayed away for several nights in a row, refusing to say where he'd been, other than that he'd been staying with his friends. Sometimes he'd had money and then he'd given her some, but other times he didn't have any at all. He didn't ever have a job, as far as she knew.

"You won't, uh, say anything about how he was looking for a job even though he didn't have a permit?" she asked. "Now I guess it doesn't matter. But, of course, he wasn't supposed to work until the permit came through."

"Then what did he live on?"

"He'd registered as a political refugee, so he got some kind of a stipend. Of course he went and studied Swedish. Otherwise he lived off of me. And naturally he did stuff in return. He cleaned and cooked and that type of thing. As soon as he'd gotten his permit arranged, he would've started working and paying me back. I'm positive about that."

"Who else did he associate with?"

"I don't know."

"You don't know? Didn't you have any friends in common?"

"No, he had a bunch of friends I didn't know. I didn't want them here. Some of them came over a couple of times, but I didn't want them sitting in my apartment when I wasn't home myself. I don't really know who they were, I wasn't interested. I was hoping he'd drop them as soon as he got a job."

"Do you know if they did any drugs?"

"Not that I know of."

"Did Hassan?"

"I don't think so. Not here at home, anyway. He didn't even drink alcohol."

"He didn't say anything about where he was going when he left?"

"You mean that last time? No, oh no. We had such a big fight. He kicked me and shut me in the kitchen. When I came out of the kitchen, he was gone. I locked the door and went to bed. I slept straight through until the police came."

We thanked Margareta and she promised to call if she remembered anything else. We were eager to find Hassan's friends and she'd said they all used to meet at a pizzeria on Svea Street. One time she'd picked him up there and he'd been furious. We decided to check it out immediately.

In the stairwell, Katrin said, "I don't suppose it could have been her? Betrayed and rejected? Ran after him with a knife?"

"Who knows? But the buddies are probably a better lead in that case."

We had a hard time visualizing Margareta Åström hunting her lover with a knife in her hand all the way to the South Sation. If it had happened at home in the kitchen, with the kitchen knife, it would have been a different story.

But why the South Station, anyway?

We had to get hold of his friends, then maybe we'd have the answer.

We knew which restaurant Margareta had indicated and that the friend who introduced Hassan to Sweden was named Hamid. Margareta didn't know where Hamid lived anymore because he'd broken up with her girlfriend.

The Immigration Department must have had all of the information, codified and entered in the computer. If you've got a person-number, it's really impossible to slip through the cracks. But the Immigration Department has privacy regulations and never discloses anything about individual cases to the press.

We didn't feel we could come as journalists to the pizzeria. Nor would it be easy for me as a Swede to pop up as some kind of a pal.

But for Katrin, on the other hand.

So each of us went in alone.

Our plan was for me to go in first. If there weren't any Arabic-speaking North Africans inside, I'd go out again and Katrin wouldn't have to show herself. If something seemed promising in there, I'd stay at a table near the door. Katrin would wait for a few minutes, then go in and sit down in the vicinity of Hassan's countrymen. Next it would be a question of her drawing their attention, which didn't turn out to be especially difficult.

After that came the preliminaries: what their names were

and what her name was and where they came from and what they were doing here and what she did. Then silence, a kind of awkwardness. Of course it wasn't a pick-up she was after, and maybe that's not what they wanted either. They asked if she'd like something to drink. When the conversation had progressed that far, Katrin started talking about Hamid who had broken up with her girlfriend and how the girlfriend really wanted to find him. Everyone knew Hamid, but no one knew where he was for the moment. Katrin mentioned that he'd had a friend who, I don't know if you've heard, but maybe you know about that terrible...?

No one knew. No one knew Hassan.

Everyone looked blank and surprised when his name was mentioned.

One day there was a boy who seemed more serious than the rest. He left his group and came over to Katrin's table, sitting down beside her. He asked:

"Did Margareta send you?"

"Oh no. I have a friend named Agneta who used to live with Hamid, you know. Margareta was Hassan's girlfriend. He's the one who died."

The boy looked at her with almost luminous eyes. His face betrayed no emotion.

"You weren't sent by Agneta. What do you want?"

Katrin measured him with a glance and figured the safest thing in this situation was to say: "I want to know how Hassan died."

"Why?"

"Because it's a horrible crime and no one wants to see it happen again."

"Are you from the police? The Immigration Department? Welfare?"

"No way."

She still didn't want to put all her cards on the table and bring me into the picture. She continued, "Don't you wonder yourself who did it? You knew Hassan, didn't you?"

"Of course," he said. "But you've got to be quiet. You can't just go around asking like this."

"Why not?"

"Because we don't know what happened to Hassan and everyone's afraid. Everybody thinks it could happen to him next time."

"Then he wasn't involved in anything? Maybe it was revenge for something, retaliation."

The boy shook his head adamantly.

"Nobody knows why it happened to him. That's why everyone's afraid. He was just butchered like an animal in that park, in the mud. There are lots of things going on—gangs, dangerous people. But no one who Hassan had anything to do with."

"Isn't there anyone at all you suspect?" asked Katrin. "Didn't he have any enemies at all? Or any drug abuse?"

"No enemy. None. He was a good guy; he was nice to Margareta. That's why we're afraid. If he got murdered because he was an Arab, not because he was Hassan—you know? It could be political—some Swedes are against immigrants. Or like that guy in Norway who was murdered by Zionists. There've been others too. It might not have been *Hassan* who got murdered, it could've just been a North African guy, someone they call a darkie, who they wanted to get rid of. They could do it to any one of us next time. You get what I mean, don't you?"

Katrin saw exactly what he meant, but none of us yet understood what a significant lead to the murderer lay in that lengthening of his final thought.

"Hassan was an immigrant," continued the boy. "There are Swedes who think, damn immigrants, go home."

He grabbed hold of her arm.

"You have to realize *we* want to know? Who should we defend ourselves against? There are lots of people mad at us, but a terrible maniac is out to murder us!"

"You don't happen to know where I could find Hamid," wondered Katrin.

"I am Hamid," said the boy. "Hassan was my friend."

We didn't get much further with the case of Hassan Abdel Karim, immigrant, twenty-eight, and neither did the police, as far as we knew.

25

Our reconstruction went like this:

After the argument with Margareta which ended about 1:00 am, Hassan went back to the train station. He didn't have anywhere special to go, it was cold, and he'd run away from home dressed exactly as he'd been at the time. He took the first commuter train into town, which also happened to be the last one of the night. For some reason, he didn't ride any further than the South Station. The last train from Huddinge stopped there at 1:38 am.

He might have left with someone he met on the train. Naturally, the police questioned both the driver and the conductor. However, it turned out (according to press reports that we verified) that they'd never noticed Hassan. This wasn't so remarkable, considering he was only on board the train for ten minutes and apparently didn't make any trouble.

He got off at the South Station. The station guard had been busy cleaning up and hadn't noticed who all went by. He hadn't opened the door to Timmermans Street, just locked it up at closing time.

It's also possible that Hassan didn't take the train at all, but instead hitchhiked into town, and that's how he met his assassin. If so, we had to ask whether it could have been a homosexual episode, but nothing else in the case indicated this. Hassan was definitely not gay, and usually it's the victim who is, not the assailant, when such matters become violent.

He was found just before five o'clock by Elin Axelsson.

And that was all we knew.

STHEN CARLSSON, 67
Member of Parliament (Socialist)

Married, two grown sons with their own families.

Carlsson was living temporarily at the Parliament Hotel. Had been elected to Parliament in 1958; was a native of Östergötland, which he represented. Regular occupation: welding, later on, being an ombudsperson. Well liked by colleagues and other members of his party. Participated on the taxation and energy committees. A diligent and reliable party member, good behind-the-scenes worker. Abstainer from alcohol and smoking.

Carlsson was found murdered in a women's restroom at the Sergel's Square subway station. The discovery was made by the bathroom's cleaning woman, who at first considered the victim a member of the so-called "clientele." He was identified in the ambulance on the way to the mortuary. The criminal police were already involved.

Carlsson's life had been taken through repeated blows in the stomach area with a sharp instrument. Some of the wounds had punctured the left lung, resulting in death.

Suspects:

The "clientele" at Sergel's Square?

A drug pusher, caught in the act by Carlsson?

A political enemy, a terrorist group?

The obituary written by a friend in the party had said, "Sthen Carlsson was known for his strong social empathy. He was often observed at Sergel's Square, where he would talk to the outcasts of society and try to help them. Some bourgeois newspapers wrote about these efforts sarcastically, comparing him to William Gladstone, whose conversations and active concern with prostitutes were misunderstood by the Victorian public."

His wife: "He was the nicest man alive. I always said it would end badly if he didn't get out of politics. He shouldn't have run again. I begged him to stay home this year. He was retired anyway and there were plenty of others who could have gone in his place. But he didn't want to listen to me. He had his duty, he said. If only he'd done as I asked!"

† † †

The air was fresh, chilly.

"It's going to snow over Easter," said Sthen Carlsson to his secretary.

She looked up from her typewriter with a grimace.

"Do you really think so?"

"As sure as the amen in church."

He left her doorway and went back to his room across the corridor. He thumbed through the papers on his desk.

"Do you think you'll have time to do this memorandum tonight, Mona?"

She didn't answer and he walked back to her door. The secretary was sitting with plugs in her ears from the dictation machine, concentrating furiously on the transcription. He went up behind her, putting his hand on her shoulder.

"Oh, Mona—"

She cried out, turning around. Shut off the button and took out the plugs. "God, you startled me! Don't you ever do that again!"

"You got scared?"

He sat down on the edge of the desk, smiling warmly into her eyes.

"You do want this letter sent off before Easter, don't you? I'm in a terrible hurry, dear Sthen. Please don't talk to me while I'm trying to work if you want to get this job done right away."

He pouted with his mouth and got up.

"It's just that there's this little memo here that I absolutely have to get typed up. You see, I'm going to take it home this week to work on. The text has got to be clear."

28

She leaned back in her chair, sighing.

"I just don't have the time. Please try to understand."

"It's got to be done."

"Then you'll have to ask somebody else."

"Mona, we have an agreement."

"Well, OK, put it there on top of the pile. And for god-sakes leave me alone while I'm working!"

Humiliated, he wandered off towards the Parliament Restaurant. Damned uppity woman, that one! And she wasn't even pretty! At least forty, gray hair, glasses. He had to get his letter on its way before Easter to be able to finish that part up, and he needed his memo to work on over vacation. He'd be visiting a lot of people in his home town during the holiday and needed to have all of his papers in order, all of his figures clarified. Of course he couldn't talk to the department managers without having everything ready. This was the kind of thing she didn't understand. How pressing everything was and how each project needed to be done in its proper time. He had to mimeograph the memo and distribute it to all of the affected parties in the district. Then the boys in their turn had to take the matter up with their own departments.

Tomorrow, the trip home. Relax on Sunday, dig a little in the yard if the weather held, prune the bushes. Monday, he had to talk to Berglund at the workshop clubhouse. Go over when it was appropriate for him to come, what he ought to say. Tuesday, the bank, be direct with Josefsson, it's got to be finished and executed that day. Preferably, he should have it memorized, so he could talk with the numbers in his head. Yes, Josefsson—the bank. On Wednesday, Hasselbom and in the evening, Rigmor and Sture Gustafsson at home for bridge. Thursday, Maundy Thursday. Stop by and wish his chums a pleasant holiday. They'd remember it later. Finally relax the whole damn Easter, maybe go to church, he probably owed it to Pastor Holmqvist on Easter Sunday, anyway. Had to give his regards so as to be remembered.

It was nice, considering all of this, to have one free evening in Stockholm without any commitments.

He checked his watch. It was 2:00. He had time to take a walk before the work meeting. He wasn't expected there, it was the civil service committee presenting a report about subsidies for housing maintenance. Nothing from his desk.

He stood for a moment in the doorway to Drottning Street, looking around.

The sun was flowing right down into the depths of the street. Chairs and tables had appeared cautiously outside the Theater Restaurant. He looked up, shading his eyes with his hand. He felt young, eager for adventure. Spring had come once again, and once again, he was feeling it—in his legs, in his loins, in his head—he laughed and didn't know why. At the sun? At spring? At his age, and the fact that he still responded to spring like a calf, like a youth, like a lark, like a bee?

Persson from Grythyttan said hello as he walked by.

"You old son of a gun, can you feel how spring's come? Want to go out on the town with me?"

Persson laughed, throwing up his hands.

"Have enough to do already without getting into that. Happy Easter to you, Carlsson! See that you get home to the old lady before you go starting something."

They shook hands in the real, old-fashioned way and then each went off in his own direction.

As he'd figured, the girls were out. Girls who actually got younger every year. It wasn't just that he himself got older, the girls were really chronologically younger. Couldn't be more than thirteen, fourteen, these little ones wagging and wiggling in mini-skirts (mini-skirts? again?) with black-black eyes and red lips and bouffant hairdos. He stopped to watch them, smiling with his hands in his pockets. Pretty girls, but why did they have to go and paint themselves like that? And the older ones of all ages, even up to Mona's, poor things. They probably thought they'd get one last chance and didn't realize how the sharp sunlight revealed them—the wrinkles, the gray hair, the pale, dull complexions....

He felt like buying some ice cream and going window-shopping, it was streaming within him, springtime.... He went back to the restaurant and ordered the daily special, Baltic herring stuffed with parsley. The fillet under the breadcrumbs, he sensed suddenly, seemed to have a musty flavor—a taste like death. It stayed on his tongue so he raised his hand to call the waiter and complain. But no one noticed him, no one came, and after a while he didn't care anymore. Guessed it wasn't really that bad.

Later on in the dark restaurant, a fatigue washed over him. He thought about how he had to go back and pack, make sure Mona had done her work, sign the letter, proofread the memo. Mona said it wasn't necessary, it went directly into the computer memory of the machine and was stored there, she could check it herself—but there might be something he wanted to change and in the final analysis he had to do it himself. Then Mona would argue with him over his revisions and say they didn't really make any difference—now she'd have to run the whole thing through again from the beginning, just because he'd decided to change a few words. Oh yes, he would say then, but at least you have your machine that fast-forwards to the correction you want to make—just think when the girls had to sit and retype page after page; you should have been around then to really have something to complain about! Mona would point out bitterly that she had been around then and he would laugh, clapping her on the back, yeah, yeah old Mona, you've been around for a long time, do you remember, Mona, when we wrote by hand leaning over our desks with our quill pens, you were probably around then, too, huh Mona?

But she didn't get jokes. He almost dreaded going back and talking to her and taking care of his papers. Mona was aggressive, he would have preferred another girl. He'd happened to get Mona just because Eskilsson and Holm next door had her, so he'd ended up getting stuck with her too. She'd worked for Eskilsson for years; he loved Mona, praised her in ringing tones—undoubtedly they'd had something going on the side. If Sthen Carlsson had dared, he would have been one of the men to have Kickan Bratt for a secretary—what a cupcake! Cute and happy and polite. But there wasn't any chance of getting rid of Mona, she was unbelievably competent and he would be retiring long before her. She was still sitting with the plugs in her ears when he came back. He went over and stood behind her to see how far she'd gotten. She pretended not to notice his existence other than to raise her shoulders protectively, blocking his view. He stood there for a little while searching for something to say, something that would really put her in her place, something she'd be at a loss to answer.

He couldn't think of anything. He went into his room and there on his desk lay all of the letters, typed out.

† † †

It was 7:30 before he'd gotten his memorandum exactly the way he wanted it. By then Mona was in a sour mood. The thought struck him that he could ask her out to dinner. She'd been busy all day long, the holiday was standing right at the door, she might want to relax. But his inner self resisted giving the invitation. If she'd just been a little friendlier! If she'd shown a little enthusiasm!

A woman like her—what man would want to invite her anywhere?

Even so, there persisted sort of a feeling of duty that told him to be nice to her.

"Are you going home now?" he asked as she was packing up her things with unnecessary noise and clatter.

"Where else?"

There goes that dinner, he thought bitterly.

"I just wanted to wish you a Happy Easter. You have a son at home, right?"

"*If* he's at home, yes."

She pulled on the arm of her jacket and seemed to have put her hand in the lining because it got stuck. He stepped over and lifted the arm, holding the jacket up for her.

"Allow me?" he said. "Or maybe you're too liberated?"

She didn't answer and he realized they were going to part on bad terms for the holiday.

"Mona," he said, "you're not mad, are you? I really did have to get that memorandum done. I've got to show it to a bunch of folks at home. It just wouldn't do to have mistakes here and there."

"No, of course not." She stroked him quickly on the cheek. "Happy Easter to you, too, Sthen. Say hello to Märta and the boys, whatever their names are. See you after vacation."

"Wait a minute."

He came back with a big Easter egg, trimmed by a rosette. "For your son."

Once again, she made that grimace he disliked—acting superior. As if she had anything to feel superior about! When he'd taken the trouble...

"My son is seventeen years old."

He looked at the egg with its childish decorations.

"Oh, I see, then—"

"Oh, shoot."

She reached out her hand.

"Give it to me anyway. I know you mean well."

She bent forward and even kissed him on the cheek. Then she disappeared down the corridor with clicking heels.

What had she meant?

He felt his cheek, where it tingled and burned.

How dumb can a man be?

But maybe she had meant something! If only he hadn't been so gruff himself, if he'd just been a little forward and asked her out to dinner. She herself had indicated that her son wasn't at home. Seventeen-year-olds, did any of them ever come home nowadays? And he'd just stood there like a fool, letting her go with a silly Happy Easter!

Sthen Carlsson grabbed his coat and hurried after Mona. Maybe she wasn't really that sore. It was true she'd had a heavy workload lately and actually she was right that he exploited her. This memo would have to be redone after it'd been through the scrutiny at home. It really hadn't been necessary to get it perfectly typed up right now. She knew it and he knew it, but when you're a perfectionist, that's the way you are. He wanted everything in order before his vacation, his desk cleared off.

He was going to fight for his home town industry—to the bone, until death! God bless Mona that she'd gotten the memo typed up anyway!

Naturally, when he came out on the street, she was gone. Clouds had gathered themselves into rain, the mist was hanging low in the air. The sharp breezes from lunchtime had died down, mixing with the moisture in the atmosphere to become a raw, piercing chill. The usual Easter weather in the making? For two weeks the sun had shone, the snow had melted, the flowers bloomed, the birds chirped, the people had taken off their boots, caps and overcoats, noses had run, cheeks were flushed, laughter sounded in the air, ice cream stands opened, the parks began turning green.

Then Easter came along and ruined everything. Typical.

Sthen Carlsson was left standing indecisively under the lights on Drottning Street. Mona was already down in the subway—it would be ridiculous to try running after her. Calling her at home would be equally ridiculous. She'd think he was after something, and if she weren't after anything herself, she'd begin to question his sanity.

He had a coach ticket for the train the following morning at 11:00. He didn't really know himself why he'd decided to stay in town. Naturally, time could get away from you in parliamentary chamber, and he always found it unpleasant to rush directly from there to the train.

I'm a man of the old stock, he thought, feeling sentimental. These young boys with their rectangular briefcases and striped suits, they have no sense of time built into their lives. They can do whatever whenever. They can stay up drinking all night long, get up early the next morning and be as clear as glass and hard as stone. They can go directly from a meeting at six o'clock and sit in a cab talking over the phone about their next meeting on their way to Arlanda Airport, where they catch the plane to that next meeting. I'm not like that. Am I starting to get old, not keeping up anymore?

He was still standing on Drottning Street with his hands in his pockets. There wasn't a soul in sight. It was a little past eight and not completely dark yet, despite the grayish fog. What a dreary evening, he thought. What'll I do here, all alone in town?

Catch a movie.

Go to bed.

It was too late to go to the theater.

He kept standing indecisively, as if he were expecting someone to come up and help set him aright. He raised his shoulders and shook himself like a wet dog in the haze.

If someone did come along, it would probably be drug pushers, pimps. Now that the city has gotten like it is.

A great loneliness, almost like an agony, came over him and

he considered taking an evening train after all. Märta was waiting for him; she'd be glad if he arrived early. She'd fuss over him. A wife in the old style. He was sure she'd draw a warm bath for him whatever time he came home—she'd even use the bath thermometer to make sure the temperature was right. While he bathed, she'd make some sandwiches in the kitchen, and she'd arrange a tray for when he emerged, keeping him company even though she didn't care to eat anything herself. She'd listen while he talked and tell him what had happened since he'd been gone.

Yet there had to be some human being left in Stockholm!

The lights were on in several of his colleagues' rooms. He could look in on one of them and chat away some time. Surely somebody would be going out to eat, after all?

Or take the suitcase and go to the train—?

Then Märta would wonder. What are you doing back so early? What happened? Are you sad? Were they mean to you?

He had to laugh at the thought, but it was very realistic.

What did people do alone in the city for an evening? There must be thousands of things going on, even for someone with nothing to do? Especially for that one?

He took several hesitant steps back to the entrance of the hotel, but couldn't make the decision to ride up in the elevator. He felt dumb hanging around the lobby like a little boy, no one to play with.

Two Conservatives were on their way out, speaking loudly.

"Hey Carlsson, what are you doing standing around in the doorway?"

His laugh was hollow and cringing.

"Just came in."

"Happy Easter to you, now! Say hello to the old lady!"

He smiled stiffly at their false folksiness. Of course they didn't know a thing about his wife, or even if he had one.

He rode up to his room and glanced around, repacking the suitcase that he'd already packed and sitting down on the edge of the bed, not knowing what else to do with himself. He went over to the desk, lifted up the briefcase and shuffled through the papers he would be reading after Easter.

The investigation on civil defense?

He sat down at the desk, turned on the lamp and began to read. The letters floated together on the paper after half a page. He tried pretending that he was going to school and had an assignment, but then it got even worse.

He put the report back in his briefcase, snapping it shut with its powerful locks. It was a big, old, folding briefcase made out of leather. He was proud of it, had inherited it from his father. The little boys' flat briefcases with their silly little legs! Their status symbols!

He snorted, putting the briefcase down beside him on the floor. Father had used it to carry his lunch to work. It'd been *his* status symbol—taking a briefcase to work even though he was only a common laborer.

That thought concluded, Sthen Carlsson sat motionlessly with his hands folded in his lap. It was at times like this that he actually wished he weren't a teetotaller. But he'd promised father and mother; they'd seen enough misery around them.

If only he had someone to go out and eat with!

Sit alone with the *Evening News*, eat stringy beef and soft french fries, no!

Go to a nice restaurant, have something good.

But impossible alone.

Call Mona?

Not on your life!

There was another girl further down the corridor from his office, she was sweet. He'd talked to her several times in the doorway and on coffee breaks. Not to mention Kickan Bratt! But calling her at nine o'clock the evening before a holiday—it could be misinterpreted. Maybe get out among his colleagues. And that could have dire consequences.

Naturally, the party leader had never had a prostitute in his room, but others had, and in some cases it had become known. In other cases it had been spoken of, suspected, or else there'd been evidence that had to be paid for in order not to be published.

Who felt like bringing a prostitute up to his room, anyway?

He just wanted the company of a human being, someone to talk to, laugh and joke with. Even a man, it wasn't a question of that. What he craved was companionship. Someone who knew what he was talking about, who understood what he meant. It might be fun to have a scrap with one of the younger boys and put him in his place, but they were all at home by now in the safekeeping of their wives or partners—they'd put on their aprons and were in the midst of doing the dishes or changing the diapers. He rested his head on his hands and sat like that for a long time.Of course there was a train leaving at eleven pm. He was too late for the nine o'clock train, and if he took the late-night train, he wouldn't be home until after two. Too late to rouse Märta out of bed, and for what purpose, to miss a night's sleep?

He lifted the receiver and dialed her number.

He hung up before she answered. Then he thought maybe she'd get scared and think something horrible had happened, so he called back again.

"Were you in bed?" he asked.

"I was watching TV, but the telephone rang and nobody was there."

"Oh, that was me. It took a while, so I thought maybe you were asleep."

She hadn't even been afraid. He got irritated with her.

"So what did you want?"

"I just wanted to confirm that I'll be coming tomorrow like we said. Just so you know."

"Yes, right, but you already told me that...."

"Is everything OK at home?"

"Yes, of course. Kasparsson called from the newspaper and then there was someone from the union club, I don't remember his name. They wanted to talk to you and said they'd get in touch tomorrow."

"Good. Kiss."

"Kiss." He kept sitting there with the receiver in his hand. Now it was also too late to go to a movie. The nine o'clock show had already begun. There were only porn flicks left this time of night.

Might as well go to bed.

But then he got an idea and something drove him back out into the street one more time.

The last time.

† † †

A Swedish man in later middle age. He lay fallen forwards in the stall nearest the door, the one without a fee, his face on the toilet seat. The graffiti on the door of the stall depicted an erect penis.

He could have been taken for one of the clientele at Sergel's Square—there were all types.

The man was nicely dressed in a mixed brown ready-made suit, light blue shirt, dark red tie and brown shoes. He was wearing a thin poplin overcoat but didn't have anything on his head. The clothing was in good shape. He was bald and had been wearing glasses, which had fallen down on the floor and gotten broken. His complexion was even and ruddy and he had half a day's stubble of beard.

The dead man lay bent over the toilet as though he were praying or throwing up, his head leaning up against the raised seat. A red sludge had run along the outer edge of the toilet, discoloring his knees. The redness continued all the way down the stool and out onto the floor.

An old alcoholic who'd gone and gotten a ruptured ulcer in the middle of the night?

The smooth, healthy complexion hardly seemed to indicate that.

He was put on a stretcher with the limp mouth and wide-open eyes turned up towards the ceiling.

He hadn't thrown up; that wasn't where the blood had come from. It had come from blows to the stomach—repeated blows, delivered in rage or cold determination.

Gaping onlookers moved to the side when the man's covered corpse was carried out of the women's restroom and into the ambulance waiting on the street. The emotions lingered in the air for a long time afterwards, together with the whispered questions about who he was and why.

But it was when the police in the ambulance went through his pockets that the second shock came.

Certainly the man didn't look like a drunkard, but appearances can be deceiving. Drug pushers, for that matter, can be conscientious family men who look just like anybody else.

But this was a bit too much:

Carlsson Sthen Malte Ludvig, 150123-1912. Member of Parliament (Socialist) and chairman of the energy committee.

"It's as simple as can be," said the detective spokesman at the press conference. "Everything's written on the paper here. There isn't much else to say."

"Say it anyhow!"

"Death occurred at approximately 11:00 pm. The restroom cleaning woman was about to close for the night when she found him."

"And what was he doing in there?"

"No idea. He'd eaten one last time around 10:00 pm, a pizza."

"Where?"

"Don't know. You can find that out for yourselves."

"We will. What else?"

"Pizza, like I said, and he'd had some milk. No coffee."

"And the wound itself?"

"The wound itself, or wounds, are about ten. They go diagonally across one another. Pieces of the skin and stomach have quite literally been carved loose or left hanging like scraps. Both the liver and one lung are punctured. He didn't have a chance."

"Didn't he shriek like a pig?"

"Apparently not. In shock, pain is sometimes expressed as gasping and moaning, not in the form of a scream. Besides, the diaphragm could have been injured, you know."

It was quiet for a while.

"And this happened in the women's restroom?"

"In the entryway, actually. The trail of blood starts there. He couldn't have gone far afterwards. He fell on his knees right away. Just had time to lean over the bowl, thinking he was going to throw up. He had froth around his mouth, but he was probably dead before anything else came up."

"Could the murderer have flushed something down the toilet?"

"We don't believe the murderer was ever inside the toilet

room itself, he must have stayed in the hallway. Mrs. Palmgren was in there, you know, and she didn't see anything suspicious. It's unlikely that the murderer could have had time to go both in and out without her noticing."

The cleaning woman on duty in the restroom that night had been Violet Palmgren. She was a broad-shouldered woman in her fifties. When we met her, she was still traumatized, with tears in her eyes and a red nose.

"I just can't forgive myself! I must have seen it! But I didn't! How can you believe me?"

"Of course we believe you," said Katrin. "Why, it was a matter of seconds, how could you possibly have known that a murder was taking place right then?"

In fact, at first we didn't believe her more than halfway. She could have been paid or frightened into silence. But later, as we got better acquainted with Violet, we began to believe her more and more.

"I'm here, you know, to keep watch, that's why it's so frustrating I missed this. It seems suspicious to the police, but I really didn't see a thing. Maybe a person gets dull over time. There are lots of dopers and strange types around here, you know. They're not really allowed into the stalls. That's the reason I'm stationed here to keep guard. But sometimes they get in anyway. Like that thing they'd drawn in the one where he was kneeling. It wasn't new, you know, I should've washed it off a week ago. But it's hard when they really press down with their pens. The door might have to be repainted."

"So what happened that night?"

"Nothing at all happened until just as I was getting ready to close at 11:00 pm. I was cleaning the toilets further away. Then I heard someone come in and slide into the free stall, groaning and breathing heavily. I usually check them if I get a chance. This one sounded exactly like somebody who was drunk, and it annoyed me because it can be a hassle to get rid of them. Sometimes I've got to call the officer to come help me. This girl, I thought, went directly into the free toilet and didn't close the door. At that point I was sure she was under the influence. I

40

went over to tell her to get out and then of course I saw it was a man."

"What did you do?"

"I was angry. I went straight to my corner and set off the alarm. They arrived almost immediately. In the meantime, I went over to see if there was anything I could do. At first, you see, I didn't realize he was dead. I thought he was drunk and had gone in to make foul. I told him to get up and go away. But he didn't move. Then I realized something worse had happened."

"And the police came."

"Yes, sure, after a few minutes. They lifted him out and that was the first they saw how he was cut up with a knife. But no one knew who he was yet, of course."

"Are you positive he came in alone?"

"That's what's so terrible, that I missed it. I heard the door and I heard his steps and his panting. But it would've been too late to save him—even if I'd been standing in the doorway to meet him—thank the good Lord for that, because otherwise my conscience would bother me my whole life. Though of course maybe then I would've seen who did it."

"And he didn't scream?"

"Definitely not. Then I would've rushed over at once."

"Did you look out into the anteroom or the central hall?"

"No. But, you see, I didn't know that—"

No one else had been in the bathroom at the same time. No one who'd been in the entryway between the restroom and the subway station contacted the police. Some people who'd been in the big subway hall at the time in question reported that they hadn't seen anything unusual. Nor had the ticket-sellers noticed anything.

The simple facts were that Sthen Malte Ludvig Carlsson, sixty-seven, had gone into a women's bathroom and died of internal bleeding inflicted by somebody with a sharp object.

We also tried to get hold of Carlsson's secretary, Mona Alm, but she refused to meet with us.

"He was a perfectly ordinary older male chauvinist," she

41

said on the telephone. "Well-meaning, nice, and completely naive."

I could sense that this was Katrin's area, so I let her take over.

"Don't you want to know who did it?" she asked.

"Naturally, I want to know who did it. But I don't know anything having the least bit of relevance to this incident. I had a good mind to do it myself many times, but I am, in fact, innocent and can prove it. My son had a couple of friends over and they saw me come in at 8:30 and not go out again. Is that good enough?'1'

"Can they testify to that?"

"Yes, they can. I'd had to work late, until eight o'clock, so I gave them a lecture about men's total lack of consideration. Poor boys, it didn't have anything to do with them. They were as sweet as could be and had vacuumed and taken out the trash to surprise me."

"To get back to Carlsson," Katrin said.

"We had no private relationship at all," said Mona. "I was not his lover. There is absolutely nothing I can tell you and when I left he was still at the chancellory."

That's as far as we got with Mona, the secretary.

Now it was time to look up the dead man's wife, Mrs. Märta Carlsson in Motala.

† † †

Katrin and I took the train to Motala. It was just after the Easter holiday and the whole world was a scrubby, yellowish-gray. The police station in Motala was located right down near the train, but we carefully avoided it so as not to be questioned about our interest in the case. Here, we were the ones who would be doing the questioning. We'd called and made an appointment to visit Mrs. Carlsson, presenting ourselves as exactly what we were, a pair of serious freelance journalists.

It was one of her sons who'd answered the phone, asking what the hell we wanted, and, when we'd introduced ourselves as journalists, couldn't we let a poor widow mourn her husband in peace? Damn hyenas, etc. etc. Katrin had been the one to call because we figured Mrs. Carlsson would rather talk to a woman, but now I grabbed the receiver, man to man. I said in a tough way that I was just as upset as he was, and what my wife and I wanted to do was write a penetrating analysis of the departed Carlsson's achievements and services, a formal obituary that would bring out his commitment to the poorer and weaker members of society. The son took the bait and wondered which newspaper I represented. I'd wished I could have in good conscience at least answered *The Workers Paper* in Malmö. But I knew it could be checked up on, so I told it like it was, that Katrin and I freelanced to spare ourselves having to write the kind of superficial drivel catering to the public that the evening press put out for the sake of competition. Instead, we wanted to do in-depth commentary that we could sell to the serious press. We presented the whole thing as a political/personal project and said nothing about our interest in the murder itself, so as not to appear vulgar. The Carlsson son said he would talk to his mother, which he did, and then returned with a time for an interview.

So we slipped discreetly past Motala's police station and over and under viaducts that had replaced the inner town in the glorious sixties. Now the community was struggling like all the others with layoffs and unemployment. A sharp wind swept symbolically over the soft hills (artificial) with their tulips that had been kicked apart. Formerly, a central district of wooden houses had occupied the area.

We were on foot, asking directions as we went. It wasn't far. The house was a single-level home from the forties, one of the first that workers had been able to acquire with their own money. The flower garden was swarming with crocuses and snowdrops. The door was opened almost before we got a chance to ring the bell, and there was a scent of freshly baked bread coming from within.

The woman who answered the door was little and chubby, with a tight permanent in her gray hair. She was drying her hands on her apron while behind her shoulders, a tall man was looming up in the entryway to the living room. Before she had time to get a syllable out, he stepped forward, saying:

"Carlsson!"

"Skafte," we introduced ourselves. Mrs. Carlsson looked nervously between us and her son and we didn't really know which one of them to address. But it was Mrs. Carlsson who showed us in through the opening to the living room, which had a curtain, not a door, and invited us to take a seat on an upholstered piece of furniture in neo-rococo. Old-fashioned, pleasant, a bit exaggerated. Katrin admired the potted plants and Mrs. Carlsson commented on each and every one of them. The son and I stood with our hands behind our backs checking each other out.

"Terrible tragedy," I said.

"It doesn't make any sense at all," said the Carlsson son. "That goddamned pack of murderers at Sergel's Square ought to be shot. His whole life, the old man worked for this fucking society, to give people a chance, and this was the thanks he got! Bullshit."

There wasn't much answer to that.

"Have the police dug up any clues yet?" I asked.

"Ha!" he shouted. "Do you think they're trying?"

"Yes—"

"I don't know what opinion you represent, or what party," he continued. "You don't represent any particular newspaper, right?"

"No."

"But you certainly know which side you're on?"

"Oh, for sure."

"Good. Then I can tell you in confidence that there must be one of those damned international drug syndicates behind this. Think about it! Who else?"

Now Katrin and Mrs. Carlsson turned, coming up to us, and he quit talking as his eyes met his mother's. We sat down and Mrs. Carlsson went out to get the coffee.

"This is awful," said Katrin. "What a dreadful blow for you mother!" He nodded and started moving away again.

"Carlsson—what's your first name?" I asked.

"My name's Tommy."

"Yes, Tommy thinks there's a drug syndicate behind this," I said quickly.

"How so?"

"It happened down at Sergel's Square, of course, and you know very well what kinds of people tend to hang around there. When my father came along, he must have stumbled upon something. So he was silenced."

It sounded a bit tame after Tommy Carlsson's strong introduction. Just then, his mother returned and he restrained himself, seeming to swallow his rage.

"Please help yourselves," said Mrs. Carlsson shyly.

Katrin gave her a friendly smile. A shadow drew across Mrs. Carlsson's face and a tear dropped out of the corner of her eye. She bit her lip and took out a handkerchief.

"I'm sorry..." she said.

Katrin lay her hand spontaneously over hers.

"We understand," she said. "Forgive us for coming and imposing. We just wanted so much to see how he lived. And if possible, we want to write a fine article about him, to let others know what a good man he was."

Mrs. Carlsson sobbed quietly. Katrin put her arm around her shoulders and mumbled warmly and sympathetically. Tommy Carlsson glared at me across the coffee table and looked like he was sitting on a time bomb.

"You said something just now about drugs. Do you have any hard evidence in that direction? Did your father mention anything to you, for example?"

"Oh, the old man never caught on how hellish it is," Tommy said. "He lived in his own little world. A nice, good world, you know? He remembered the thirties and how shitty everything had been for the workers. We've come a long ways since then, in terms of our standard of living. That's all he saw, and he thought everything was still going forward. Didn't see what the bourgeois parties are up to, never realized they're in the process of destroying everything that's been built. He was an old-time socialist, you know, didn't see the bigger picture like you and I. He didn't see that the whole capitalist structure has to be changed."

"Do you believe anything political lay behind his death?"

Tommy fell silent, looking rather confused.

"Morality has been broken down by the bourgeoisie," he said. "You know perfectly well how it is. It pays better to work

45

under the table and speculate in property than to make an honest living. Organized crime is spreading like never before. Illegal money gets laundered while common wage-earners see their real income shrinking."

"Had your father uncovered something?" I asked desperately.

Mrs. Carlsson laughed apologetically.

"Please, Tommy, can't you be quiet for a little while?" she said. "Do you really think our guests are interested in hearing all of this? They're here, you know, to write an article about Dad."

The voice was low and soft, but it cut through Tommy's barrage of words like a thread through butter. With a bit of show, he stopped talking, gave me a glance and poured some coffee.

"Tommy's theory is awfully interesting," I said to Mrs. Carlsson. "But it's so general, I mean, I don't suppose your husband could have had any personal enemies?"

"Everybody liked him," Mrs. Carlsson answered. "He entered political life as a teenager, in the thirties. It was during the war, and we hadn't met yet."

She told a simple and charming story about love, children, work and political struggle, with more and more progress over time, but nothing that shed any light on the meaningless murder of her spouse. We didn't have a tape recorder with us, but both Katrin and I had scratch pads that we used to take notes.

"They say he called you up that night?" asked Katrin.

"He called as usual. Said he'd be coming the next day."

"Did he mention anything about where he intended to go that evening?"

"He didn't say anything about himself. Just asked about me, if I was OK. That's the way he was."

Tommy, who was sitting on the couch, stuck out his chin as his mother sobbed again in her handkerchief.

"Where were you that night, Tommy?" asked Katrin. "Were you at home with your mother?"

"Tommy doesn't live here," Mrs. Carlsson answered for him. "Tommy lives with his girlfriend out in Öster. I suppose you folks were home too, expecting Dad to be coming back for Easter vacation, right Tommy?"

"Of course," said Tommy. "*What do you mean?*" He faced Katrin.

"No, nothing," said Katrin. "I was just wondering whether you'd also spoken with your father that night?"

He shrugged his shoulders and Mrs. Carlsson smiled apologetically.

"Tommy's so active politically," she said. "And Rosemarie, his girlfriend, is too."

"Naturally we wonder, like both of you, what happened after that conversation," said Katrin, leaning forward. "He didn't say anything earlier that might help explain—? Something he mentioned, maybe just in passing? Someone he'd gotten acquainted with?"

"Not that I remember," said Mrs. Carlsson. "I still can't believe it's true. I keep thinking he's going to be back again and every time the phone rings I think it's him. And that he'll say, 'I was just kidding, you knew that, didn't you?'"

She hid her face in her hands and Tommy fidgeted. Then she looked up again, trying to hold back her tears.

"It must have been some lunatic," she said. "It can't have been anyone he knew, surely you understand that? He was just so nice. Everybody liked him. He argued sometimes with those right-wing types, but not even they would actually—"

"They have their henchmen," said Tommy bitterly.

We tried carefully one more time to bring out what Sthen Carlsson had said when he called, and if he'd had some definite, personal enemy who might conceivably have been after him. But everything kept coming back to the same point—that it must have been a maniac, probably someone drunk or on drugs, maybe someone Carlsson had exposed committing a crime and who'd dealt the blows in order to silence him.

Of course that left the field wide open, infinite. There were any number of people like that out on the streets.

"Hassan," Katrin said suddenly on the train back to Stockholm.

"Who, did you say?"

"Hassan. The boy in Bergsgruvan."

47

"Margareta Åström's boyfriend?"

"Yes. I was just speculating about the common denominator between Hassan and Sthen. Because there is one, isn't there?"

I didn't know what to answer. Was there?

"Drugs?"

"Hassan didn't do drugs."

"But he could have dealt."

"He didn't have any money. He mooched off Margareta."

"He might've had money stashed away somewhere. Or he could have come upon something too. He could have threatened to reveal a drug pusher, exactly like Sthen Carlsson."

Our eyes met. This, finally, might be a clue to a clue.

MARTIN BJÖRKBOM, 45
Journalist and playwright, unmarried

Björkbom was active as a cultural journalist for several Stockholm newspapers. As a fairly well known figure, he was featured now and then in the weekly magazines' gossip columns, usually without the company of women. He lived alone with his cat in an Östermalm apartment. Björkbom was versatile both literarily and musically. He had a large circle of friends and an even larger number of acquaintances, but very few intimate companions.

Björkbom was found murdered in his home after he'd failed to show up for his appointments for three days, which worried his friends, who knew him to be punctual and reliable. Neighbors had heard the cat screaming for several days but hadn't given it much thought. The cat was a Siamese and known to be noisy; the neighbors had complained before. When the police made their entrance into the apartment, Björkbom was found lying prostrate in the living room, seemingly on his way to the telephone. His clothes were in disarray and the apartment was a mess.

Cause of death: repeated stabs with a sharp weapon in the stomach and abdomen.

Suspects: various intellecutal adversaries?

Björkbom was not known to be gay, but it was possible he'd been killed by some unknown man out of jealousy or anger.

† † †

Once again, it was time for the premiere and the review.

He'd already known how the play would be before he'd even seen it. And he'd seen it prior to this evening, suffering through a final dress rehearsal whose painfulness could only be compared with the volume of the actors' voices. He'd had to force himself *not* to resort to the hackneyed old phrase, "weak arguments, strong voices" in his review, certain that it would come out anyway in one of the others.

He was right.

He'd written a drama himself that had played during the winter—unfortunately not an especially long run, although it had been acclaimed by several of Stockholm's theater critics. The public hadn't understood the play, unobtrusive and low-key as it was, with an emphasis on the psychological interplay between the actors. It had proven to be too subtle for an audience accustomed during the past two decades to a theatrical style in which the leads shouted their lines right into the spectator's face, often with the help of cheering barkers. That type of theater bored him to death and he couldn't in good conscience neglect to point out how deficient he found it to be. Its origins had to be respected: the morality plays of the middle ages, Brecht, and political underground theater. But the simple leftist propaganda of the sixties, which had been new and fresh then, continued on into the eighties after the public had long since grown tired of it, after it had become petrified in stereotype and calcified cliché; this was something he couldn't regret more. Where had the nuances gone? The interaction? The sensitive innuendos? One more dressed-up clown yelling slogans over the footlights to the audience, and he would...

He detested the amateurism within the art, the philosophy that everything is equally good, everything equally important. After all, great art is that which has been created by great artists. When the little artists came in—the little craftsmen, the opportunistic advantage-takers, the uneducated amateurs, the political extremists, the navel-contemplating housewives, the immature youths, the shrieking female mafia—then there could only be one result.

He was sorry sometimes that he had to be firm in his attack on all pseudo-art. But there was no other way. A man has duties to himself, to his conscience, and to his circle of readers, even if that duty might be inopportune and make him unpopular in other circles. He admired and readily supported the new theater, which was vigorous, seething—what he was against was the old, institutionalized theater's rigid forms, with its omniscient decrees from above, its communist model for democracy. The hot new left stood closer to his own sense of values despite the fact that he characterized himself as having conservative tastes. Not only did he despise the established theater's fossilized quasi-revolution, but he was also bothered by the conservatives' cynical courtship of mass culture's most vulgar products, which they equated with serious art.

As if the terms could ever be equal in a competition between wood lice and dragonflies!

Tonight, it would definitely be an evening of wood lice. He was obligated to be there, and he would be seen.

Although he found the weekly magazines boorish, he considered it useful to be photographed and featured in them. The more people recognized his face, the more they would listen to his message. Unfortunately these were the prevailing conditions.

He surveyed himself in the mirror.

He was aware that a heaviness had begun forming under his jaw lately. His face had always been long and narrow, virile. His chin had been solid and definite, somewhat protruding. Now, unmistakably, the skin right in the joint between his chin and throat was beginning to sag. He raised his chin, stroking the skin with his hands, feeling it firm and tight under his fingers. But as soon as he relaxed and lowered his chin to a natural level, there it was again, baggy. It lay in wrinkles that were already defined. It wasn't more than a little while ago—not over half a year ago!—that everything had been taut. His skin had still closed around his jawbone and throat. Now there was a bag; he could take hold of it between his thumb and index finger like a fat woman can do with the spare tire around her waist.

Little drops of sweat broke out on his forehead, not because he was holding that one wrinkle in his hand—many had worse—but because this was the first step of an irreversible process.

He'd noticed it in people his age.

He'd seen thirty-year-olds with pot-bellies, thinning scalps and breadth around the rear-end at a time when he could still be taken for a teenager. He'd known he would never experience the same fate. Certain people had an earlier aging process genetically and they simply encouraged it by being slack and listless, eating and drinking too much, sinking into their fat and uniting themselves with it. They didn't *have* loose flesh, they *were* it. He himself had always been slender and toned up. He felt compassion for the others, but never any fear of becoming like them. He was simply a different kind of person.

Nowadays the men his age, between forty and fifty, had left behind the earlier days of beer binges and sitting around with the family, but their laziness manifested itself in a new way—as an unwillingness to take care of themselves. Their personal grooming seemed to be limited to public tooth-picking, and he shuddered to see pale-white, middle-aged men with a bald patch and long, tangled, gray-sprinkled locks hanging down to their shoulders, worn jeans and corduroy jackets. There was something of the old-style community teacher about this look, a paraded folksiness, as if it would be an insult to the masses to distinguish oneself from them through better grooming and hygiene. He had many colleagues in that category.

He felt an instinctive disgust for unkempt men, could never associate comfortably with them. He felt like they were laughing at him over his possibly exaggerated aestheticism. It was the same way with blue-collar workers. They were tough men who might consider him as a weakling because he occupied himself with education and culture.

He scrutinized himself in the mirror. Actually, he looked like a corporate executive, but the wrinkle wasn't very deeply creased yet. If he smiled and lifted his chin up a little, the sagging under his cheeks wasn't visible at all. If only he remembered to raise his chin a tad, it wouldn't be noticed.

This wasn't the real problem. Today, maybe no one would see anything, nor perhaps next week. But aging was on its way. It was going to creep up on him and the process would never go in the opposite direction. However long he succeeded in hiding

52

his chin line, it was there—and one day it would be a part of his being, something to be taken for granted as though it had always existed. He'd meet people, people he hadn't yet encountered, who'd know him solely as the man with chin bags, for they would never have seen him as he was before. Although the bags hardly showed yet, with time they would become an integral part of his person, a characteristic associated specifically with him.

For an instant he was seized by a sorrow so intense that more than anything else, he felt like staying home from the premiere. It seemed as if everyone would just be staring at his chin—how many had noticed it already? Was it something people were pointing out to each other? "Did you see Martin, don't you think he's gotten a double chin recently?" "No, not a double chin, more like a little bagginess." "Yes, he's gotten sort of flabby."

He closed his eyes, wishing everything away. He couldn't identify with the face in the mirror. His face had always been thin and—no, it was hopeless. He opened his eyes and examined the image in the mirror again. Was there anything he could do with his hair to get another look? Women usually tried that—although it was always obvious and actually quite pathetic, just tending to emphasize what they were trying to conceal. Even more pathetic were balding men's attempts to cover their skulls with all kinds of intricate loops that were displaced by the slightest breath of wind, held down with water and styling gel, really stuck down behind one ear after their origin from a low part all the way over by the other ear. He was embarrassed just seeing them, at their lack of dignity—their cowardice in not daring to stand up for who they were and how they looked.

Himself, then?

Indeed, yes, his hair lay where it should. Nicely kept, trimmed every third week.

But that damned chin line! When he stood completely straight in front of the mirror, it was apparent that there was something *under* his chin which had never been there before. The angle had changed from sharp to blunt.

He could also begin wearing higher collars on his shirts.

But this might be noticed, exactly like the balding men's hair loops, and taken for what it was, a sign of weakness and aging vanity.

A polo collar was another good idea. But there were probably quite a few others who'd tried that trick already.

An unbuttoned V-neck would undoubtedly make his throat seem more narrow and draw attention away from the jaw and chin.

But god, he hated unbuttoned shirts—hairy or not-hairy chests, they were both just as bad! He'd rather die than show himself in public with hair on his chest. It would mark him forever as one of those pseudo-intellectuals who try to be cool by appearing down-to-earth. The only thing missing would be the Jesus medallion!

He'd rather stand out as an old-timer.

And using a scarf or necktie would be just too, too affected.

Make-up he didn't even want to consider.

With that he'd come full circle and was back to the root of the problem, unsolved.

He stroked himself one more time in front of the hall mirror. If he kept his neck straight, it wasn't really perceptible. But checking his profile in the back mirror, there it was again—hanging down in the middle like the keel of a rowboat, that bit of loose skin.

It was definitely worse from the side. But of course you never see yourself like that. You view yourself from the front, and when he did that, only the bags furthest back between his cheeks and chin were noticeable. Maybe he could get some new glasses that would catch people's eyes—dark, powerful glasses. The rimless kind were beginning to be a little commonplace anyway, turning up on every Tom, Dick and Harry. It might be worth it to pay the optician a visit.

Actually it was only when he lowered his head—chin against throat—that the wrinkle appeared. You generally go around your head raised, of course, outside in public. You lower your head at work, leaning over the desk, and at home, with your nose in a book or eating at the table. The human being is simply not designed to keep the chin up in all of these situations—like the cartoon characters with lifted arms holding

54

a book up in the air. Maybe there are a couple of people who read like that, but certainly not the one for whom literature, the written and spoken word, is profession, hobby and life.

But on the other hand, it wasn't a problem yet at the theater. *There*, if nowhere else, you actually do sit with your head tipped upwards, the throat stretched, tight and intent as a bird's. Assuming, of course, that you're sitting in the orchestra seats, but that can always be arranged.

The cat came up, wanting to say goodbye. A beautiful, brown-masked Siamese.

"You don't get to come with me, Utrillo!"

Sometimes he came along to the office. Martin carried him in a basket, wishing he were a larger animal that could be taken on a leash. The simplest thing, of course, would be to get a dog; dogs were led with leashes, no problem. But a *dog*? They smell bad. Force themselves on you. Press. Humiliate themselves. Obey, fawn. Need attention. And are miserably rash when they're in heat.

A cat takes care of itself, with discretion and dignity. It was unpleasant carrying Utrillo by hand in a basket. Sometimes he meowed and silly old ladies had to stop and fuss over him. Little girls came up asking what the cat's name was. As if it made any difference to them. Dogs were so much more anonymous on the streets. Naturally, since there were so many more dogs there. What if the cat had been willing to lie across his shoulders like a shawl?

Imagine walking around on the city streets with a cat draped like a shawl over his shoulders! The critter did it at home, came and lay like a shawl while he was sitting and reading. Utrillo enjoyed that! But the cat pushed his head forwards, causing wrinkles—he would have to watch out for that. It could be the cat's fault.

At the same time, it was impossible to push the cat away.

A dilemma!

Solve the dilemma, get a dog.

He bent down and petted the cat, who was winding himself around his legs, crying.

"Utrillo, we agree about this. You don't like the basket. And I look ridiculous carrying it. Neither one of us likes the basket."

The cat abruptly gave up, turning its back on him and disappearing with a raised tail.

Martin met his own good-bye smile in the mirror. The smile deepened and his teeth were even and white.

Vale, victor!

† † †

He decided to go alone. Let them wonder! He invited it. The play was just as bad as he'd expected. Maybe even a little bit worse. The acting may have been even more pathetic. In his review, written after the dress rehearsal, he'd pointed out the difference in quality between the small, free, fierce, aggressive groups who stood for survival in a more and more regimented society and the state-supported, conventionally provocative art. For a moment it had crossed his mind that his own review was conventionally provocative, that he had merely burped up currently fashionable opinions. But he'd suppressed the thought, for the review would be published in one of the largest and most respected daily newspapers, the one everybody read nowadays.

Going to the play and the party afterwards was pure show. Posing in front of the camera. Waving, smiling, hugging friends.

Eva Svenberg came up and rubbed shoulders with him, an actress who'd gone to the dogs. It was said that she got the roles she, despite everything, still managed to get because she'd once been lovers with a certain producer. She didn't have a part in this play.

"Oh, so you sat this one out?" asked Martin, and she answered:

"Horrible performance, wasn't it? These days I choose my roles myself."

The deadly response he'd had on the tip of his tongue didn't get out before she left again, hurrying off into the crowd. It didn't really bother him that he hadn't gotten a chance to put her in her place. She was already there, poor thing.

"Well, what did you think? Wasn't it good?" Dagg-Marie, short for Dagmar Maria, the PR-woman for the theater who popped up everywhere, always exuberant, always enthusiastic, always sparklingly happy. He got a headache just looking at her. But she tracked him down, seeking his approval. She was one of those he could murder without even giving a damn, yet he was also moved by a certain feeling of pity and affection for her.

"Did you really think so?"

"I thought it was brilliant. We need more theater like this!"

He turned away from her and raised his chin several degrees as he was approached by Magnus Westerlund, the new oracle for the new newspaper. A dangerous man—sharp-edged, with a soft tongue, but out for the kill.

"Hey, old chap!"

"Why, look who's here! It's been a long time!"

Handshakes, pats on the back, then a photographer came up and Martin saw the malicious smile on the pursuing gossip-journalist's face:

"Just friends, or...?"

"Not even friends," said Magnus, measuring a blow to Martin's stomach. Martin didn't bother to answer.

The reporter—he knew her well! A magpie! Long blond curls, red lips, fluttering clothes, taller than most men, laughing, always laughing—she drew near again. He didn't want to look at her. She came up and pulled on his arm.He'd just barely had time to turn his back and now when she tugged at him, he had to act surprised that she was still there. "Hi, Martin Björkbom," she said with familiarity.

He eyed her coldly.

"I don't believe we are acquainted, Miss," he answered.

Her obtrusiveness repulsed him, but it wasn't only that. He was quite sure she worked for one of the most obnoxious women's magazines—famous people's divorces and new romances, parties and balls, parties and balls...

"Who's the guy I saw you with?"

She was also rude!

"Look, I'm here to see a play. It really is the stage which interests me. Not the people swarming around out here. I suppose that's more your department."

She was still hanging onto his arm.

"You wrote a play with a similar theme a year or so ago, didn't you?"

57

"Certainly not. I wrote a play with a completely different theme."

"Is that right, you know, I saw it and I thought they were very similar. What do you say we have lunch sometime and an interview?"

He made a quick calculation. The woman undoubtedly had contacts.

"For which magazine?"

She named the women's magazine and he pulled back his arm.

"We have a very large circle of readers," she appealed. "Many of them wonder how you live."

He shuddered.

"Well, how do you live yourself? What do you live on?"

She showed big, white teeth in a smirk.

"People's flesh, and you?"

"My dear, I think we can terminate this conversation," he said. "If you'd been a recognized journalist, there's no question I'd have granted you an interview."

He noticed that her smile stiffened to a grimace. Maybe it was less than well-considered to hit so hard. But the woman really wasn't going to leave him alone and she'd scarcely be able to do anything for him. Write a gossip column with insinuations about his private life? It could only be insinuations, after all. He would neither affirm nor deny and nobody else would either. He kept his private life to himself, and they could write whatever they wanted, but they didn't know a thing about it. The public would have to be content with guessing.

The Great Actor emerged, wanting praise, as always. For lack of a mane, he shook his whole head, tossing it from side to side. His penetrating bawl could be heard over the crowd's hum. He was full of self-admiration for his interpretation of the role. Martin would have preferred to avoid him, but the Great One had spotted him and was making his way forward.

"What did you think, old buddy? Well? What did you think?"

"Wait till the newspaper comes out tomorrow."

"Come on, be a pal! Say something! You can whisper, anyway, OK?"

A circle of admirers gathered around them, including the faded actress who'd been trying to make herself noticed. She said something to the actor, but he ignored her, continuing to develop his plea with Martin.

"You were super, Hugo! The way you sort of underplayed—"

"Hey, Björkbom, that was a different kit and caboodle, huh? This is what theater should be. You have to think of the audience, too, really give them something!"

"It was like when I played Millicent," continued the actress persistently. "I applied that technique too, kind of concentrating on—"

The actor became aware of her and blinked for a moment as if he didn't know who she was. Maybe he really didn't recognize her. Martin took advantage of the reprieve to try to contact a friend, an actor about his age who hadn't been in the play. The actor had also caught sight of Martin above several heads in the crowd and was heading over, waving his hand. Martin turned away from the rivaling actors and went in that direction.

An arm got stuck in under his own and a voice was heard very close by.

"Hi."

A soft, quiet "hi." He looked to the side. A small girl, a complete stranger.

"Hi."

"You don't know who I am..."

"No idea."

"You write reviews."

"Yes."

"I've read all of your articles. I think you write very well."

"Thank you."

"Especially what you've said about stagnation within the institutionalized theater and the renewal that's needed and that's coming from the outside, from the independent groups. Wasn't it atrocious tonight?"

For the first time since he'd left home, he smiled.

"Disgusting."

"Wasn't it gross when he stood there yelling right out at the audience? I can't stand it when they treat us like nursery school kids, but that's what they're doing in these productions. Haven't they realized that the sixties are over?"

He looked at her with greater interest. Little, dark, slender, with enormous gray-green eyes.

"You're definitely new here. What's your name?"

"Lila Ljungblom."

"Lilac heather blossom. That's an unusual name."

"I'm an unusual woman."

They stood facing each other, smiling at one another, and he felt an expectation he hadn't experienced for a long time.

Could she be the theater companion he'd been searching for?

"Where have you been hiding yourself?" he exclaimed. As the approaching actor arrived, he said, "My young lady, this is *my* friend!"

Painful. Just the right opportunity for that sort of...

At the same time, the magpie advanced with greedy eyes. Was she hoping to witness something as spicy as the formation of a triangle? She had her photographer in tow. He was fat and sweating freely in the glare of the lights. To make matters worse, he was dressed in a wool sweater and sporting a full beard.

The girl said nothing. She turned her face to the photographer, who took a picture.

"A budding new romance?" asked the journalist. She held up a pad with a pen poised above it.

"God, you're a fool," said the girl's clear voice. "Obviously, Mr. Björkbom and I were discussing the play."

"And who is the lady?" the journalist asked Martin.

"Do you have a new girlfriend?" asked his friend, just as interested.

"I haven't the slightest notion who she is," answered Martin, irritated.

"Lila Ljungblom," said Lila Ljungblom, smiling at the photographer.

† † †

"Hey!" said Katrin excitedly at the breakfast table.

It was a Thursday morning at the end of April. There was

warmth in the air. Spring had come early and the bushes were already green.

"Say what?"

We'd seen it on the TV news the night before. One of our most renowned critics, Martin Björkbom, forty-five, had died suddenly. He'd made a name for himself by discovering several obscure German poets and introducing Nobel Prize winner Heinrich Böll to the Swedish public, according to the news report. Martin flickered by briefly on the screen, a still photograph, thin and intellectual-looking with a hint of a middle-aged double chin. Is that so, Björkbom is dead, we'd said to each other then. He hadn't been a friend of ours, though we knew who he was—our paths had happened to cross now and then. He was a fellow who kept his distance. Katrin had stood beside him once in a cafeteria line at the Film Center, recognized him and said hello, but he'd hardly responded at all. She'd said a few words about a film guru whose lecture they'd both just enjoyed, and, she assures me, he not only refrained from answering, but even looked right through her as if she weren't there. Over her head, he interrupted her in mid-sentence to begin a conversation with a well known male journalist who was standing behind her.

"Serves him right," Katrin said. "It must have been some young woman he'd invited home and tried to do something sadistic with."

That was pure fabrication on Katrin's part, because the TV news hadn't mentioned anything about murder. However, there it was in Thursday morning's newspaper, producing Katrin's shocked gasps.

"Stabbed to death with a knife!" she shouted.

"Who?"

I tried to grab the paper away from her, but she resisted. I took the other paper and we read together, like a dialogue:

"Martin Björkbom, forty-five, noted theater critic and contributor to this newspaper was found murdered yesterday in his apartment in Östermalm. He was last—"

"—and a correspondent for this newspaper was found murdered yesterday about 4:00 pm at his home in Östermalm. His life had been taken—"

"—by several knife wounds in the stomach and abdomen!"

"Amazing!" yelled Katrin.

"Zacatecas strikes again!"

"Another knife murder!"

"Wait, it could be something else altogether. Let's go on!"

"Björkbom was last seen on Saturday at the Stockholm Theater's premiere of *Dr. Arnheim's Affairs* and since then he had not..."

"Neighbors notified the police when they heard commotion coming from the apartment and no one answered the door despite repeated attempts. The source of the noise proved to be Björkbom's cat, who—"

"Just think of the evening papers!" interrupted Katrin. "Kitty alone for three days with master's corpse. Will Pussy Måns, three years old, ever be able to forget—"

"What did you say?"

"The cat!"

"Poor creature. Well, anyway—now the police are investigating who was last seen with Björkbom. After the premiere, he was spotted with some friends at a pub in Östermalm. One of those friends is being interrogated by the police."

Katrin put down the newspaper.

"I see."

"Yes indeed," I saw it too. It was someone he knew.

"Homosexual?" asked Katrin.

I shrugged my shoulders to indicate that I didn't know anything about that area.

"If there's any reason to think so, the newspapers will certainly have a field day with their speculations. Wonder who the pal was who came home with him."

We were soon to find out.

For you see, Cilla Olsson phoned Katrin. She'd also read the news in the morning paper.

Cilla Olsson is an old friend of Katrin's—in fact, they were school chums. Cilla is an up-and-coming journalist in the magazine business. She reports mostly about famous personalities, but has her sights set on investigative journalism in the long run.

Anyhow, she'd been at the premiere. She was one of the last people to have spoken with Björkbom.

Katrin called Cilla, and Cilla called Katrin, and finally they got hold of each other. I listened in on the extension, making my comments.

"Cilla, what happened! Why, you were practically in on the act! Don't tell me you're the one who did it?"

Cilla laughed on the other end.

"God, you don't really think *I'm* the one he invited home for a tête-à-tête? He barely agreed to open his mouth to speak to me. He didn't say a thing about how he was going to be murdered, and he categorically refused to give me an interview. At least that's how I understood it. Now, unfortunately, it's too late."

"Have the police been to see you?"

"You bet! Watch out, there's probably a wiretap on the telephone."

"Tell me, what do you know?"

"The police aren't saying very much. Just a little hush-hush with their hands on their revolver holsters."

"Have you been questioned?"

"I've had a conversation, as they say. When I heard what had happened, I called the police to say I'd seen him that last night and ask them what they knew. They asked me what I knew, and we carried on like that. Now I'm going to try to write an obituary. Of course I never did get an interview, but you know, something like, 'Martin's final words to me before he died—did he have a premonition?'"

"What *were* Martin's last words to you?"

It got quiet in the receiver. I'd expected Cilla to come up with some hot new item—she was a woman who could do that. Instead she was silent. I waited, holding my breath.

"Did he say anything that—could be an indication in some way?" wondered Katrin. Cilla's voice came back.

"I don't know whether I dare say any more over the telephone," she said. "Oh, OK, I do have an alibi. He said something very personal and very cruel to me, something that I hadn't intended to forgive him for if he'd kept on living and absolutely don't intend to forgive just because he died."

"Now don't tell me you took what he said seriously?" asked Katrin. "He was mean to everybody. Me, he merely ignored, but I'm sure he's been on other people's cases and hassled them—authors and actors and other reporters. What did he say to you?"

"He expressed his opinion about my capacity as a journalist," said Cilla. "There are probably ten times as many people who read what I write compared with him. And I've never condemned any human being in my columns or anywhere else. Besides, I thought his play was flat."

"I bet that's what he couldn't take," comforted Katrin.

"Anyway, I'm not the one who was holding the knife. Too bad," added Cilla.

"What do you know about him otherwise?" continued Katrin.

"Forty-five years old, born in Gotland. Survived by an aged mother. Quite lengthy studies at universities in Lund and Germany. In recent years, he left literature and went over to drama. Especially German drama, of course; he introduced Kroetz and Strauss, but lately he'd turned away from the realistic every-day theater and gone back to his classics. His play was staged at the Little Theater last winter and all of his cronies liked it, but the audiences didn't show up."

"He didn't, I don't suppose, lean particularly to the left?" I wondered.

"What do you mean by left?" asked Cilla, and we all laughed.

"Actually," Cilla went on, "I believe he was somewhere in the middle. He went neither to the left nor the right far enough for it to be noticed; he didn't dare. He was quite a lily-livered type. Only associated with people who couldn't hurt him."

"What was the last you saw of him?"

"The last I saw, he was talking to Christer Nilsson and some little gal. I don't know where she came from. I got him and her on a couple of Hasse's shots and she gave her name as Lila Ljungblom. I asked Martin if I could get an interview with him and he said no in a very rude and cocky way, but since I'd established some kind of contact with him, nevertheless, my head editor thought I should get hold of him again to try to get him to cooperate. My boss figured we could take it on as a challenge. So I've been calling him off and on all week long, and you can imagine my surprise when—"

"Do you know anything about how he died?"

"Stabbed with a knife."

"When?"

"They don't have the autopsy results yet, but it probably happened on Saturday night. After the premiere, in other words. They say his cat was already screaming on Sunday, so most likely he was dead by then. And on Monday he was unreachable—just ask me, I started calling at 9:00 in the morning. By the way, the police have a suspect."

"Oh, who?" we shouted simultaneously.

"Ugh," said Cilla. "Apparently Christer Nilsson has admitted as much as being with Björkbom all the way to the door. The worst of it is that Christer doesn't have an alibi. And they say it was pretty messy in the apartment. Like after a struggle."

Christer Nilsson. A sensitive actor. Never any great name with audiences, still waiting after age forty for the definitive breakthrough. Brilliant role interpretations in small and quickly forgotten productions. Seldom seen on film and never on TV. Maybe one of our greatest actors right now. In a few years, he'd begin to age and everything would be too late.

"Did he have something going with Björkbom?" I asked.

"No idea. Both of them, you know, acted a bit refined and sophisticated. But Christer is an artist and Björkbom was a smart second-rater. Who knows?"

† † †

Strangely enough, it turned out to be more difficult to get hold of Christer Nilsson than the mysterious Lila Ljungblom.

After he was released, Nilsson went underground. That was typical of him—a cleverer, tougher guy would have stuck around cashing in on the advantages of having come into the limelight, where natural talent and twenty years of hard work hadn't managed to bring him. Now, suddenly, all of the magazines wanted his life story—second and third-string friends came forth to testify what a fine and good person Christer Nilsson was. He was lauded for role interpretations that no one had paid any attention to until now, and inquiries were made immediately regarding the future theater productions.

He himself was conspicuous by his absence.

On the other hand, Miss Lila Ljungblom popped up, spirited and gay. She notified the police as soon as she realized she was one of the last people to have seen Martin alive. Lila Ljungblom lived in south Stockholm, in one of the few old houses that had survived the modernizing frenzy of the seventies. We found out that she had a one-bedroom flat with a tiled stove and a wash basin but no telephone. We wrote a letter asking if we could come over to get an interview. She answered that if it didn't make any difference to us, she would just as soon meet in town; she was juggling a bit with her finances, so maybe we could take her out to lunch? It took gall to say it, but it was disarmingly honest at the same time, and of course we could deduct the expense. We all met at Tim's on Timmermans Street.

"It was right outside here!" exclaimed Katrin as we emerged from the South Station. I saw the park to the west of the station. This was where Hassan had met his fate six weeks ago. Even so, it was as though we found ourselves in a totally different city. Hassan had died on snowy slush and now we were looking at a smiling green park. The trees were still bare, but they had that brown-violet shimmer about them—every year I liked to check on the birch standing in its vale at the South Station, always being one of the first trees to burst into leaf—and the bushes were completely adorned with healthy little green foliage. Crocuses and snowdrops were already in bloom, and white and yellow narcissus were swarming in the flower bed.

We ran into Lila outside of the restaurant. She wasn't really as pretty as the newspapers had led us to believe. She looked quite ordinary and it was clear that she wasn't eighteen years old, but more like twenty-eight.

She ordered fillet of beef with morel sauce.

"Since your newpaper's paying for it anyway," she said calmly.

When we told her that we freelanced, she was surprised and offered to pay for her meal. We reassured her by pointing out that we could deduct the expenses.

"Actually, I'm deceiving you about this," she said. "I don't know anything about Martin Björkbom."

"What we wondered most was whether he'd said anything in particular to you that night," I explained. "You were apparently one of the last people who really spoke with him."

"True, but I don't know him," she said. "We'd never seen each other before, and of course we didn't see each other afterwards."

"Then how did you happen to jump on him there?" Katrin wanted to know.

"And who are you; what do you do?" I asked.

I knew approximately, because I had read an interview with her in *The Express*. But she could just as well do her part for her good lunch.

Lila studied theater history at the university. She supported herself with odd jobs as a caregiver in the home for handicapped and elderly people and through occasional small roles with independent theaters. She seemed to be somebody who barely managed to get by. Studied, worked, roamed around meeting people—no real foothold in life. With cheap rent and free meals now and then, one could probably survive for quite a while, even if that sort of existence got harder and harder to maintain in the computerized society.

"I'd gotten a free ticket to the premiere," she said. "In fact, I thought the play was very bad, but then I caught sight of Björkbom there in the crowd. I usually read what he writes and couldn't resist the opportunity to hear directly from him what he thought. Of course I would have preferred talking about it more properly—not just gabbing in the lobby, but actually sitting down and discussing, conversing. He was quite an authority, you know."

"You seem to have had a very fine rapport with him," I said rather sarcastically.

"Yes, indeed. I'd just gotten him interested when Christer Nilsson showed up, and he certainly didn't appreciate seeing me there."

"Do you know him?"

"Christer Nilsson? No, but naturally I recognized him. He's also among those I admire. I thought for a moment I could kill two flies with one blow—imagine getting to talk theater with both Martin Björkbom *and* Christer Nilsson!"

She beamed at us, and I wondered whether her innocence was genuine or feigned.

"They're both gifted men," she continued, as though she'd read my mind. "Especially Christer, perhaps. But he wasn't the least bit entertained by my company. I asked Martin if I could meet with him some other time to continue our conversation. I don't have a phone, you know, so he gave me his number and said I could call."

Here she got a little pale around the nose and set down her knife and fork.

"Did you call?" asked Katrin.

She nodded.

"When?"

"Several times. I started on Sunday."

"Did you get an answer?"

She threw me a murderous glance.

"So that's all?"

"That's it," said Lila, wiping the sauce up from her plate with a soft piece of bread.

"I just have to ask one more thing," I said. "Are you really named Lila?"

She finished chewing and swallowed before she replied: "As a matter of fact, my name is Lillian. But Ljungblom is true."

We parted outside of the restaurant, watching her go down towards Horn Street with swinging skirts. She hadn't brought us one step closer to answering the question: who did Martin go home with after the premiere?

When we finally located Christer Nilsson, it was purely by chance. We were in Stockholm's Old Town to investigate an entirely different matter and tumbled into a place on Ny Street. There he was, sitting alone in a corner. Katrin grabbed hold of my arm, nodding in his direction.

The guy looked awful. His hair was dirty and stringy and his handsome face was covered by an uneven stubble of beard. He sat clutching a bottle of red wine with both hands, staring down at the tablecloth, seemingly unaware of the surrounding world.

Most people probably wouldn't even have recognized him.

I nodded back at Katrin and we went over to his table. He looked up, appearing to have trouble focusing his eyes. He shook his head and waved his hand to get us to go away.

"Christer," said Katrin softly.

"Leave me alone," he said. "Go to hell."

I went over to the counter and ordered, letting Katrin be responsible for the initial contact with Christer. I saw her sit down beside him and put her hand on his. He was still shaking his head and drops were falling out of his nose. I'd already noticed that he was under the influence, not just of wine.

When I returned, tears were streaming down his face and getting lost in his beard. Katrin was patting him on the cheek. I'd equipped myself with red wine for Christer's sake and now I poured some into his glass. He tried directing his red-rimmed eyes at me.

"Who's that?" he asked in a grumpy tone of voice.

"That's my husband," said Katrin. "Never mind him."

I felt quite superfluous at the table. Christer sobbed gently against Katrin's shoulder and there I sat, pouring more wine to get his tongue to loosen the way his nose and eyes already had.

"Would you like for us to help you home, Christer?" I asked. "Where do you live?"

He looked at me as if he didn't comprehend a thing, then turned back to Katrin.

"My husband, you know," she said. "Should we ask him to leave?"

"Doesn't matter," said Christer, "doesn't damn well matter."

"Christer, you're terribly depressed," I tried again. "Shouldn't we help you home?" For the third time, he attempted to look at me and failed.

"Well obviously Christer's sad," Katrin took the opportunity to interject. "You know what Christer's been through lately. Lost his good friend and then got suspected on top of it."

"Exactly," said Christer, nodding.

"You really liked Martin, didn't you?" she continued.

Christer raised his head, wiping his nose with the back of his hand.

"He was—buddy. Martin, we've known each other for twenty years. Could always call. Stuck together if anything happened."

"I know," said Katrin, and her hand closed around his.

"Martin was a friend like that for you?" I asked, and Christer nodded.

"He was a guy who knew how to live. Did his own thing, went his own way. Was his own man. Never went along with anything he didn't believe in."

"Just like you."

"That's right. And here I sit, drunk and alone and old and rotten. That's what happens when you think you're somebody. You get a knife in yourself or else you sit around like me."

"You're a fantastic actor, Christer," said Katrin quietly.

"Why, everybody knows that. Ask anyone."

"Who the hell are you to say so? I know damn well how good I am! Who the devil are you, you cunt?"

Katrin recoiled and I bent forward, grabbing hold of his shoulder and saying:

"Hey Christer, take it easy now, huh?"

Katrin moved farther away and folded her arms.

"Come on, Christer, she didn't mean anything! Cool it, OK? Sure as hell you're a good actor!"

He relaxed a little and it was as though he suddenly noticed me. Katrin was moved to the obscure place in his consciousness that I had just occupied.

"OK," he said. "It's just that I can't stand being patronized. You see, Martin was a damn fine fellow. A pal. He was a guy you could always count on."

"You must have been one of the last people to see him," I said.

"Don't start jabbering like a goddamned cop," he answered with an ironic glint in his eyes.

"No, shit, that's not what I mean. I mean, you were friends up until the very end, right? You and he."

"That's for sure," said Christer.

"Did you talk about anything in particular that night?"

"He had that little girl tagging along. But we decided to get a beer anyway, so we went to the bar there by his place and met these two other guys, I mean guys who lived there and they all used to meet at the bar now and then. Throw darts and stuff."

The men had reported themselves and been cleared from the list of suspects. They were a ship broker and a bank clerk from Östermalm, some of the regular patrons of the bar, who didn't have anything to do with Björkbom privately.

"So who was the girl?"

"We got rid of her. Martin saw, you know, what she was after. Clinging broad. He said she could call sometime, and then we left."

"Was it Martin, perhaps, who supplied your drugs?" I wondered.

Christer watched me speechlessly for a moment. Then he took aim with his fist. I managed to duck and Katrin ducked in the opposite direction. Left behind was Christer, lying halfway across the table as the bottle of wine toppled to the floor. A waiter came up to the table.

"I'm going to have to ask you to leave," he said. "OK," answered Katrin, standing up. "We're just trying to get our friend home."

I went around the table and, with the waiter's help, lifted Christer to a standing position. The only hitch was we didn't know where he lived. If worst came to worst, we could take him home with us.

Christer seemed to sober up when we came out on the street. At the same time he collapsed, becoming somehow weaker.

"Sorry I'm being such a bastard," he said. "But it's just too much all at once."

"Did Martin buy your stuff?" I asked once again.

"You're crazy," he answered with some of the aggression back in his voice. "All that goddamned punk ever touched was sherry and vintage wine!"

We stashed him in a cab and I sat beside Christer in the back while Katrin took a place on the front seat. The driver

71

asked where we were going.

"Where do you live, Christer?"

He just mumbled. We had to take him home with us. By the time we got there, he was already asleep. I dragged him into the bathroom, got as many clothes off of him as I could, and put him in the shower. When I'd rinsed him off, I lay him down on the couch.

It was a subdued Christer Nilsson who met us the next morning. He knocked softly on our bedroom door, and when I called out a reply, he stuck his head in shyly. "Oh, it's you guys," he said. I had to laugh.

"Where did you think you were?"

"No idea. May I borrow some things to shave with?"

Clean-shaven, he wanted to make us breakfast and pay for his keep. We assured him that it'd been a pleasure to put him up.

Katrin warmed up again in response to his bashful charm and friendliness. Now he related more coherently how Martin Björkbom had been one of his very oldest friends. The death had been a hard blow for him, intensified and aggravated by his being suspected at first of the murder.

"But it *wasn't* me," he said, fixing his bloodshot blue eyes on us. "I swear! We left from the bar together and I wanted to come on in with him. But Martin said he was tired; we could chat some other time."

"Was there anything between you and Martin?"

Christer shook himself.

"What do you mean, between us?"

"Was he gay?"

Christer looked me in the eyes for a long time before answering.

"*We* didn't have anything going, anyway. Not like that. If that's what you mean."

"Was he with others?"

"Hell," said Christer, "I don't know. We never went into that. We didn't talk about such things. He kept his distance, you know. Maybe he was like King Gustav III, only turned on by old ladies."

"Well, somebody's got to know what turned him on," I said, irritated. "He must have had something going with somebody at some time."

"Not necessarily," said Christer. "Some people simply aren't interested. There are old spinsters who've never been with a man, and old bachelors too."

Even so, his theory sounded improbable. This was Martin Björkbom we were talking about, not some simple country boy who lived with his parents.

"Who do you think could have murdered Martin?"

He looked tormented.

"I think he'd already invited someone over. That's why he didn't let me come in. And this person—wanted something different from him."

It was quiet around the table. Christer swallowed hard and we all probably saw the same image in our minds....

"Christer, did Martin provide you with anything?"

"No, like I said," answered Christer emphatically. "Martin didn't have anything to do with stuff like that. Besides, you're wrong if you think I do drugs. It was just that one time. I swear."

"Where did you get it?"

"Oh, it's as easy as can be. You've got to know that."He was right there. And yet, was this where the connection lay? Hassan Karim—Sthen Carlsson—Martin Björkbom? Did each case somehow involve drugs?Christer got up and thanked us. He begged our pardon a thousand times for troubling us. He embraced us both warmly in parting. We watched him walk to the subway after he left our house.

"Poor guy," said Katrin. "He's so damn talented, why does he have to have such a hard time?"

"Maybe he has to have such a hard time because he's so damn talented," I suggested.

"And you can't do a thing about it, either."

We both felt a little sad after the meeting with Christer. Not just because of his own situation. But also because he seemed to be the first and only person who mourned Martin Björkbom, as far as we knew, aside from an aged mother in Gotland.

CURT SAMUELSSON, 34
Computer systems analyst, salesman.
Married, two children.

Found lying near an exercise trail along Mört Lake in Täby. Had gone to a business dinner the evening before with Japanese visitors and not come home all night. Was discovered by two joggers at 6:34 am on a Sunday morning in the beginning of June.

His wife broke down when she was informed. She didn't know her husband had had any enemies. The marriage had been happy. His wife was employed part-time as a physical therapist at Danderyd Hospital. For two years, they'd lived in their own house. Good financial situation.

Suspects:

The wife?

The Japanese businessmen?

Some third person whom Samuelsson met after he left the Japanese clients, according to their report, on Svea Avenue about 2:45 am?

Cause of death: repeated stabs in the stomach and kidneys with a sharp object. Had not been robbed, was not gay. An exhibitionist? Unlikely, according to his wife. The sex life between the spouses had been good.

† † †

The day had begun well. It was one of the first hot days in June, when the summer burns like a welding flame. The windows were open, the Venetian blinds pulled down, and the heat already strong at 6:30 am when Curt put his arm around Inger from behind and cuddled up next to her. She was still as-

74

leep and protested half-heartedly. He pressed himself closer. Her drowsy resistance changed into contented acceptance. His hands gently held her breasts (they'd gotten smaller after the children, small and saggy) and her response came when he slowly entered her from behind.

Saturday and Sunday mornings were practically the only times they had—the other days they had to get up quickly; dressing and eating breakfast, getting the kids to day-care. Curt often came home late in the evenings, so often that the issue of whether it was she who'd gotten moody and bitchy in her old age or he who neglected her and the children had become one of their recurring arguments.

Curt couldn't help it that he enjoyed his work. The pleasure was an extra bonus beyond everything else he found satisfying about his job. It was a difficult field, but he loved it. He'd been in it since the beginning, when people used to talk about computing machines, and the machines in question were as big as houses. Now it was down to micro-chips and the whole thing was still progressing, with new innovations all the time, continual development. He could work day and night and never get tired of it!

The computer was going to take over everything and it still had a long ways to go; not even a fraction of humanity's knowledge was stored on computer yet. Curt had his entire life ahead of him, full of exciting and interesting work, and he could hardly wait to plunge into every new project.

Inger ought to be grateful. Not everybody had husbands who were as happy with their jobs or earned as much money. Two years ago, they'd been able to sell the condominium in Akalla and invest that amount in the house in Täby. On paper, he was a millionaire! They had it made where they lived now. Inger got to be with the kids and still go out and work half the day—meet other adults, get the stimulation she needed—and the children had a good day-care sitter. Many people would consider her privileged. When she complained about his not being at home, he'd learned to turn a deaf ear. He didn't really have anything against her going out and entertaining herself on her own; her mother lived in Täby and was always willing to babysit.

Actually, there weren't any problems at all.

Especially not on a Saturday morning in June with the hot sun and two sweating bodies in an accelerating embrace and the whole day ahead of them, the whole day—

Before they climaxed, they heard the children's voices, shrill and sharp and nearby, and they had to rush the last part. When the door opened, Curt lay panting beside Inger as she stroked the sweat off of his face and tried to force her own breathing to be calm and even. Her heart was still pounding like a jackhammer.

"Mama, Patrik hit me!"

Rickard jumped into bed, with Patrik after him. "Papa! He took my radio-car!"

Patrik caught hold of Rickard by the heel and punched him on the head. Rickard started howling. Inger moaned and crawled under the covers, pulling them over her head. Curt sat up in bed, trying to come between Rickard and Patrik.

"Goddammit, kids! Can't you leave us alone one single Saturday morning?"

"Don't swear at them," mumbled Inger from under the covers. "They pick it up so easily."

So a Saturday morning that began better than most had become a completely ordinary day.

They brought breakfast out onto the patio where the sun was shining from the south. Inger, wearing her bathrobe, was afraid she was getting a headache. The abrupt transition from the sun-golden, sweat-glossy morning to the usual yelling and ruckus had made her clammy.

Inger's mother, Barbro, came over for lunch. Curt played with the children and took the chance to get some telephoning done while the women prepared the food. After lunch, the boys wanted to go swimming. Curt protested—the water was still too cold. But when the mercury in the thermometer nudged 30°C, he had to give in to the children's whining. Barbro was also eager to get outdoors. She worked at an office in town and valued her weekends, wanting to make the most of every minute. Inger had planned to stay home and clean house, but

Barbro said that was out of the question, instead they could all three help out when they got back. All three!

At the lake, Curt chased the jubilant boys in and out of the water while Inger and Barbro sunbathed on the beach. After they'd come home and were having coffee on the patio, Curt said:

"I'll be leaving again at 8:00."

"What did you say?" asked Inger.

"Yes, you know," answered Curt. "The Japanese clients."

"What Japanese?"

"The Japanese. I told you before, have you already forgotten?"

"I don't know what you're talking about."

Inger's voice sounded a little thin, as though she was ready to cry. Barbro straightened up in her deck chair.

"Honey, I'm sure I told you about it. You must not have been listening. Hasse called earlier, while you were fixing lunch. It's absolutely imperative that I take care of these guys tonight. There's a super-big order in the works."

"Why doesn't Hasse go, then? He's the boss, you know."

"He's had them all week long—now it's my turn."

"Kalle Nicklasson, then?" asked Inger sharply. "Or else Bosse?"

Curt got up and left the table. He slammed the patio door behind him as he went inside. Barbro and Inger sat quietly, listening to his movements in the house. A little while later, they heard him go out through the garage door and right after that came the clatter of the lawn mower.

Both of the women rolled their eyes upwards, exchanging wry expressions. Barbro started to say something, but Inger waved the words away with her hands.

"I don't have the energy to fuss. It's too hot."

While Inger was cooking dinner, the subject came up again. She called for Curt to come and help with the potatoes, but he wasn't there. She went out into the garden and he wasn't there, either. The children were playing in the sandbox.

"Kids, have you seen Papa?"

They hadn't seen him. Barbro took the bait immediately.

"Where did he say he was going?"

"I don't know. Mama, will you go see if he's up there?"

Curt was standing in the bedroom busily changing his clothes.

"So, you're going out tonight?"

He didn't bother answering the obvious.

"If you want a babysitter, I think you could say so beforehand and not just take it for granted."

"We don't need a sitter," said Curt, being unnecessarily short.

"Why not?"

"Inger isn't coming."

Her mouth narrowed and she pivoted on her heels. In the kitchen, Inger had gone about doing the potatoes herself. Barbro rolled up her sleeves and began stacking dishes in the sink.

"You don't have to, Mama, I'm going to run the dishwasher."

Inger recognized her mother's clatter and knew what it meant—pent-up anger that she didn't dare express.

"And what is Curt going to do this evening that you aren't invited?"

"Oh, I don't know. He has so many meetings and conferences."

Whistling softly, with his keys jingling in his pants pockets, he walked past the kitchen door.

"Bye honey! Bye Barbro!"

"And where are you going, may I ask?"

He ignored his mother-in-law, coming up to Inger and embracing her. Inger brought her hands up to her face to push him away. He blew some strands of hair off of her forehead. Inger pulled back, nodding her head in Barbro's direction. She walked in front of Curt into the living room, closing the door.

"Did you really have to go and start trouble when Mama's here? Now she'll be harping about it as soon as you're gone!"

"What do you mean, trouble?"

"Well, where are you going that's so important, Saturday night and all?"

"How many times do I have to tell you we have Japanese

78

clients in town and it's my job to take them out?"

"Oh, I see, your job. Are you getting overtime pay?"

"Don't be such a damned nag! You like it that I earn good money, don't you?"

"I'd like it better if you were home one evening with the chidren!"

"OK, so you expect me to say I can't take out the Japs because I have to read stories to my children! Paternity leave, huh! What do you suppose Hasse would have to say about that?"

"Maybe he could go out with his Japanese himself?"

"He's had them all week long and he asked me."

"Couldn't he just as easily have asked somebody else?"

"Indeed, yes he could, and then that fellow would have been in good standing and gotten the bonus if the contract comes through. Shit, don't you see I have to stay ahead? Don't you realize that's what counts? I wonder what you'd say if I just sat there from nine to five and came home with a salary but no extras—you might have to work full-time yourself!"

"Don't blame me that I have to stay home half the day instead of getting a decent job!"

The children were standing with their noses pressed up against the patio door, listening hard. Little Rickard knocked on the window; Patrik pulled his arms to drag him back to the sandbox and Rickard screamed.

Inger gave up rather than continue the quarrel with the boys outside and Barbro probably eavesdropping in the hallway.

"Aren't you at least going to stay and eat with us?"

"When'll dinner be ready?"

"You could have helped, you know!"

"Well, I didn't this time! What's your mother here for?"

"Why don't you just go eat at some tacky restaurant with your Japanese," shouted Inger. "Go ahead and leave! I suppose it just ends up on the expense account anyway! And why can't I come too, are you all going out to a porn club, or what?"

"You know very well," said Curt, "that the Japanese never have women along on business dinners. It just isn't appropriate. Please try to understand?"

He smiled and took her around the waist, pressing where

79

he knew she liked it. Inger pushed his hand away.

"So when'll you be home?"

"I don't know yet."

The argument had lost its sting, but nothing had been resolved. He would go out and she would accommodate, exactly as if they hadn't talked at all, precisely as though nothing had happened. Inger turned her back on him and went to the patio door. The children were swinging and everything was peaceful and happy.

When she turned around again, Curt had left the room. He was adjusting the knot in his tie in front of the hall mirror. Barbro slammed the oven door, hard. Curt and Inger heard it and exchanged a glance, bursting into laughter. He took the opportunity to put his arms around her.

"Don't sulk anymore."

He pinched her breast and she moved away. Then he left.

† † †

It wasn't far from Mört Lake that Roger and Lasse found the corpse.

They'd been jogging together for a couple of years, every morning; their feet knew the path by rote. They didn't see the rocks and trees they rushed past. Their legs took the curves automatically.

He was lying a little ways from the trail but was completely visible. The feet were in neat black shoes, with thundercloud-blue socks sticking out.

"Hey, what the hell? It's a drunk."

"I guess we'd better move him. He can't just lie here like this."

They stood hesitantly, looking down at the protruding feet.

"Hey, let's leave him be. He'll probably get going himself once he wakes up."

"Someone could come along and trip."

"He doesn't seem like the type to get drunk out in the forest."

They couldn't see more than the lower legs, the well-polished shoes, the stockings that matched in color with the light summer suit. The upper body was almost concealed by the luxuriant grass.

"Maybe we should call the police."

"Oh, let's try and wake him up first." Lasse kicked the guy, quite hard, on the lower shin.

"Come on, man! Time to get up!"

There wasn't any movement. The leg he'd kicked was rigid. Lasse looked up, gazing unsteadily at Roger.

"You try."

Roger felt his uncertainty. The man's face was turned towards the ground, one hand was stretched out. They noticed an expensive-looking digital watch on his wrist.

"It wasn't robbery, anyway," said Roger timidly.

"Should we try to turn him over?"

"I've never seen a dead person before. I think we ought to get the cops."

"In any case, we should check—"

Lasse bent forward and turned the man face up. Then he saw the ants.

"He's lying on a goddamned anthill!"

But it wasn't an anthill. The ants had come there, enticed by the fresh blood that had run out of the man's cut-up, hacked-apart front side. The weapon had been a narrow, sharp-edged knife, which struck repeatedly, directly from the front and from underneath, towards the stomach, the kidneys, the diaphragm and the lower part of the lung.

Death had been torturous but mercifully quick.

Nothing appeared to be stolen.

Ring, watch, wallet remained. The wallet contained three hundred kronor in bills and three different bank cards, one private and two distributed by the company. The ID-card confirmed: Samuelsson, Curt Edvin, 480316-7254, programmer, Täby.

Katrin and I were abroad for a couple of weeks in June (visits to the theater and restaurants in London—imagine seeing Elizabeth Taylor!) so we nearly missed the story about Curt. It had already blown over by the time we returned. Since Curt's homicide wasn't some murder of a girl that could set the senses on fire, it soon disappeared from the news. A friend told us about it when we came home from London, knowing of our interest in murder in general and, nowadays, knife murder in particular. He hadn't gotten the idea of linking it up with Hassan, Sthen and Martin, except as another unsolved knife murder. Approximately one knife murder per week occurs in the greater Stockholm area, usually on Friday night, and usually involving people who have been drinking together. The motive is jealousy. The Curt-homicide definitely didn't belong in that category. Nor was there any reason to connect it with drugs, and therefore the newspapers had missed the possible tie-in with Hassan and Sthen.

We were sitting down in the Central Station having a beer, and our friend was relating what had been happening in the city during our absence. It wasn't really that much. Record temperatures, heat waves, water pollution and nude bathers. The cases of arson in Solna had been cleared up. Cases of murder, well... not many. Mostly booze parties where the perpetrator was hauled in immediately. And then that guy out in Täby, strange story, but couldn't it maybe have been his wife?

"What's this?" we wondered, our ears pricking up. And he gave the account.

Another friend of mine who's a crime reporter had gotten hold of one of the Japanese businessmen the next day and interviewed him. He offered us the material for what it was worth. An edited version had already been published in his local rag.

"It looked the devil like *harakiri*," he said, shuddering. "It was a gruesome murder. I've never trusted the Japanese; they're crafty somehow. I think they're involved."

"But *harakiri* means suicide," Katrin explained. "You can't perform *harakiri* on someone else."

My friend knew this. But he maintained that *harakiri* was Japanese—that's how they do it in Japan.

Katrin pointed out that there are also plenty of knife homicides right here in good old Sweden.

"I mean the nature of the knife itself," said my friend. "Because the police, you see, presented it as something special. The type of knife that was used. So thin, so narrow, almost like sheet-metal punched into a knife—hardly any thickness at all to the blade. Stabbed in every direction."

Katrin's and my eyes met and locked into each other's. We didn't have to say a word, we knew we were both thinking the same thing.

Hassansthenmartin.

"Some kind of stiletto, you mean?" asked Katrin, appearing completely nonchalant. "Did the investigators say anything else about it? Had the same murder weapon ever been used before or anything?"

"No," said the friend, "but the police could certainly be hushing something up. Were you thinking of anything in particular?"

We assured him that we were just spinning around in quite general terms.

We got his interview recorded on tape. It was in English:

"We've been in Sweden for a week. What a beautiful country! So clean!"

"You're all here as representatives of your firm?"

"We represent a company in the computer field that's in the process of negotiating with Swedish computer specialists about possibly working together to sell components—"

"Last night you were out with a Swedish agent, Curt Samuelsson?"

"That's right."

"A Saturday night? Business dinner?"

"What do you do in Sweden on a Saturday night, sir? We're a little perplexed. We've heard a lot about Sweden, you know, the freedom, the openness—Swedish women's, shall we say, goodwill? We've found that it corresponded poorly with reality."

The young Japanese man laughed politely to hide his disappointment.

"One night, we were invited to the home of the firm's director. Charming wife. Exquisite daughter. The house so tastefully—at ten o'clock, everything was over. We were back at our hotel. Indeed, the next day we asked ourselves well, what do you do in Stockholm?"

"What do you do?"

"What do you do if you have no family. Or wife along. Like us. Entertainment."

"Oh, I see."

"The next evening we went to a very elegant cabaret. Stylish furnishings, fine food, amazingly energetic performance. Everything was over by one o'clock."

"But during the days, weren't you all involved in bargaining talks?"

"Of course! But we had also hoped to get a chance to see more of your lovely city. We inquired in discreet terms and some gentlemen from the company were kind enough to show us what we wanted to see."

"And on Saturday night?"

"Then, as you know, we were out with Mr. Curt. We were a bit indecisive and he came into town to meet us at the hotel so we could all go out together."

"What time was it?"

"He came about eight o'clock."

"Then?"

"Then we proceeded to go out. Your town is radiantly beautiful! The light, the sunlight over the water very late at night!"

"Where did you go?"

"We went to a restaurant and ate. Then we wondered if there were any girls. He said he didn't know any, but there must surely be places. We'd heard that from other businessmen who've been here before. And eventually we did find a place."

"What kind of place?"

"A strip club."

"What did you do there?"

"We sat for a few hours. We really wanted to meet some of the girls personally. We asked our friend Curt to arrange it. He spoke with some of the girls and they joined us at our table."

"How many girls?"

"Three. There are three of us, you know."

"But what about your friend Curt?"

"He didn't want a girl. He stayed at the table and talked,

helping us with the translation and so on. We don't know any Swedish, you see, and the girls didn't know much English. We laughed and told stories, that kind of thing. We compared Japanese women with European women. There was a little disagreement over which were best."

"There was a disagreement? Serious?"

"Oh no, not at all. Joking. Mr. Curt observed that Japanese women are known for being submissive and wanting to please men. That annoyed the Swedish girls. They insisted that they placed greater emphasis on independence and having their own money. They made it clear they didn't let men tell them what to do. We pointed out that there are also some men, of course, who prefer dominant women and besides, there's one area where the Europeans greatly surpass the Japanese, namely with respect to the forms of the body. Their bosoms! Which they show! Even openly, on the beaches!"

"Did you sit there for a long time?"

"Until two, two-thirty or so."

"And then?"

"Sir, we are gentlemen."

"You, maybe, but I'm a reporter. Where did you go after that?"

"We three went to our respective hotel rooms."

"Each by yourselves?"

"Naturally."

"I mean, did you go alone to your hotel rooms?"

"Not actually alone."

"The girls came too?"

"Of course. They left this morning. Then we slept. The firm called to remind us about a meeting tomorrow, and then the police arrived. We regret the tragedy that happened to our friend Mr. Curt. We couldn't even suspect, when we parted—"

"Just a second, only a couple more questions. Do you know where Curt Samuelsson went after you all split up?"

"No."

"Where and when did you go your separate ways?"

"As I said, we came out of the club about two-thirty. It was already light, the sun was high in the sky. A bird was singing in a park near a church. It was divinely beautiful. You must be aware how valuable your undisturbed nature is?"

"And so that's where you and he parted company?"

"Yes. Not far from that church. We took a taxi back to our hotel. Mr. Curt said he wanted to go for a walk."

"And he was alone?"

"Yes, right then."

After a little moment of silence, he added, "I turned around when I stepped into the cab. Then I saw Mr. Curt heading back towards the club."

Next Katrin and I directed our attention to the owner of the club, or more accurately, his spokesman. This was a dumb fellow barely over twenty years old whose hair was already thinning, with sloping shoulders and an anxious smile. He was apparently chosen as the spokesman because of his unfavorable appearance and idiotic manner—no one would believe him capable of anything. We knew where the owners of the club were; they resided someplace else entirely and had definitely not been in the vicinity of the club on the night in question. Nor could they have known that Curt would be going there, since the visit happened on impulse—the Japanese men's impulse, not Curt's.

"Yeah, I remember the guy, the cops were here asking about it, weren't they? Why? Are you going to write something?" the man asked hopefully.

"We often do special articles for the men's magazines," I encouraged him. "Of course, we don't use our real names. But if you read the usual publications, then you've probably run across us several times."

What I said was completely true, and we satisfied his curiousity a little on that point before I pressed further. He watched Katrin the whole time and didn't look me in the eyes once.

"So you remember him and the three Japanese?" I asked. "You saw if they met anyone here in the club?"

"No, I didn't see that."

"Were they sitting by themselves the whole time? Didn't they talk to anybody else?"

"I don't remember."

"Did they ask about girls?"

"Well—no."

"There must be girls here, right?"

"There aren't any girls working here," said the man, blinking. "It's just me and the guy who shows the film. Yeah, and then the girl who serves, of course. And the girls who perform, if that's what you mean, but they don't associate with the audience—that's strictly forbidden. We have netting at the edge of the stage."

"Come on," I said. "We don't give a hoot what your employees do after work. The only thing I want to know is whether some girls started talking with the Japanese guys, just by chance. They could, you know, have been female guests."

He smiled broadly and we smelled his bad breath. He answered:

"Yes, now I remember. As a matter of fact, a few did look in towards the end of the evening."

"Do you know what their names were?"

He pretended to think. Katrin watched him, smiling, and he blushed, turning away from her.

"Ewa, Tanja and Git," he said.

"Do you know them?"

"Well, not exactly. I know who they are."

"This could be great stuff!" I said, prompting him. "Imagine if I could get an interview with the girls, 'We were the last ones to see Curt alive.'"

"Yeah, but he didn't have anything to do with them," said the man.

"How do you know?"

"Well, it's true that the girls were here, but they just sat and flirted with the Japanese. They didn't pay any attention to the fourth fellow."

"Are you sure?"

"Sure, man. They left right before I closed, the whole gang. The girls had each hitched up with their own Japanese guy. What's the deal, the cops and a bunch of you folks from the press have all been here asking about it already, what else is there to say?"

"We're trying to get a new perspective," replied Katrin, smiling.

"I think he met up with some maniac after he left," said the man flatly. "He wasn't with anyone here, girl or guy."

"But he did come back again!" Katrin burst out.

"He did not!"

"He didn't?"

"Nobody came back. I closed after they left, they were the last ones to go. If you don't believe me, just ask the cops, they've been here checking everything out!"

We really did believe him.

"Are you absolutely positive he didn't come back? He could have forgotten something, maybe, that he just came and picked up."

The guy pinched his mouth together, shaking his head.

"He didn't come back. Ask Nielsen, who showed the film. Ask Gertrud, who served. Ask—"

"We believe you."

The three girls were very willing to cooperate. They admitted that they'd slipped into the club to, as they said, see if they could meet someone. According to Ewa, there were lots of foreign tourists in town during the summer, and she was interested in practicing her English. Git and Tanja agreed. They'd met three Japanese businessmen in the company of a Swede, and been invited to take a seat at their table. They hadn't seen any harm in that. The Japanese had expressed quite a bit of prejudice about women and the girls had reprimanded them. But it hadn't been a serious dispute, more like a playful discussion. When they all left the locale, the Japanese offered the girls a ride because they were going in the same direction. The lone Swede said he wanted to take a walk and they didn't see where he went. Git had a vague impression that he turned around and went back towards the club, but she wasn't sure. Upon arriving at the hotel, the Japanese invited them for a parting drink and one thing led to another. There was never any talk of monetary compensation. Rather, they had wanted to demonstrate the Swedish women's freedom to make their own choices about their bodies. They had left the hotel, each by themselves, between six and seven in the morning.

And there the trail ended.

Curt had turned around on the street outside of the club and walked back towards it. At that point it was almost three in the morning, and a bird was singing in Adolf Fredrik's cemetery. Curt disappeared and was found again several hours later on the jogging trail at Mört Lake.

But he'd been somewhere in the meantime, and with somebody.

† † †

Curt's boss, Hasse, didn't have time to meet with us or talk over the telephone. He was a busy man, letting his secretary speak for him. We hung around outside his office building until we got hold of him physically. He was in his forties, skinny and bald. His eyes shone with joy and an eagerness for work.

"Pardon me," said Katrin, as she stepped right in front of him.

He hardly saw her, moving aside so she wouldn't trip over him and getting within reach of his car. But there I was, standing on the sidewalk.

"Hey, man," he said, "what the hell's going on?"

"Please sir," said Katrin, who'd caught up and grabbed his arm. "Just a couple of little questions?"

He looked around as though he expected someone to come and rescue him. Several guys he'd had in tow were waiting nearby, but none of them dared make the first move forward.

"You must be Hasse?" said Katrin.

Quick as lightning, I tossed out my press card and he softened a bit.

"Yes, what is it?" he asked.

"Curt Samuelsson," countered Katrin.

For a moment, he stood completely still.

"Curt Samuelsson?" he asked, as if tasting the words. "Curt...I know I've heard the name before."

"He used to work for you. Negotiated with the Japanese clients."

"Shit, of course!" yelled Hasse. "You'll have to talk to Bosse Persson about that contract, he's the one in charge now. Hey Bosse, can you come here for a minute?"

A man freed himself from the pack and approached.

I tried to keep him away, but he'd already joined us. That same type of striped suit as the others and the same diplomat's briefcase. Bosse was a powerful guy, well-built and broad-shouldered, with thick, blond, curly hair. Katrin focused her attention on him for one instant and that was enough for Hasse. With a polite smile, he lifted up my hand, which was lying on his shoulder, glided into the car parked at the curb and was gone.

Bosse had to do. He was full of enthusiasm about his own accomplishments. Unfortunately, the deal had reached a deadlock, he explained, because the Japanese businessmen had been unfavorably affected by what had happened to Curt and all of the resulting questions. Just in general, the whole thing had made a poor impression, which Bosse regretted. He didn't want Sweden to appear to be a lawless country; he was afraid the foreign visitors would get the wrong idea. Just between us, he could confide that Curt really hadn't been any great shakes in the field. In fact, it was questionable whether he would have succeeded in landing the contract anyway. Even if Bosse didn't want to say so directly, it could be interpreted as a stroke of luck that he had gotten to take over. Now he was setting it up in a completely different way and would be traveling to Japan the following week to tackle it from a new angle.

"Had you been involved in this deal before Curt died?"

"We'd all been working on it. But now I'm the one responsible."

"You," said Katrin, "what were you doing that night?"

Bosse laughed, pounding her on the back.

"Hiding out at Mört Lake, huh? So as to nab my rival?"

Katrin looked embarrassed.

"OK," she said. "Then where were you?"

"On a Saturday night?" shouted Bosse. "Where do you think?"

Katrin raised her shoulders in surprise, and I didn't know either what to guess. There's a lot to choose from, and if it were as his tone of voice suggested, there would hardly have been any witnesses.

"Playing golf, of course!" he yelled. "At Södertälje Golf Club! Where else?"

"Did you and Curt ever see each other socially?" I asked. "Were you friends?"

Bosse shook his blond curls.

"No, not really. You don't get a chance for that kind of stuff on this job. We got together when we had to, for work and so on. But you don't have time to associate personally."

"Had you ever been to his house? Did you know his wife?"

"Met her at some party given by the company. Cute gal, big rump."

"But not personally?"

"Didn't have time, like I said."

"Do you know if anyone else at the company used to meet with him privately?"

"Or her," inserted Katrin.

Bosse smiled compassionately.

"Obviously, you two don't know a thing about this kind of job. Here you're always on the go, man, otherwise you might as well hang it up. That's the law of survival."

"In the computer field," smiled Katrin.

"Exactly, you've got it. It just doesn't wash to take time out for sitting around at the opera bar shooting the breeze and drinking red wine," he said. "Around here we work. Hard."

We felt a little depressed after that volley.

It took a while before we got in touch with Inger. The next muder had already occurred by then. It was one of those murders that disappear quite rapidly from the news. If the police drew any parallels with the Curt-murder, they didn't say so. The homicide after Curt's was the fifth, but the victims came from such different social classes and living situations that a connection wasn't readily apparent. Naturally, there was no *direct* relationship and the victims had never met one another.

Inger was lying on a lawn chair in her yard when we came over. She was wearing a halter top and cut-off jeans. In her thirties, attractive, and a bit heavy around the bottom, Inger looked like a real woman. She had a visor over her eyes that she pushed up on her forehead when we came. She made a gesture towards a couple of other chairs but didn't offer us anything. She didn't say anything, either. She just took note of who we were and leaned back in her chair again. It was as if she'd forgotten we were sitting there.

I looked at Katrin, using body-language to indicate that she should begin the questioning. The sisterly bond, so to speak. Katrin shook her head and positioned herself exactly like Inger, stretching her legs out in front of her, leaning her head back and closing her eyes.

So there I sat, being the only person awake in the party.

"Nice place you have out here," I said encouragingly to Inger.

Almost imperceptibly, she moistened her lips as a sign that she'd heard.

"Your—Curt must have liked this house too," I bumbled along.

"Yes."

She answered calmly, clearly and without revealing any emotion. She made it damned difficult for me to continue, and I kicked Katrin on the leg. Katrin drew herself together but didn't open her eyes.

"How long have you been living out here?" I continued.

"Two years."

"Are you planning to stay, or...?"

"Yes, I probably will."

Now Katrin joined in from the side:

"It must be nice to have your mother living so close. Does she take care of the children during the day?"

"No, Mama works full-time herself. But now that Curt isn't here anymore, we've decided she'll move in so we can share the mortgage payments. The children go to a day-care sitter not far from here."

"It must be difficult for you without Curt."

"Oh yes," said Inger. "Of course I miss him. But he was so seldom at home. I'm surprised how little I notice the difference. Of course you need a man, but you can always get one, you know. Here at home, there really isn't such a big change."

"What about the children? Don't they miss their Papa?"

"Oh yes, of course. It was rough right at first. But there are two of us for them, you see, and I get more help from Mama than I ever did from Curt."

It seemed, in other words, as though she had mostly gained by the trade. Wasn't there any way this woman could be reached? Didn't she miss her husband at all?

Katrin moved her chair a little closer to Inger's.

"It must have been terrible for you in the beginning," she said. "When you realized he wouldn't be coming back."

Inger's mouth narrowed.

"When I realized he wouldn't be coming back," she repeated. "Naturally, at first I got mad. I thought that he had, well, you know. They did find him right away—I hadn't had time to start calling around yet. Then everything happened so fast, somehow I never got a chance to deal with it. The hearing, more questioning, the funeral, and all of the hyenas who ran around here snooping and hiding in the bushes. Taken altogether, it was like a nightmare. In a way, Curt ended up being the smallest part. I don't know whether you can understand. I just didn't get to be in peace and mourn him. Someone was always sucking on my sorrow like a parasite. The whole time I was more angry than sad, just because I didn't get to be left alone. And then all of the insinuations about what he'd done. Sure, he'd been to the strip club—that fact is evident. But he didn't go with those prostitutes. The Japanese took care of them. No one knows what happened to Curt, and that's what still makes it so strange. Like it never got a natural ending. You're both thinking what a hard-boiled devil I am. Aren't you?"

Suddenly she sat up, pushing the visor high on her forehead and looking directly at us with her clear eyes. First Katrin, then me.

"I noticed it as soon as you two came, how you thought I was a damned bitch. Instead of weeping and wailing like I ought

93

to, I'm sitting here so cool and collected. My oh my, what a lousy widow!"

"Oh no," I said, while Katrin, as usual when the exposures come, just leaned forward and smiled warmly, as though she'd been expecting it all along.

"But I'm telling you this is the only way I can live," said Inger. "I think it's because they destroyed my sorrow. I didn't get to keep it for myself; I was forced to try to encapsulate it. Until finally it disappeared."

"Don't you think it's dangerous to suppress your feelings like that?" I asked.

Inger abruptly showed her teeth at me.

"Dangerous or not, I'm not the one who did it! They're the ones who forced themselves on me, remember that. Just like you're doing right now! If you think it's dangerous, then leave me alone!"

Katrin laughed and Inger laughed too. Katrin had done it again—broken the ice, come closer. She's so smart, I don't know how she does it!

"Of course the police have asked you this a thousand times," she said, "but anyway. So Curt was meeting with some business contacts about an agreement with a computer firm in Japan. Could he have had any rivals for this deal, or anything like that?"

"He could very well, but the settlement hadn't been written yet, you know. This part was just preliminary and the contract itself would have been drawn up on Monday, if everything had gone smoothly."

"Did Curt have any foreign friends?"

Inger looked surprised.

"Him, no! Well, there's a Greek fellow who lives three houses away, and you could probably say they were friends. But otherwise, Curt wasn't especially fond of foreigners. All you have to do is look at the crime statistics," she said, pinching her mouth together again.

"Did he do anything to stop foreign criminals?"

"He didn't have time for that," she answered quickly. "He had his hands full with his job. He just grumbled a little, the way

94

people do."

"About drug dealers and so forth?"

"Yes, that kind of thing."

"You haven't heard whether the investigators secured any clues from the car?"

"They kept it for a week, but they haven't said anything to me, at least."

"What do you *believe* yourself?" wondered Katrin. "Do you have any feelings about what *might* have happened?"

"They must have gone to the lake together," said Inger.

"Yes."

"But if it were somebody he thought looked suspicious, or who he caught doing something illegal, he'd never have let them in as a hitchhiker."

"No. Unless the person in question were already threatening him with a knife. In order to be driven someplace."

A shudder went through my spine because I sensed that this was important—we were on our way somewhere.

"But the car was still there," said Inger calmly.

"Yes?"

"If a criminal had wanted the car to get away, why would he do that to Curt and then just leave the car behind? Where did he go afterwards?"

She was right about that. I felt stuck. But even so, there was something that had burned when we spoke about the possibility, something I'd had within reach that had slipped away again—

"Have you heard about this new knife homicide yet?" asked Katrin.

"No, which one?"

"This Torsten, the young man from Jordbro."

Inger snorted loudly and scornfully.

"I doubt that was murder! That must have been gangs! It happens all the time, punkers and skinheads or whatever they are. Just hoods, the bastards! Don't mix Curt up with them!"

She was probably right. There didn't seem to be any connection between the neat Curt with his orderly economy and the next name on the list.

No connection, that is, besides the cause of death being exactly the same and the murder apparently having happened in the same way.

TORSTEN GRAHN, 20
Retail stocker

Grahn was a twenty-year-old youth who visited Gröna Lund Amusement Park along with two friends one night the week before the Swedish solstice celebrations. An exchange of opinions arose between Grahn and his friends and some other young men while they were all waiting for the bus at the #47 stop. A fight broke out which resulted in Grahn's death.

All of those involved protested their innocence and a murder weapon could not be recovered at the site, nor within the area of Djurgården Park, which was searched with a fine-toothed comb that night and the following morning. Witnesses had not been able to determine who had dealt the fatal blow.

The autopsy revealed that Grahn had died as a result of deep wounds in the stomach and diaphragm. Grahn was alive during his transport by ambulance to South Hospital, but died during the ensuing operation. He was not able to give any coherent testimony.

Grahn left a mother and a stepfather with whom he had been living, as well as a girlfriend, Sussie Engman, eighteen, employed in retail.

† † †

He is—Superman!

Sailing through the air, pow, pow! His fist strikes—there! Bam! Crash! Kapow, kapow!

He runs forward in a crouched position, his fists clenched, his mouth twisted in a warped grimace. His eyes are shooting lightning.

His machete slices through the air. Swish!

No, that's wrong. Superman, not Tarzan.

Oh, shit, both are just as funky, just as old-timey. Who the hell is Superman? Who cares about him? Clark Kent?

Though the film was good.

There are other guys nowadays, tougher. Guys who really don't ask first. Who just take what they want—

Like this for example:

You see a babe you dig. Nice body. Instead of maybe first bullshitting with the chick and so on, pretending to like her, you go up from behind and take hold of her shoulder and turn her around.

He jabbed a little in the air to see how it would work. Like this—you reach out your right paw, putting it on her right shoulder. That must be how it goes. Press down on it and she loses her balance a little and has to turn around. For sure, her left shoulder won't work. He stands up again, shutting his eyes while he practices the grip. Imagines a young woman in front of him.

And it'd be a real girl, not that damned whiny and bitchy Sussie.

"Can't we move in together, Totte? Why don't you want to be with me, Totte?"

That's the way it always sounded.

Sussie had a nice pad and sometimes he did sleep over, but hell, *live* together? Let her rule and decide? Like Mom?

Guys who let girls tell them what to do hadn't figured out what counts. They hadn't realized what makes the world go around.

Like Rolle, for example. Sat there letting Mom nag year in and year out. Instead of *acting*!

Oh no.

Not Tarzan. Not Superman. Maybe a stone-hard Vietnam soldier, GI on the hunt after gooks in the jungle. His uniform is camouflaged. Over his helmet there's a net he can stick twigs into. The bayonet is drawn. Quiet! What was that? A bird? It *sounded* like a bird, but it might have been the enemy, sending a signal! They're everywhere in the bushes the teeming throng of enemies all with the same yellow faces and the same false expressions with slanted eyes straggling hair you don't *know* but he's sneaking up behind you soundlessly, invisibly, inaudibly he *is* there. You don't know until you wake up and you're dead, aaaow! The cloth rips on your back it's the knife the sharp knife the stabbing with a double edge you hardly feel it until it's *there* you writhe in double paroxyms on the ground barf shit on your-self scream bawl parrots chatter in the trees monkeys shriek no hell now there's something wrong again but this is El Salvador for godsakes.

Or Honduras or Guatemala or whatever.

Little yellow people. Or brown.They're filling up the world.

Damn, the yankees have got to take a stand. Too bad John Wayne is dead.

He stopped and took a deep breath after getting through his death struggle.

He found himself in Jordbro Mall.

Sussie was at work in the ICA food store to the right. Just as well she didn't catch sight of him. She might start ragging. He should be at his job. Her mom had fixed him up with a job. He hadn't wanted it. But Sussie's mom had said he could go there and say hello from her someday when he didn't have anything else to do and so he'd done it. A stocking job—driving a truck, loading it and driving it away, then some girls sat and marked prices. At times it was really cool. Could josh with the girls, scare them. Hunt them with the truck—shit, it was cool. Pretend that it was a tank rolling over the burned fields the air with napalm, little blue puffs of smoke still rising up. There came the Americans in their tanks. The pipes were sticking out like long, fucking cocks hunting around searching for targets to shoot at. No one in sight. Just the burned wood. The smoke from it. The ground had stripes, hell that was strange the trees had stood in rows like they were newly planted could that be true? Damn, what difference did it make. The tanks came and the girls were on their way to the well, they didn't comprehend a thing, had never been around this before, talked with little chirping voices like Chinese kee ho lang kang. The tanks are coming around the corner and the girl doesn't know a thing—who does she see there but Bruce Lee!He wanted to buy some beer, but then he'd have to ride into Handen where his mom worked and she might see him and start making a fuss. But after all, didn't he do what he damn well pleased? His buddies were probably there. They hadn't shown up yet. They weren't anywhere. Maybe still snoozing at home. Sussie woke him up this morning, goddammit, wanted him to get up and go to work. He shouldn't ever stay over with her. She was forever bitching and moaning! Totte do this Totte not like that Totte why don't you talk to me Totte can't you help me out a little? Damn Swedish girls! They should be like in the Orient! Quiet obedient always on their knees. Just crack the whip and they come. There you can handle your women. What the hell kind of bullshit was going on over here, anyway? Even the Turkish girls were better. But of course you can't ever get to them. Totally unfair, the Turks are always after the Swedish girls, feeling and squeezing and shouting and chasing, always a damned thrill for them with the Swedish girls, don't leave the girls alone for a minute but do they ever let anyone get near their own, huh? Oh no, they have to sit nicely at home waiting while the guys are out on the town being rowdy, hell it could make you gag. He got royally pissed off whenever he thought about it. Really, they ought to be taught. He ought to show them. You can't just come up here and treat Swedish broads one way and Turkish ones another. In that case you might as well stay home, right? No one made them come! If Turkish girls are so damned good then stay home in Turkey for godsakes and lay Turkish girls then if they're so fucking good, though a little short-legged, huh, not really as cute, huh, so Swedish cunt isbetter, huh? Bullshit! He stopped, raising his upper lip over his teeth in a cruel expression. The Turkish commander-in-chief was standing in front of him. The little thin black moustache bore witness to sadism and torture. He made an almost imperceptible movement backwards with his head and the whip coiled like a snake at his feet. Small, even, white teeth could be seen under the moustache. His eyes were completely black and the tip of his tongue played in the corner of his mouth.

"You confess?"

The Turkish officer came one step closer.

"You confess, you treacherous dog?"

The blond viking was steadfast. He closed his eyes when the whip came whizzing past. But it didn't strike him. It just knocked the cigarette out of the mouth of the soldier sitting at the corner of the table and a low, urgent laugh oozed from the chief interrogator.

"Maybe you wanna talk now?"

He didn't even condescend to answer.

"Abdul! Ergün!"

The two soldiers who had just been sitting and smoking strode up. They carried strangely-shaped metal instruments in their hands that looked like screws, but no, they were something electrical. Instinctively he backed up a step and put his hand over his groin, because he knew, of course, that that's what they were after—

"Watch out!" said a mother with a baby carriage who was walking by. He had recoiled so violently that he'd run into her. He pretended he'd done it on purpose. It felt funky to have made a fool of himself. The child in the carriage looked Turkish, goddammit; he tried to think of something to say about it, but she was on her way again before he could come up with anything good.

He might just as well ride in to Handen. The weather was fine, just a few clouds floating by. He could take a bottle down to the lake with him and go swimming.

In Handen, it was clear sailing. He was glad when he got carded in the liquor store. It was nice to be able to flip out his ID. He smiled with the corners of his mouth at the old woman who'd asked. The pistol was completely loose in its holster and he could have twirled it around his pointing finger. His hat was still on.

"OK, babe."

She tossed her head, the little whore. He knew how to handle them. Wait till he got her outside. Then she'd pant and beg for more. But it was never his style to have the same broad more than once. While she stood there with her hands pressed against her heart and her eyes full of tears, he mounted his faithful roan and rode down main street, out of town—forever. Old men watched him with clouded gazes and respect in their voices, "There he rides, the man we called—"

No, wait. That was a shitty way to go. Dull. Better with action! He swept his six-pack into the bag and gave her a daring smile, looking her in the eyes. She was already far away, attending to the next customer. Abruptly, he pivoted on his heels and walked away. Small sparks flew from his spurs. The revolving doors spun for a long time after he'd come out onto the dusty street.

There, as he'd expected, he met up with Kenny and Kricke. It had cleared up after the rain just in time for Friday night. They ducked when they went past the News Department so Totte's mom wouldn't see them if she was there.

Down at the lake, they were free.

† † †

In the movies, they died neatly. Not much blood, no pain and no terrible sounds. A cry, a few spasms and everything was over. Torsten had time to think of that before something went wrong inside his body and everything began spilling out of the wrong place. Then the images in his mind got more and more red and jerky and one moment he thought he saw a very beautiful horse spring forth out of burning grass, take a big leap into the air and disappear to the left of his visual field. Sitting on the horse's back was a person leaning forwards who was holding tightly onto the mane, probably an Indian.

The horse and rider disappeared out of Torsten's view. Actually, it was Torsten's field of vision which no longer existed. He lost consciousness and during the operation an hour later, he died.

"It doesn't surprise me one bit," said Roland Larsson bitterly. "I always said it would end badly for that boy."

His wife was still standing by the door she'd just closed behind the visiting policeman.

It was just as she'd heard. They always came in person when something happened. They didn't call. She hadn't known whether it was true. She would rather have thought they'd call. That's what they'd done the other times Torsten had gotten in trouble—been seen at places where he wasn't supposed to be and with friends he shouldn't be hanging around. Sometimes he'd been given a ride home. Always a little ashamed, a little obstinate on those occasions. And Roland had gotten mad.

This time Roland kept his mask on as long as the policeman was there. Clicked his tongue, drew in deep sighs and even held her hand.

Now he was sitting in his usual chair as she went to the window to watch the policeman get into the car waiting outside.

There would have to be more conversations, more questions. Naturally. And then the funeral. This was only the first session.

She still couldn't believe it. It was only a day since it all started—if they could just set the clock back twenty-four hours, it wouldn't even have happened.

She stood at the window until the police car had driven away.

"Is that all you have to say to me when my son has died?"

Roland rustled with the newspaper, trying to pretend he was reading.

"I've always said that—"

"And you're still saying it when he's lying dead in the mortuary with a knife in him! You cold, heartless monster!"

She turned to him with flaming eyes. Roland raised the paper into the air as though to shield himself from a blow.

"Oh boy! I can sure see where he got his temperament!"

She shoved her way past him, blind with tears. She made it to the bedroom before her sobbing broke loose. She fell headlong across the bed, howling and weeping loudly. There were no thoughts inside of her, only wailing and crying. A human being had existed who existed no more, a feeling was fluttering freely in the air, care and concern weren't needed any longer.

If only he'd killed himself driving! That could be accepted as fate, as God's will. But not being murdered! Stabbed to death with a knife! That was weak, cruel, it was against the law and against the rules of the game.

Roland came into the room. He stopped, watching her

while she roared her sorrow to the ceiling. She turned over on her stomach and buried her head in the pillow to avoid seeing him.

He came closer, putting his hand on her shoulder. He cleared his throat.

"Do you want to talk about it?" he asked.

She hadn't locked the door. She had to get out, he had to get out, they couldn't be in the same room together! Never again. Nagging at Totte, hassling Totte. Jealous! Would even compare who'd gotten the biggest piece of meat and complain that it was unfair. Roland, a grown man! Jealous of a little boy!

She screamed loudly to drown him out and prevent his awkward words from reaching her.

"OK," said Roland. "So this is how you're going to take it, huh?"

He left the bedroom, slamming the door.

He'd turned on the TV when she came back out. It was a rerun of an American comedy with dubbed-in laughter. She shut it off and looked at him with dry eyes.

"You're leaving now, you bastard," she said.

"Hey honey! I know you—"

He stood up halfway to push her to the side and turn the TV on again.

"Out, I said! Out!"

He had to hit her in order to protect himself. She tumbled backwards, yelling, falling onto the TV; it teetered and rolled over with a crash.

"Now look what the hell you've done!"

"Your old TV! You care more about it than you do about Totte!"

She came over and they stood facing each other in a duel of life and death.

"For heaven's sake, calm yourself down now."

"Out of my house! Get lost!"

"*Your* house? Is this supposed to be *your* house?"

He was strong, but greater than his strength was her rage against Fate, against a bloodthirsty God who had so easily, so easily nipped off Torsten Grahn's life and let, for example, Roland Larsson keep his.

"If you'd ever been like a father to him! If you hadn't let him go off the way he did!"

"I see, so now I suppose that's my fault too? Thank you very much!"

"It *is* your fault! You never got along with him!"

"But dammit, he wasn't my kid! The boy was crazy! Took after his father, always getting into trouble! Just like his mom!"

A vase flew through the air, just missing his ear. The TV lay on the floor smelling like rotten eggs. Four thousand kronor if it couldn't be repaired.

"You know you're just as damn nuts as him! Breaking furniture—you're out of your mind! What could become of him with a mother like that?"

She grabbed him with her bare hands.

He understood it wasn't her fault, so he didn't hit her harder than he had to in order to defend himself.

† † †

Little, thin as a rail. Dressed completely in black. Short black skirt, black lace stockings, black high-heeled pumps, black tee-shirt, open black leather jacket. Her hair was a mixture of black and red and her eyes were thoroughly black—around the edges and in the middle. The small face looked tired and defiant at the same time.

"You might as well come in, I guess. Though I don't really have time. I have to go to work. I took time off just for this."

She showed us into her living room, which was furnished with a sofa set and lots of green plants.

"What a pleasant home," said Katrin spontaneously.

She broke into a smile.

"I like puttering around with my plants," she said. "Here's my paradise tree. It's eighteen years old. My mom took a cutting the same week I was born. It's been mine ever since."

"It's very nice," said Katrin. "Hope it lives a long time."

The little face drew together and got blank.

"Please have a seat," she said. "I didn't make any coffee, but if you'd like some..."

We'd brought a carton of cherries and that made her

happy. She arranged them in a bowl and munched her way through our conversation.

"It's hard to believe it's true," she said. "That Totte!"

"Were you two very close?"

"What do you mean?"

"Well, was there anything between you?"

"I guess there was, whenever he remembered. It was sort of off and on."

"Would you say you were going together?"

She sighed deeply and thought for a minute.

"I don't know. He was strange, Totte. Sometimes so super-sweet—I'd think, now everything's settled, he's going to move in pretty soon. He'd buy things for the apartment, for example. Like the stereo over there, that's his. He got it and kept it here at my place because they already had one at his house. Now I don't know what to do with it. Do I have to give it back?"

She addressed the question to me. It was a fine speaker system, certainly worth several thousand kronor.

"If I were you, I wouldn't worry about it. Just don't sell it, in case someone comes around asking about it. Wait and see what happens."

"He was going to buy a video, too. But he hadn't gotten a chance to yet."

"Too bad."

"Yeah, though really it's not that important. Really it's worse that Totte's dead." Her eyes were big and totally dark.

"Do you know who he met that night?"

"I didn't even know where he was. Typical Totte! I thought we were going to get together. That's what he'd said: I'll be in touch on Friday, he said. So I waited around here and had bought some shrimp and strawberries and thought we'd have a cozy evening together, Totte might have brought some wine. He's *allowed* to buy it," she pointed out seriously.

"So then he didn't show up?"

"Yeah, he just didn't come. Didn't call either. Of course I got awfully depressed. I called Iris at home, that's his mom, and she said she thought he'd gone to Gröna Lund Amusement Park. His poor mama!" she continued on the next breath. "It's almost even worse for her. She knew him much better. He was her own child," she added as explanation.

"Yes," we agreed.

"And that terrible old man she lives with!"

Sussie clenched her fists.

"If it were me, I would've kicked that jerk out a long time ago! If I were Totte, I would've moved! At least he got away from him over here!"

Her black eyes sparked full of hatred.

"You should see him! What a nauseating old bastard! Just sits in front of the TV shouting at Totte and Iris all day long! Shit!"

She spit out a cherry pit so vehemently that it sailed over the sofa set, landing in the opposite corner of the room. Sussie giggled. Katrin joined in.

"Though actually, I think she has gotten rid of him now," continued Sussie contentedly. "They way he acted when Totte died! It was unreal! The worst I've ever heard! Jumped on his own wife when her child had just died! You know that old man's got to be crazy!"

We were aware of the cold facts.

"What happened after that?"

"She kicked him out, you better believe. Now he's going around whimpering and begging to come back. Typical!"

"How did Torsten and Roland get along?"

"Not at all, of course! The old man was so jealous that Iris hardly dared talk to Totte without him getting mad. He used to count meatballs."

Sussie giggled again with her hand over her mouth.

"If only Totte had lived a little longer, he absolutely would've moved in here," she said with a sigh. "That's what's so awful. That that's all he ever got out of life, living with that old man."

"But he had you, anyway," said Katrin comfortingly. "It must have felt good for him to have you and this nice home to come to."

Sussie lit up.

"Do you really think so?"

"I think it must have meant a lot to him," I said after an elbow from Katrin. "But you know how it is, young guys like to live the single life too. Some of them get in too deep."

"I know Kenny and Kricke," said Sussie softly. "There's nothing bad about them. They've been here with flowers; they were really sorry."

"It wasn't their fault either," said Katrin.

She gave Sussie a hug and the girl pressed herself close.

"We'll let you know if we hear anything," I said as we left. "And you too, OK?"

Like a straight black line, she stood in the doorway until we'd gone. She raised her hand in a little military salute as we disappeared around the corner of the stairway.

† † †

We met Kenny and Kricke about a week later—half ready to cry and glancing fearfully over their shoulders.

Naturally, nothing was their fault.

They never meant for it to be like this, never.

It just turned out that way. It wasn't Torsten's fault, either. It was those others, the dagos.

Everything had gone wrong, even though the day had begun so well. The weather had been nice after several days of rain. They'd sat down in the field at Rudan Lake and drunk the beer Totte'd bought plus a little bottle Kircke'd had in his possession. It hadn't really been that much. They weren't actually ever even drunk. They'd taken off their shirts and lain and sunned themselves in the grass, listening to music because Kenny had had his stereo along. The music had been loud; some uptight old ladies had told them to shut it off and just for that, of course, they'd turned it up even higher, so the atmosphere had gotten rather intense but super-cool. There were some girls who'd come over and talked about what they were going to do that night. Hang out at Gröna Lund Amusement Park, thought the girls, but Totte, Kenny and Kricke weren't especially into that. After a while the girls left because they were going home to get ready.

That evening, they did ride in to Gröna Lund after all—what else was there to do? They brought the stereo along and there was a hot mood on the train, though some old hags frowned about it.

And Totte was a super-good guy. The best. It was typical that the dagos went after him, of all people. Totte who was so for real. But it was typical. It happened like this:

They arrived in the city about nine at night. It was Friday, so there were quite a few people around. Masses of people camping out and the types who swarm around downtown with their big backpacks and things, they really looked ridiculous, thought Kricke anyway. They'd teased a few of them a little, in sport. These people ought to be able to take it! If you rig yourself out like that, going around with your whole house on your back, then you'd better be willing to tolerate a lot. It's a free country, people can certainly put up with a joke! Anyway it was all just in fun.

Totte had happened to kick someone's backpack and the man who it belonged to had gotten mad—typical—and started arguing. Actually, you couldn't really say Totte kicked it, more like he happened to bump into it as he walked by. But the old man had gotten furious just because of that and he up and started hollering and then a bunch of other old snooty types jumped up too. You know how it is, they don't really dare say anything, but as soon as *one* says something, then all of the others have to start shouting too. So anyhow these old folks started to complain.

"Let's split," said Totte then, and they split before the cops could come. They laughed loud and hard when they left, and Totte turned around in the entryway, pretending he had a machine gun and was mowing down those old women and men. How they'd roared about that, Kenny and Kricke, because as a matter of fact one old lady did get super-scared and started screaming and thought he really did have a machine gun, shit what a riot Totte had been. They got on the bus the same way—with the machine gun, that is—it was tough. The bus driver yelled some nonsense about you can get off if you don't stop making trouble, boys! and I'm not driving unless you come up here and show your tickets! Actually, they did all have bus passes, but like, it was electric. So the hassle went on for a while until finally some old lady started griping because the driver wasn't driving and an old man and several others thought it was funky that the driver wasn't driving and that they had to suffer just because he couldn't keep order. Then he opened the back door and told Totte, Kenny and Kricke to get off, but of course they just burst out laughing and then that old man said if he didn't drive, he'd report him to the bus company and so he started driving.

He was black.

"It's mostly blacks, you know, who drive the buses and they don't know how it is in Sweden, they don't get it at all, but they shouldn't think they can boss us around and tell us what to do or whether to pay on the bus or not. That's probably what that old man thought too, and that's why he was going to report the black guy," explained Kenny.

"So we got off at Djurgården Park, but it wasn't really live there. Really we should have been in Gothenburg digging the Stones, damn what old farts when you think about it, but they're still hip anyway! Think of us when we're forty," said Kricke, laughing uproariously, "wonder if we'll have any teeth left by then, huh?"

"Haha—you'll be living in a row house and have an old lady and a shit-job, don't think *you're* ever going to amount to anything," said Kenny with unexpected venom but Kricke turned to him and said no, he'd rather off himself with drugs before thirty.

The police statement had indicated that none of the boys abused drugs.

We asked them to continue telling us about the last day in Torsten Grahn's life.

"There wasn't anything special happening on the stage, just some old folk dancers. Everyone who could, you know, was down at Ullevi grooving with the Stones so there wasn't much left to go for in Stockholm. But it was OK for one time, you might as well hang out at Djurgården as anyplace else. What's there to do in town in the summer, anyway? There's really nothing! What can you do?"

We agreed that there wasn't so terribly much to do.

We'd gotten hold of the boys the week after the solstice celebrations and our dismal conversation was taking place against a backdrop of steady, gray, pouring summer rain. Curt

Samuelsson had been dead for a month. We'd been in London and come home and begun following up on the Curt-case. Then the murder of Torsten Grahn had occurred, which appeared at first to be one of the usual gang fights. These pathetically dressed-up children who, fortified by drinks and video films, go out to conquer the world and each other. Three boys from Jordbro—Torsten Grahn, Kent Johansson and Rickard (Kricke) Lindgren—had ridden into Stockholm to go to Gröna Lund. They were slightly intoxicated and wearing jeans, tee-shirts, hats and boots. They hadn't really wanted anything more than have it a little cool. Torsten Grahn was twenty years old and employed as a stocker with Åhlens department store in Jordbro. He'd felt a little out of sorts that morning and hadn't gone to work. Kent Johansson was nineteen years old and unemployed. Rickard Lindgren, twenty, was a construction worker on vacation.

None of the boys had problems with drug dependency, although they had told the police, and told us, that they often used to buy something on the weekends because it was such a bummer if you weren't drunk.

"So you were all at Gröna Lund. What happened then?"

"Well, there wasn't much action. And we didn't have anymore to drink. Then Totte got it into his head that he wanted a girl."

"His girlfriend wasn't along?"

"No, he didn't go out with her, she just bitched! Though it wasn't really like that. He didn't really want to get a girl. Just be tough and make himself a little awesome, try to impress. So that the girls'd notice him. He called out at some of the girls, stuff like that. And ran up and started, you know, jumping in front of them."

"Jumping in front of them?"

"Yeah, getting in their way so they couldn't go forward. And asking where they were going and if they wanted to go with him. Like that."

The black grouse's mating dance, or was it the capercaillie's? My ornithology isn't what it ought to be.

"Some of them got mad but some thought he was pretty sharp. They stopped and talked and Totte asked where they were going but none of them actually came with us. Though one girl did get really pissed off, she almost slapped him. That made Totte so damned mad, of course, that he shoved her. Then she ran away. We ran after her and told her to stop and come back so we could fuck her."

Kenny was telling the story and now we saw that he was truly incensed, his voice shook, he clenched his fists and stuck out his chin.

"Did you really mean that?"

"If we'd gotten hold of her, sure. Shit, you should've seen her, she was going to give it to Totte! That broad was crazy as hell."

"Maybe she didn't like his advances?"

"Advances, my ass, it was just in fun, you know! She can take it if she goes out! What was she doing at Gröna Lund, then, don't people step out to have a good time, huh? Lucky for her I didn't get a hold of her, or she would have found out!"

Tears of rage and hatred rose in Kenny's eyes.

"You didn't catch her, any of you?"

"No, man, she booked and we were after her, but we didn't catch her. She probably snuck into the women's can. We waited outside for a while, but we couldn't stand around all night so we split."

"None of you saw her again?"

"How should I know, there are shitloads of girls milling around out there. Besides, it was her own fault."

"Did you accost any others?"

"We didn't damn well accost anyone!"

"What did you do after that?"

"Nothing. Just the ride home, of course."

"Actually, there wasn't anything to fight about," explained Kenny. "I mean people want to fight, so they fight and then they say it was because of this or that. But really they make it all up. They pretend the other guy picked the fight just so they get to kick some ass."

"Is that what happened in the fight with Torsten, too?"

Kenny and Kricke searched each other's faces.

"I don't know."

"Me neither."

112

"I don't know what happened."

"I wasn't looking right then."

"Yes, but for heaven's sake, boys, what's the hang-up? You're not afraid, are you? Do you think someone's going to get revenge? Is that it?"

"Hey, man, that's bullshit! We're the ones who'll get revenge in that case! Wait'll I get hold of that damned dago who—"

"You really didn't see anything?"

"It was pretty dark, you know. And we were looking for the bus, seeing if it was going to come."

"Totte was standing off to the side a little, sort of by himself. And they jumped on him."

"We've told the cops about this a *million times*!"

"Well, one more time, please. Was it just you and the Chileans or were there others, too?"

"Others. There must have been twenty or so people standing around. Some of them were sitting on the bench and there are lots of trees, you know, so you can't see, really big trees. Some people were sitting by the trees. And it was quite dark, I mean pretty dark, not really, but like bluish."

"And you were all standing there waiting, perfectly calm?"

"No, we were probably being a little rowdy. We were pretending we'd caught sight of some Indians."

"And actually you really had."

Silence. The boys looked at each other.

"Shit, you're right! And actually we really had!"

Kricke started laughing and his friend was quick to chime in.

"We thought they'd torture us but like, we'd torture them first."

"Yes?"

"So we'd sneak up and take one of 'em by surprise from behind. But then one of 'em noticed and he turned around and—"

The boy's face got blank. His gaze was far away.

"Yes?"

"No. He didn't have a knife. Everyone was just kidding around. We grabbed a hold and fought a little. But it wasn't serious because we were waiting for the bus, you see, so we were going to quit as soon as it got there."

"And what did the other people do who were there?"

"Some of them moved up closer. They saw us fighting. Maybe they wanted to join in."

"Anyone you remember?"

"No, it was so dark. And there was a little wind, so the leaves were fluttering, they sort of made shadows. And sounds in the trees. Then Totte fell down and right then the bus came and everybody just ran. And the leaves were like, fluttering. We ran too, but not very far; of course we thought Totte'd catch up so we didn't stop and wait for him."

"Why did you run at all?"

"I don't know. Oh yeah, there was someone running. And a girl was screaming. And it got like that, I don't know why. Everyone was running. And Totte wasn't coming so we stopped and then we saw—"

They were six altogether. The police hadn't gotten anywhere with them. They didn't speak Swedish, so they'd had a Spanish interpreter along for the police interrogation. We met them at the Workers Adult Education school on Svea Avenue. Their Swedish teacher insisted on being included in the conversation and helping us translate. It's possible we would have gotten further with them in private, but at the same time we got the feeling there wasn't any further to go—that they were telling the truth, and they really hadn't been holding any knife. We realized that they didn't understand a thing. They'd moved here from oppression and injustice. They'd been attacked by big, blond vikings—on a lark, but could they perceive it that way? As a result, they'd been taken in for questioning in connection with a knife murder.

We couldn't ignore the possibility that knife homicides and sudden assaults from behind were not unknown phenomena for them. They came from a country where people disappeared in strange ways and were unrecognizable when found. Some who went under the guise of refugees were actually criminals whom the government wanted to get rid of. Others who weren't criminals to begin with turned to crime after what they'd been through.

These boys hardly seemed to comprehend what had happened to them at Djurgården. They hadn't been in Sweden more than a few months. They'd gotten their money and gone out that night, had some fun, shot at the targets and ridden the roller coaster. Hadn't talked to any girls; their Swedish wasn't good enough. All six had stayed together the whole time. While they were waiting for the bus into town, these three Swedish boys had come along and started yelling at them. They hadn't been able to understand what was being said or what was wanted. But when the Swedes seemed aggressive, one of them turned around and took aim with a karate chop. Then the Swedes backed off. All three appeared to be very angry. Juan Felipe and his friends looked around for a way out. The Swedish boys came up to them again, shouting. So they ran. They saw him falling. None of them had a knife, none of them had ever had a knife.

"What other people were there?"

"Several others. One girl who started screaming terribly. She was with a boy who took her away from there. Several other people, maybe three or four. Some older people."

"Older?"

"Yes, not old, but older, not teenagers. Adults."

"Someone must have been holding that knife."

"Yes."

"He yelled and stepped back when I set up that karate chop. I know karate," added Juan Felipe, and a smile brushed across his face.

"But you didn't hit him?"

"No, he pulled back. I didn't go after him. One of his friends came at me from another direction and put up his fists and wanted to fight. But my friend got in between. I didn't see where the first boy went—his friend was facing us then."

Kricke.

"And his other friend shouted something, I don't know what. Everything happened so fast. Then the bus came and the girl started screaming and everyone started running. We ran

115

too. Then the police came and took us. But we have no knife."

He raised his hands as an invitation for us to search him. We refrained. The police had conducted body-searches and none of the Chileans had had any weapons. Nothing they could have thrown away was recovered either.

Therefore they had to be released.

† † †

"Can you see any connection between the murders?" asked Katrin.

"According to the police, there isn't a tie-in," I objected.

"Don't be an idiot!" she snorted. "We took this job on because we did see a connection and wanted to figure it out, right?"

"Should we make up the classic list?" I asked. "Like in the old whodunnit detective stories? You know—motive, time, method and what else is there?"

"The catch, of course, is," said Katrin gloomily, "that you have to have a whole list of suspects to mark off against the list."

We cracked a smile at each other, a bit long-faced.

"I suppose we could start by making a list of the victims," I suggested, "and seeing if they have any common denominators. Maybe we could proceed from there."

"Do they have anything at all in common?" wondered Katrin. "Besides all of them being men."

"That fact is undeniable," I acknowledged. "But is it relevant? Unfortunately, men are subjected to more violent crime than women. That holds true in general, as far as I know, both historically and geographically."

"Don't say that," protested Katrin. "Think of all the battered wives, all the rapes and assaults on women..."

It was an illogical objection, which I couldn't help pointing out to her.

"Katrin, right here we have five clear cases of men who've been murdered in a brutal and bestial way. However many assaults and rapes of women may occur in other places, it doesn't affect *our* statistic."

"No, you're right about that," she had to admit.

"Now, what do we know about these cases? What do they all have in common besides being men?"

I got out a piece of paper and a pen and began scribbling while we talked:

Hassan Abdel Karim
Sthen Carlsson
Martin Björkbom
Curt Samuelsson
Torsten Grahn

"They seem to be all types," I said thoughtfully. "Swedes and foreigners."

"Young and old."

"Rich and poor."

"Fat and thin?"

"They must have something in common, something!"

"A prick," said Katrin, giggling.

"Katrin, a hideous tragedy in five acts has been played out right before our eyes; it's a question of people having died. I don't understand how you can sit there and laugh."

She straightened up a little.

"I'm sorry, honey," she said. "It's probably just that I'm a little nervous. There really isn't anything to laugh about."

She sat down on the armrest of my chair and put her arm around my neck. We bent forward, studying the list together.

"They all seem to have been murdered during the night," suggested Katrin.

"Yes, but that's not so strange. That's generally how it is except with organized crime, robbery and so on, which for obvious reasons occur in public places. Most personal murders happen in private. And at night."

She bit her lip.

"But you don't want to characterize these as personal murders, do you? For if so, the connection between them would disappear."

She reminded me that up until now we'd been talking about organized crime, the drug syndicate. But there was something about the actual style of the murders that made it difficult to believe they represented gangster executions. Those murders are usually clean, discreet—a surreptitious plastic bag, a

117

drowned body. These murders were spectacular, almost as if the murderer *wanted* to be seen—a different type of gang? One compulsively preoccupied with murdering for pleasure?

I threw the idea out to Katrin.

"You mean," she said, "some maniacs? Who get together and commit these kinds of crimes in order to give each other a thrill, impress one another—?"

"Yes," I said.

I felt a cold horror sneaking up on me from behind. It was as though "the case" had suddenly become real. I heard the russle of leaves at Djurgården, saw their blue-black shadows. We were getting close to something that would soon reveal its true face.

"It's possible," I continued slowly. "Could it be homosexual after all?"

"Leob and Leopold," said Katrin.

We were starting to get excited. We set up a bigger list, like this:

	age	occupation	income	marital status
Karim	28	student	unemployed none(?)	live-in partner
Carlsson	67	politician	high	married
Björkbom	45	writer	medium	single
Samuelsson	34	computer man	high	married
Grahn	20	retail stocker	low	single

"We can probably rule out the wives and partners as suspects right away, don't you think?" asked Katrin. "Even if it were a matter of jealousy or revenge in one particular case, it's ridiculous to imagine a whole mafia of women running after unfaithful men."

"Who said they were unfaithful?"

We studied the list again.

"Well, I guess no one said so. Was there a mistress in any of the cases?"

"Old man Carlsson seems to have cast his glances, if we can

believe his secretary."

"We should definitely believe her," said Katrin adamantly. "Björkbom didn't have any woman at all, as far as we know. But even disregarding him, can you picture a female mafia consisting of the competent Mona, the exploited Margareta Åström—"

"Also competent!" interjected Katrin.

"The cool, controlled Inger Samuelsson—"

"Competent! Competent!"

There I got stuck. But neither Björkbom's cat nor Torsten's brave little Sussie seemed particularly competent, which I pointed out to Katrin.

"There's another way," she said. "There's something else we can do by relying on our own competence."

"The police don't inform us about anything," I protested. "We've already tried. We get nothing beyond the routine press statements. And we've interviewed everyone we could find."

"Since we can't get any further there, it seems as though we'll have to wait for the next case."

"But it's impossible to know whether it's a case or not until some time has passed."

"Or else we could search it out ourselves and investigate it," she said.

"That certainly wouldn't be easy!"

"No, obviously it isn't easy. But we can't just let this thing go. Good Lord, we're not going to leave it like this? Put it aside?"

"Then what are you suggesting?"

"That we set a trap for the murderer or murderers."

I had to laugh. I patted her on the back and ruffled her hair.

"Baby! How do you figure on doing that?"

"We'll probably have to send out some bait," she said with a narrow smile.

"And where will we get that?"

I looked around, but soon I realized what she meant.

"Are you talking about me? Am I supposed to be some kind of—?"

She nodded happily.

"Oh, I see. And how is that going to work, from a purely practical point of view?"

She still had that dumb smile and didn't answer.

"Do you mean I'm supposed to stand out on Malmskillnads Street with a rose between my teeth and look inviting?"

"I don't know. I haven't worked out all of the details yet. But so far there isn't a married detective on the list, so why not you?"

"Thanks a lot."

Actually, it wasn't so much that I was afraid, even if it had been feasible. It was actually quite an entertaining idea she'd come up with. To catch the murderer right in the act! Katrin hidden in the vicinity with a loaded camera, both the story and the photos...

But the prerequisite for a surprise maneuver like that is, of course, that you have someone to suspect and therefore surprise.

I told her this.

"I know," answered Katrin. "We have to think a little harder. There must be a way to solve that last problem."

PER GUSTAVSSON, 32
Psychologist, Vaxholm

Gustavsson worked at a psychiatric out-patient clinic in Vaxholm. The team consisted of psychologists, medical and psychiatric nurses, doctors, counselors, secretaries and caretakers.

Not long before his death, Gustavsson commented in a newspaper interview:

"Our view is that psychological difficulties can be the result of various social problems. One example is the threat of unemployment hanging over many residents of Vaxholm, which ends up meaning more patients with problems. We have no magic wand to change people's lives. But we can help and guide people in their struggle to change their own lives."

Gustavsson died the same day in July that his vacation was to begin. After work, he had dined with his live-in partner and the children in their shared home. Then, in anticipation of his vacation, he had gone to the marina to make an inspection of his sailboat. When he didn't return that night, his fiancée went out looking for him. She found Gustavsson on board the boat, murdered, with signs of a struggle. Death had been caused by repeated blows with a sharp, pointed object that had punctured the lungs and spleen. It was established that death occurred about 10 pm, which is before darkness sets in that time of year.

People had come and gone in the marina, but no direct witnesses of the crime or of any suspicious activities reported themselves. The relationship with his partner, Lena Dahl, a social worker employed in Akersberga, was allegedly good. The older child was hers from a previous relationship. According to the statement, no reason for jealousy between the parties existed.

Suspects:
The three patients of the day?
Some other patient?
If so, was that patient also guilty of the other crimes?

† † †

The man came in with his head turned to the side. He reached the tips of his fingers out as he gave his greeting, but looked away towards the other wall. His hair hung down, concealing his face.

"Bengt Wallin."

"Hi, Bengt! Have a seat!"

This wasn't the man's first visit. It looked like it was going to be just as tough, just as slow as both of the earlier ones.

There was no doubt that the man had problems. An old bachelor close to sixty, known in town as something of an eccentric. Quiet career at the bank, quietly alcoholic, quiet hobbies: fishing, stamp collecting. Now he was being replaced by a computer and an early retirement was waiting at the door. He had been sent to Per for a diagnosis. The employer hadn't wanted him to get any treatment, much less to recover. Bengt Wallin would be granted a pension quietly and discreetly for "psychological insufficiency."

Now he was sitting with his head bowed, one leg pulled up and his narrow hands clasped around his knee. His hair was long, thick and scraggly. Usually, he had it brushed back in an outdated fifties style, but now it had fallen down from the anchor behind his ear and was hanging in a sweep that almost covered his face.

Long, beautiful, slender hands. His neck bent, his hair an indefinite beige color, thick and unwashed. Worn brown suit and red-checked bow tie.

"Well, how's it going?"

The man made a little gesture with his hands but didn't answer. If he would at least lift up his head! As if the thought had taken the form of a telepathic message, Bengt Wallin looked up, stroking his hair behind his ear. He stuck his chin out defiantly.

"Not too bad, it's going about like always. And would keep

on going if there weren't so much garbage and fuss about everything."

He didn't know he'd been dismissed. He knew the department was going to be computerized, and had expressed his uneasiness about the change. He'd been sent to a course that he couldn't pass and had asked for another job he'd be able to do. There wasn't anything else besides what the typing girls did, and you couldn't offer that to a grown man, not even Bengt Wallin. There'd been a little arguing and a scene with the boss and then he'd been put on sick leave and that's where he was now. Per knew Bengt Wallin wasn't welcome back at the bank.

"Nice that summer's here, huh?"

"I'd really like to get back to work."

"Take the chance to rest up a bit. It's vacation time anyway, right?"

"In that case I want to be on vacation. I don't want to be on sick leave."

"Do you generally travel during the summer?"

"Before, I used to vacation with my mother most of the time, but she's passed away now. Sometimes I visit my older sister, and otherwise I stay home and go fishing."

Mama's boy, latent homosexual. Latent?

"Maybe you have some friends in town that you get together with?"

"A few. Not that many."

"Would you like to tell me about it?"

"Why?"

"I just thought if you wanted to."

Silence. Bengt Wallin snuck a look at his watch and Per snuck a look at his. The silence continued.

"If there isn't anything else, maybe I can go now?"

Bengt Wallin stood up with his feet neatly side by side, his hands hanging loosely down from his shoulders.

"Stay a little while longer. We aren't in any hurry."

A deep sigh and an open look at the watch.

"Were you going someplace?"

He observed an almost elated glimmer in Bengt Wallin's eyes. Here sat a man who'd gotten his chance, who'd seen the door open.

"Well, it's Friday."

"So?"

The glimmer died down.

"I thought maybe you'd want to go home early, doctor."

"Me? No, not at all, I'll be here as long as you want."

It was cruel and he knew it, he saw the man droop. Per bent forward.

"We have a great deal left to talk about, don't we?"

"But why?"

"If I'm going to be able to help you."

Thin hands warding him off in the air.

"I don't want any help."

"You need some help to be able to keep on working. You need help coming to terms with yourself so that you can function on the job again. I'm here to help you, OK?"

"I really don't understand how," said Bengt Wallin hesitantly. "I'm sorry about that trouble at work but of course it's all cleared up now. We've talked the whole thing over. Now it's just some new work assignments that have got to be arranged. You say I'm supposed to have problems, but I don't really understand what you mean, doctor."

Per took in a deep breath. Bengt Wallin forestalled him:

"If you mean I take a drink now and then, I can certainly put your mind at ease on that point, doctor. It never happens on the job. I have a nip sometimes to unwind and calm my nerves. And then on Friday, of course, when I relax. But I've never neglected my job because of it. Never stayed home from work. That's for sure. You can check."

When they'd gotten rid of him at the bank, it'd probably be smooth sailing for Bengt Wallin to drink day and night, no reason to keep himself sober anymore.

The bank director's secretary had asked Per to understand. Wallin was fifty-eight. It was a matter of time. And efficiency demanded more than Bengt Wallin could offer. After all, the bank wasn't a protected workshop for handicapped people.

"I know you do your job very well," said Per warmly. "That's not it. The question is whether you're sad, anxious. If there's anything else you'd rather be doing."

An obliging smile lit up Bengt Wallin's face.

"There's a lot, as a matter of fact! I have plenty of interests, you know. But work is one thing and hobbies another. I'm lucky to have both."

"How would you like to spend your time if you didn't work?"

"Why are you asking me this, doctor? I've worked ever since I was eighteen and took my graduation exam. What else would I have done? I've done my job for forty years, what difference does it make if I'd rather have been doing something else?"

Still smiling in a friendly way, but with a sharp tone of voice, he got halfway up from the chair:

"It was nice of you to see me, doctor, but I still don't quite understand what it's supposed to be good for. I'd really just as soon be going home."

"Bengt," said Per slowly, trying to look him in the eyes. "Is there anything you haven't told me? Anything you'd like to say? Ought to say?"

And why did the man persist in calling him doctor? Even though he'd asked him to say Per?

Wallin flung the long fringe of hair up and ran his fingers through it. Immediately, it fell down over his eye again. His voice got harder.

"I just want to be left alone," he said. "I haven't done anything wrong. I just want to be left in peace to mind my own business."

Per leaned back in the chair.

"Sure," he said. "Take it easy, Bengt. We'll have a little vacation, huh? And then we'll get together again. Feeling fit and healthy this fall. OK?"

He got up and reached out his hand. The other took it, dropping it quickly.

"Get a good rest, now," said Per, tapping him on the shoulder. "Swimming and sunshine, so you get strong for this fall."

He knew, if he thought about it, that Bengt Wallin would spend the summer huddled up in his rowboat out on the lake when he wasn't alone in his two-room apartment, making frequent visits to the liquor store as long as his money held out.

"Promise me, Bengt!" he said, taking the other's hand again and trying to keep hold of it. "Do me this favor! A nice walk in the sun every day. Do you promise?"

Bengt Wallin opened his mouth and breathed through it, but neither yes nor no was audible from his lips.

Per went over to see Sonja in order to get a preview of the next patient—that way it was easier to achieve natural rapport during the introductions. He'd already looked at the card Sonja had prepared: Andersson, Irene, 380415-1961, secretary, unmarried.

She was quite good-looking, slim, dyed blond hair, lines around her mouth and eyes. Tired, well-dressed, very tense. She didn't have a referral; she'd called up herself asking for an appointment.

Irene Andersson settled down in the patient's chair, arranging her legs and skirt. She watched him attentively as though she expected to begin taking shorthand.

"I need some help."

She said it quickly, quietly.

"What's the matter?"

"I can't take it anymore. I can't stand it. I can't go on like this."

"Why don't you tell me about it."

She tossed up her head and made a gesture over her hair, almost like Bengt Wallin.

"What good does talking do? It doesn't change a thing. Everything's still just the same. I've screamed at the walls and it didn't help—everything was still just the same, I had to get up and go on. Nothing ever changes."

"Screaming at the walls isn't especially constructive," he said, taking a pen up from the desk.

"I know," she said. "Everything still stays exactly the same. What I'd like is to get some tablets, some kind of strong pills. Valium or whatever. To calm me down so I can cope."

"We don't just write out prescriptions on request," he said, irritated. "If you'd like some help, you'll have to tell me what you want help with; I can't just sit here and guess. Otherwise I don't know why you came."

"Then where should I go? Where is there to go? I've been to the doctor, there's nothing wrong. The minister is putting me on the waiting list for counseling at the City Mission. My friends are all in the same boat as I, we can't be any help to each other. Should I go out on the dance floor and offer myself? What do you do when you're not allowed to get close to anyone, rely on anyone, you're just expected to love your work and take care of yourself? That's how it's supposed to be, right? Not needing anyone but yourself and your work?"

Her eyes were completely wide open so as to hold back the tears.

Per sighed even deeper.

One of those.

"We do have a certain responsibility for our own lives," he said. "Maybe you agree with that?"

She watched him steadily.

"You're dissatisfied with your life right now," he continued. "It hasn't gone exactly the way you intended."

"Nothing has gone as I intended!"

"But you can't demand that either."

"I most certainly can if it's my own responsibility! If I shape my own life myself, then why can't I? If everything depends on me, than I *can* demand that something turn out like I want it to myself!"

He got confused.

"Now look, if you'd listen to me..."

She fell silent. Her eyes shone. She looked as though she was just waiting to catch him in contradictions.

"Ingrid," he said, squinting at his papers. "In very concrete terms, what is the nature of your problem?"

"I can't stand my job. I hate my work. I've done the same thing for twenty years and I can't get any further. They won't let me advance because I'm so competent. They want to keep me where I am."

"But you chose this work yourself, right?"

"Did I?"

"You must have. Why else would you be doing it?

"What do you know about my freedom of choice? What do

you know about my needs?"

"I don't know a thing if you don't tell me. If you've made the wrong choice and you aren't happy anymore, then obviously you have to do something about it. Talk with the union at your job. I don't honestly know how I'm going to be able to help you."

She snorted.

"No, of course not. Apparently, I'm on the wrong track again."

His lips narrowed.

"Apparently. I'd be glad to help you if I could. But it's difficult when the patient has such a negative attitude."

"Why shouldn't I be negative? Does a person always have to be charming and smile?"

"If you can't handle your job, then my advice is to look for something else. You might also request a transfer or shorter working hours. Either the Labor Exchange or your union representative is the proper authority. Remember, we live in hard times. We can't just pick and choose. Some people would be thankful to have a job."

"A minute ago, you said I chose it myself and it was my own fault if I chose wrong. Now you're saying I don't get to choose at all. Which way do you want to have it?"

The aggravation struck him down like a falling bird. He felt like banging his fist on the desk. She was trapping him with her tricky questions, her sharp turns! What did she have to complain about? She ought to be grateful she had a job when so many were unemployed!

"I can't solve your problems for you," he snapped. "You've got to do that yourself. I can only help you see what you've done wrong, what path you should take in the future."

"Tell me then."

"I can't just tell you. It's something you've got to arrive at yourself."

"But right now, I need help immediately—to be put on sick leave, pills, whatever. I can't stand to be there. I can't bear it. I'm crazy, can't you see that? I'm a Swedish woman who doesn't love her job, I must be crazy. Please write me a prescription for some pills, anything. I can't go to work day after day and be quiet and obedient and cheerful. I've had two big breakdowns these past winters and couldn't even get sick leave—my blood tests were normal. I can't make it through another winter."

"But it's summer now. I guess you'll just have to wait until this winter and then contact a doctor."

"That's what I did last year right before it happened; they stuck me in the finger and said I was fine and told me to go back to work but three days later I collapsed."

He couldn't hide his smile.

"Well, I guess you'll have to call right then. When you notice it's happening."

"I can't call *then*!"

"Surely you can get to the telephone, can't you? Don't you get up and eat?"

"No, I don't get up and eat."

"There must be someone who brings you food?"

"Nobody brings me any food."

He couldn't keep a straight face, the conversation was getting so absurd. What did this woman want? What was she looking for? Was she just plain lazy, trying to get her vacation extended? On the form it said she was a secretary; that certainly wasn't a bad job? At her age, she ought to be getting a decent salary. Did she have trouble working together with the others? Menopausal problems? Single—there was probably some man in the background; maybe that's where the shoe was pinching.

He couldn't help smiling slightly. She said she stayed in bed and went without food and he saw her in front of him, still just as angry, with a tight-lipped mouth. Who would dare go in with food for her? Who'd—?

She jumped up out of the chair, grabbed her purse, and in the next instant she was gone. He heard her thundering heavily down the stairs. Sonja looked in from her hole.

"What was that?"

"Hysterical woman. Couldn't come to the point."

Sonja gave him a strange look.

"But she must have been sad?"

"She was so aggressive I couldn't get any contact with her.

It's probably just as well she goes and thinks things over. Maybe she'll come back after she's calmed down."

There was half an hour left of the woman's time and the next patient hadn't arrived yet. It would be nice to take a stroll around town, but he was afraid he'd run into her. It was dumb to have let her run off like that. He should have called Sonja in and asked her to comfort the woman. Maybe given her sick leave for a couple of days; she was obviously extremely unstable. But in these particular kinds of situations, he maintained that it was best for the patient to attend work as usual.

He went out to the kitchenette and put on the coffee. He and Sonja drank a cup together. His colleague Nils still had a patient. Sonja was very quiet. Was she taking that woman's side in some way?

"If something's bothering you, you might as well tell me, Sonja."

He thought she'd have something to say to him but after a long inhalation, she just answered:

"It'll be nice to be on vacation."

He looked at his watch.

"Just one more, then we can clear out."

She nodded.

"So where are you going for your vacation?" she asked.

"You ought to know. We always take off in the boat with the kids. And you?"

"Maybe Rhodes. Or else Crete."

"I think Sweden is its most beautiful this time of year."

"That's for sure. But then, we're here all the time."

"There's no finer place on earth than Vaxholm in the summer. Rhodes! Good Lord!"

Sonja got a little red in the face.

"Why not have both? I'm in Vaxholm fifty weeks a year, so I really don't see why there's anything wrong with spending a couple of weeks in Greece. There's an archipelago there, too!"

Was he about to get into an argument with Sonja now, too? It must be the heat. Some kind of pre-vacation jitters. It'd been a messy spring, with lines of patients—stressed and unhappy people, unemployment, alcoholism, difficulties with cohabitation...

It wasn't so surprising if you got a touch of the trouble yourself.

Just one more, then vacation!

For the boy named Alexander Rosander, half the course is already run.

The other half lies ahead. At twelve years old he is 157 centimeters tall (five-foot-one), weighs 72 kilograms (159 pounds) and has breasts like a girl.

Per took the papers out and scanned through them before the boy came in.

Alexander really should have been at a child psychiatrist's office, where the school doctor had referred him, but there was no such office within range for an overweight, awkward twelve-year-old to go without Mama—and that was exactly the point, that he should undertake something without Mama, because otherwise it was useless. Per knew his mother followed Alexander to the door and let him go with a silent hug. She was probably waiting for him outside around the corner. That couldn't be helped. During their first conversation, she'd been with Alexander and spoken for him to Per. The boy had stared sullenly at the floor and, as soon as Per directed a question to him, looked up and caught his mother's eye.

"Hi Alex," said Per when Alexander came in.

"Hi."

"Are you having summer vacation now?"

The boy glowered and clicked his tongue.

Alexander Rosander was academically gifted and lousy in P.E. His attendance at school had been a daily ordeal for six years. Now he was on his way to the upper grades, where it'd probably get even worse.

Per leaned back in the classic doctor pose with his fingertips meeting each other. Of course the case wasn't hopeless. No child was a hopeless case. First and foremost, a strict diet and regular exercise. The only natural feeling of self-worth that could exist within the pale, fat body in front of him was a recognition of superior intelligence, and that was extremely dangerous for a heavy boy in the higher grades.

Per cupped his hands around his face, rubbing his eyes. Alexander gnawed indifferently on a fingernail.

"How've things been at school lately, would you say?"

"So so."

"Has it gotten any better?"

"I don't know."

"Hasn't it gotten a little better since you started coming here?"

Alexander shook his head.

"Now they tease me about that, too."

"They tease you for coming here?"

"Of course. They think I'm nuts. I'm whacko, loony-tunes."

The boy distorted his fat face in a disgusting grimace. Per closed his eyes. When he opened them again, Alexander's face had resumed its usual non-expression.

"Is that how you feel about it? Do you want to be funny so everybody laughs at you?"

"I don't have to be funny. They laugh at me anyway."

"But then what do you want, Alexander? What do you want to do?"

Bitter question, bitter answer:

"I might just prefer looking like Dracula."

Per covered his chin with his hand.

"Why?"

"Then they probably wouldn't laugh. Then they'd probably watch out for me a little."

The hint of a smile fluttered by, gleaming in a bright blue eye and disappearing again.

"Which would you like best, Alex? That they were afraid of you or liked you?"

The smile came back again, strong and sure. Then it died abruptly.

"Don't you want to talk about it?"

"No."

"You don't want to tell me?"

"No."

"Maybe we could continue with this a little anyway. If you were Dracula, what would you do?"

"I don't know."

"What do you like about Dracula? Is he dangerous? Does he have any friends? Does he have power?"

"It really doesn't make any difference," said the boy contemptuously. "Of course he isn't real anyway. What matters is that they're afraid of him but not of me. They do what they want to me—they yell and shove and shout dirty words and the girls just laugh. But if they were *afraid* of me—"

He raised his upper lip above his teeth, revealing a strong, healthy bite.

"Or maybe I could be a werewolf," he suggested.

"Do you believe that?"

The boy observed him pityingly. "I *know* I'm really not."

"Isn't there anything that you aren't yet but could become? OK, Alex, we know what you are. We know you have a number of problems and your classmates tease you about them. You may not be able to get your classmates to quit teasing you as long as these problems remain. But is there anything you could change about yourself in order to make things different? I don't mean being like Dracula, because that's unrealistic, both you and I know that. Becoming a werewolf is also unrealistic. Each of those escapes involves fantasies and dreams. But think about it, Alex. Isn't there something you really *can* do that would change your situation?"

He saw the glimmer fade in the boy's eyes. Alexander collapsed, becoming inert.

"Can't you think of anything?"

"No."

"You know how the doctor spoke with you about certain things she could help you with. I can ask her to come in for a minute if you like, she's here today too."

"No!"

The boy grabbed hold of the armrests on the chair. His mouth was wide open, his eyes full of tears.

"Mama!" he cried.

"Your mother isn't here. Let's talk man to man."

"You just want to trick me!" the boy shrieked.

"What do you mean? Trick? Me?"

"Don't think you're so smart!" shouted Alexander fiercely.

133

"Of course I know what you want! I'm supposed to diet, I'm supposed to exercise. I'm supposed to be like *them*!"

"I didn't mean that at all..."

"If I'm like them, they'll stop teasing me! When I'm the same, they'll stop teasing me! You're just the same yourself, you're laughing at me too," yelled Alexander.

"Alex, listen."

The boy threw his hands over his ears, shaking his head.

"Please, Alex. I didn't mean at all that you should be like them."

"You did too!"

"No, of course not. You have the right to be yourself. You're fine the way you are. It's just that you should—"

"Exercise and get thin."

"It'd be easier for you, Alexander; you'd have less trouble in school."

The boy relaxed, sniffling through his nose.

"I don't want to hang around with them anyway."

"Then what do you want?"

"I don't know."

"Alexander, I don't think we're going to get any further today. How about if we take a summer vacation? What do you say?"

The boy's expression was as sharp as an adult's, and scornful.

"If that's what you want."

Per got up, raising his hand to pat the boy on the shoulder but withdrawing the gesture again. There wasn't actually any sympathy between them. He didn't especially like this heavy boy. He could understand why the classmates acted the way they did. It was almost always like that; there was something about the victim that irritated, provoked—

Maybe it wasn't weakness at all; maybe, on the contrary, it was a strength. Maybe it was the strength to dare to be different, dare to be oneself, refuse to change in order to be appropriate that had to be punished.

Per's hand sank down.

"Bye," he said. "Have a nice summer." In the shelter of the doorway, Alexander Rosander made an obscene gesture.

He walked home. Vaxholm was a wonderful summer town. It was happiness to live and work here.

He paused in the gate, looking at his home. The house was blue with white trim, embedded in the most luxuriant leafy green. The blossoming was over now, the white clouds of fragrance were gone. But the foliage was deep and rich after the long rains.

Lena was already home. She was sitting in the garden with Jenny close by, picking strawberries. They waved at Per when he came in through the gate. The baby was sleeping on a blanket on the lawn, naked as could be except for a little sunhat.

"We can eat out here," said Lena. "If you go get it."

"What are we having?"

"Herring and potatoes, OK? The potatoes are ready, I put a towel over them. They're on the stove. If you go fix the rest, you're a sweetheart."

Jenny jumped up and followed him in. She helped get out the knives and forks.

Per had a sudden impulse to pick the child up and hug her. Jenny wiggled, wanting down. She was six years old and doing a job, she didn't want to be treated like a baby.

Lena looked up from the strawberries, smiling at him when he and Jenny returned with the food.

"How was your day?"

He set everything down before answering. Took a seat and poured some beer into his and Lena's glasses.

"A little rough. I'm glad it's over!"

Lena, finished with the strawberries, wiped her fingers on the seat of her pants. They laughed.

"Do I have to go in and wash my hands?"

"You have to, Mama!" yelled Jenny haughtily.

"You don't have to," said Per.

Jenny started picking at the strawberries and he lifted her down onto the yard. She stuck her tongue out at him, but he didn't notice.

"The people you run across!" he said. "A typical last day. There was one woman who was so—"

"You didn't get in a fight, did you?"

"No, but it was unpleasant. I never did understand what she wanted. She begged for Valium, but that can't really have been what she was looking for."

"Housewife?" asked Lena.

"No, strangely enough, she had a job. Seemed completely independent."

"How odd."

"It sure was."

Lena worked at a social welfare office in Åkersberga and had a completely different clientele: overworked single mothers, immigrant teenagers caught between cultures, homeless alcoholics.

"Well, did she get some Valium?"

"You can't just give it to them."

He took his serving of the freshly boiled dill potatoes, the herring, the sour cream. There were chives growing in the ground beside them.

"Jenny! Run in and get the scissors, dear!"

"Some people are really spoiled," said Lena. "Think of all those who are going without jobs! You could have told her that."

"Absolutely, like this man, you know the one I mean. There isn't going to be a place for him after his vacation and if he isn't disturbed now, he certainly will be then."

"I think I know who you mean," said Lena. "What's going to become of him?"

"Who knows? He's probably too old to get into a protected workshop. He doesn't even realize anything's wrong. Just puts on his blinders. That's what his mental illness is."

"Not those scissors, Jenny, those are the sewing scissors!"

"I'll go," said Lena.

The baby on the lawn was moving and Jenny squatted down, watching him. Per smiled and waved at his son, who was swinging his arms in the air. Lena came out with the kitchen scissors. Some small white clouds darted across the sky, blocking the sun for a moment.

"It's not going to rain, is it?" wondered Per.

"Don't believe so. Haven't I promised you a beautiful summer this year?"

"I'm going down to trim the boat later so everything's ready for tomorrow morning.

"I've done two loads of laundry today," said Lena. "I think everything's ready from this end."

"It really isn't that important," Per put in. "We can go home whenever we want."

"Yes, but it's no fun having to." Lena ducked in and came back with strawberries and cream.

Then they drank coffee. Per showered and changed.

"Well, I'll be going for my walk. Bye for now."

He turned around in the gate and saw the young mother with the baby in her arms looking like a painting by Carl Larsson. The slightly older child peeking out from behind her. They were standing on a gravel pathway in front of a blue house with white trim, surrounded by greenery. The young woman raised her hand, waving to him.

"See you later!" she called.

But they didn't.

Lena went in and put the children to bed, sitting with Jenny until she'd gone to sleep. Meanwhile, the sun was setting and the air had become a warm orange. Lena put a shawl over her shoulders and went out into the garden. She picked up the embroidery she'd left on the garden table, along with Jenny's little clogs that were still sitting on the lawn. Lena stood for a minute looking around in the garden. The cherry tree bent its loaded branches over the neighbor's fence. The air was still heavy with the day's warmth, but a light breeze had come up from the water.

Per ought to be coming home soon.

He'd said he was just going to trim the sail. But he'd been gone for three hours now.

He could have met some friend and gone out for a beer. But in that case, he should have called. The grass was moist under her feet. She couldn't see the sun anymore; it was hanging behind the trees, but the sky was still orange and rose.

She breathed in the peacefulness around her.

Per had to be coming home soon.

Lena put Jenny's little shoes on the porch and the embroidery in her crafts basket. She slid her feet into some sandals and ran the few steps down the street. When she came to the bluff, she stopped, taking in the view to the north over the bay. Down below, the boats were moored in a row almost right against the bluff; there was only a thin wooden dock in between. During the day, there were usually swimmers further out. Now it was quiet and still. Per's *Mamba* was tied like always to the dock. She couldn't see whether he'd actually done anything to it. In any event, he didn't seem to be on board right now.

What if he wasn't still down there?

Though of course there wasn't much left to do. She'd looked through the pantry herself and packed up the baskets they'd be taking along.

Lena went down the bluff and out onto the dock. It was chilly so close to the water. She wrapped the shawl more tightly around herself, wishing she'd changed into long pants. There was nobody on the dock. The waves were knocking against the hulls of the boats. The sky was blue-gray out over the bay but still rose-colored in the corner along the mainland.

Shivering, with her arms crossed over her chest, she went further out towards the *Mamba*, which was winding around its mooring.

Apparently Per wasn't on the boat.

She went past, all the way out on the dock, and turned around.

It was just as empty everywhere.

But on the way back, when she came to the crook in the dock and saw the *Mamba* from a new perspective, she saw something that shouldn't be there at all. If Per was still on board, he absolutely should not be lying face-down with his hands stretched out as though he'd tried to drag himself forward using his nails, not huddled up in that strangely unnatural and rigid position, not with his head twisted like that. And not with blood around his mouth!

While she ran to call for help and be with the children, one thought formed itself and rolled forward in printed words before her eyes:

"If Per is dead, can the children and I keep on living in the house?"

† † †

Afterwards, the following was recorded:

The police called on Alexander Rosander, twelve, in his parents' home. The boy shouted with delight and practically swung from the chandelier when he was informed about the murder. He wanted to go to the mortuary immediately and identify the body; he interrogated the police in minute detail about the character of the wounds and the number of blows, wanting to know whether there had been much blood and if the death throes had been difficult.

The boy was obviously unbalanced with a strong need for self-centered action. His mother assured them that he'd been lying in his bed at 9:00 pm, but the boy denied her statement with meaningful gestures and by shaking his head.

"Imagine if I'd known," said Alexander wistfully to the assistant detective as he and the police matron were leaving the home.

"Known what? Is there something you're aware of that you haven't said?"

A lingering smile glided over the boy's face.

"That maybe I was the last one."

"The last what?"

"Maybe the last one to see him alive. Except the murderer."

The boy had beautiful eyes, deep blue and surrounded by long lashes. Now they were shining divinely.

Bengt Wallin had been out fishing on Friday night. He brought a small bottle out and two cod and a cancerous pike in. The police were waiting for him in the harbor. He secured his rowboat, taking along the gear and the plastic bag with the fish. When he caught sight of the two uniformed officers sitting in their car, he turned pale and had to lean up against something.

"I didn't do anything."

139

He lifted his head definatly when they approached him.

"Where have you been all night?"

"Out fishing. I didn't do anything. Look here."

He showed the cod and the pike. The police wrinkled their noses at the smell.

"That pike died of disease. Get rid of it."

"But where?"

They looked around and agreed that he should keep it until he got home.

He'd thrown the bottle into the lake. That might be illegal, but the police didn't very well turn out for—?

"You're a patient of Per Gustavsson's?"

A bitter little movement around the mouth.

"So what's he done now?"

"He's gone and gotten himself murdered."

Bengt Wallin began shaking uncontrollably. They drove him home and told him to take it easy and not to worry. He had trouble unlocking the door, and once inside, he went directly to the reserve bottle he'd stashed in the pantry.

Irene Andersson couldn't be reached. She answered neither the telephone nor repeated rings at the doorbell. Finally, the police let themselves in with the master key. Irene Andersson was found unconscious in her bed and quickly transported to the hospital to have her stomach pumped. She was still unconscious when the newspapers went to press.

It wasn't said straight out, but strongly implied, that the crime had been committed by Irene Andersson, forty-four, in an attack of mental disorientation. Therefore, she'd tried to take her own life. No one knew what had occurred between Irene and Per, but there was lively speculation about the different possibilities:

He'd jumped on her with sexual/aggressive intentions and been rejected/encouraged.

She'd jumped on him with sexual/aggressive intentions and been rejected/encouraged.

An endless number of variations could be gleaned from these premises, and the newspapers reveled in them. This wasn't the usual sex maniac who attacked young girls in the summertime on their way home from a dance. If a mature woman had assaulted a virtuous young man with deadly results, it could sell twice as many copies of the paper.

Irene Andersson wasn't in any condition herself to answer questions, but her actions during the day were reconstructed step by step:

Between ten and eleven o'clock, she'd had an appointment to talk to Per Gustavsson. However, she left his office by 10:40 am. She went to the pharmacy and bought a large bottle of aspirin and another box of aspirin with codeine. The pharmacist's assistant remembered her because at first she'd wanted more of the codeine tablets, which couldn't, however, be sold in greater quantities. Later that day, Irene was seen at the liquor store, where she bought a bottle of Explorer vodka and then apparently went home. When the police broke into her apartment, the curtains were drawn, the telephone jack was pulled out of the wall and Irene Andersson was lying unconscious in her bed. She'd vomited off and on but finally gone to sleep.

The Explorer was empty, as were the bottle of aspirin and the box.

Another version: the woman was extremely groggy but awake when the police made their entrance. She started screaming and ordering them to go away immediately. When she was urged to calm down, she broke into abusive language. The ambulance was called and she was brought to the hospital to get her stomach pumped. Meanwhile, unconsciousness resumed and at the present time she couldn't be interrogated.

The conclusion was easy to draw.

One thing was clear—we had to get an interview with Irene Andersson. If she was the one who'd murdered the whole gang, it'd be a scoop. I reminded myself of a thought Christer Nilsson had thrown out with regard to Martin Bjorkbom: there are old bachelors, like old spinsters, who've never had normal sexual relations. When they reached a certain age, it could break loose within them, in some way or another.

Irene Andersson might be one of those.

*

141

We had to meet her, feel her pulse, find out if she'd been in the vicinity when any of the previous murders had taken place.

There was only one way.

"You have to go and visit her, Katrin."

"Me? Why me, specifically?"

"You're a woman. She'll accept you."

"She might just as readily accept you because you're a man."

From what we understood, her condition had improved, at least physically. Irene was awake and out of danger but she wasn't being cooperative.

Soon the newspapers got tired of the story. They just announced that a woman had been questioned about Gustavsson's murder and then put it aside. Irene was discharged from the hospital and stayed home for a while. She was still on sick leave and could really enjoy her extra vacation on the bluffs of the North Harbor. We found her there one day in July, hardly a stone's throw away from the place where Per Gustavsson had been murdered.

We sat down in the grass on either side of her.

"Hi," I said.

She looked at me coldly and then closed her eyes.

Katrin employed her usual method—ignoring the victim as she made herself comfortable. Then we lay there. Pretty soon, Irene got up and went into the water. When she came back, she took her towel and was about to move to another spot on the beach.

"Wait," said Katrin.

Irene stiffened again.

"Excuse me for imposing," continued Katrin, "but I think I recognize you. Aren't you the one who—"

"Go away," said Irene, turning her back on her.

But in so doing, she ended up facing me. Up close she didn't actually look as old and harried as she'd seemed in the newspaper photos. The suicide attempt and the resulting holiday had apparently been good for her.

Or was it the murder that had been good for her?

Maybe all of the murders had been good for her?

"Excuse me," said Katrin. "I really didn't mean to offend you."

Irene waited, on guard.

"Didn't you work at a legal firm on Birger Jarls Street?" continued Katrin. "I got some training there once, and I'm sure I've seen you before."

Irene relaxed noticeably.

"No," she said. "But I've worked right nearby. Maybe we've seen each other in town."

"Did you used to eat at Rendez-Vous?"

"The best restaurant in the city," answered Irene.

"But don't tell anyone, keep it a secret!"

"Their filet mignon!"

"Carne asada!"

They laughed and the tension in Irene's figure almost completely disappeared. But she was still holding her towel, and now she grabbed her swimming bag with the other hand.

"Nice to see you. I've got to be running along."

"No, stay and talk, the man here doesn't bite."

Irene stood hesitantly and I sensed that it was my turn.

"Do you live here in Vaxholm?" I asked. "Or are you just out for the day?"

"I live here."

"A fantastic place in the summer."

"Yes."

She was still standing in front of us and Katrin and I were looking up at her from a rather strange angle. Nice legs.

"Wasn't this where—" I began.

"Quiet!" shouted Katrin, putting her hand over my mouth.

"He's so tactless," she continued, turning to Irene. "He can never keep his mouth shut."

Irene had tightened up again.

"Yes, what is it?" she asked.

Katrin let go of my mouth and I sat up straighter.

"My wife is a little violent," I said. "I got it into my head just now that you were the wife, or the partner, of that doctor who met with such misfortune recently. But now I see I'm wrong. Pardon me."

"No," said Irene with almost unmoving lips, "I'm not the wife. Or the partner."

"I'm sorry. I don't know what made me associate you with that story. Excuse me," I blathered on.

Irene sat down, eyeing me frostily.

"What do you want?" she asked.

Katrin's head drooped.

"That was a ghastly story," I continued. "He was quite well known in town, I imagine? In such a little place as this."

"What do you want?" she asked again. "Are you journalists? Which newspaper?"

"No paper," answered Katrin quietly. "We just want to know who had reason to kill him."

I saw Irene's knuckles blanch as they squeezed the swimming bag.

"I did."

"Did you know him very well?"

"I didn't know him at all," she answered.

We exchanged a glance.

"Then I don't understand..."

"You understand enough," she said bitterly. "Isn't that why you're sitting by me? The poor mental case Irene A. But I didn't know Per Gustavsson and I've never had a thing to do with him, except that one time when I went and asked him for help and he didn't have any help to give. Why should he? No hired expert can help. There's just one thing, one single thing that helps."

"What's that?" asked Katrin.

"They say it's work," she said, laughing quietly to herself. "And since I worked so hard and was so competent and still didn't get anywhere or do anything, then it had to be my own fault."

The conversation was beginning to get absurd and perhaps Irene Andersson was mentally ill after all. If she were to break down and confess, all of a sudden, we'd have to be prepared to take care of her. Meanwhile, Katrin ignored my signals, watching Irene attentively as she went on:

"Suddenly, when I hit bottom, I saw clearly. When I woke up and they were trying to force the same damned life on me all over again. They said the responsibility was mine; they tried to brainwash me into believing that I myself had chosen to live alone and work like a dog. Now I don't give a shit. I do what I please."

"And Per Gustavsson?"

"What about him?" Irene looked at me with polite surprise.

"He got murdered."

"He certainly did."

"Don't you know anything about it?"

"How should I? He was murdered on Friday night, and I was already lying in bed by then."

"I don't believe the police are totally convinced of that," I tried.

"Well, I don't give a damn," said Irene. "I have a clear conscience."

"Do they suspect anyone else?"

"I don't know," said Irene. "If I'd had a knife in my purse when I was up there with him, maybe, when he sat and laughed and thought my problems were ridiculous. Maybe then and maybe if I hadn't been a lady, in spite of everything, I might have done it. But I didn't have any knife other than the one at home in the kitchen drawer and I don't go around with that. I thought this was all in the police report?"

"Of course, but—"

"It's so stupid you can't believe it," said Irene heatedly. "In other words, I'm supposed to have rushed down his stairway—which I did—and home to get the knife. No, gone to the pharmacy and the liquor store and then home to get the knife—a knife with a double edge, a stiletto—and with that in hand, I'm supposed to have gone to his boat, for of course I knew which one it was and where it was kept and he happened by chance to be on it right then and he happened to be alone. Ugh, go jump in the bay."

She flung herself down on her stomach in the grass, covering her head with both arms.

Katrin's and my eyes met over her back.

"Well," I said.

"Go to hell," she repeated, a little stronger.

"No fine lady talks like that," I said, quite offended.

"Well that's how it is," said Irene. "Now I'm not a lady anymore, I'm a woman. And I want to live and to be left in peace."

We felt a little dejected after that conversation with Irene. Not for her sake, but for ours.

"Do you think it was her?"

"No."

"I don't either."

"Maybe she knew one of the others, though? Maybe Samuelsson or Björkbom, but what would she have been doing there? She didn't have anything to do with the theater premiere, did she?"

"Do we know that?"

"We don't know anything, she could have been his secret lover. They're about the same age. He broke up with her and in a desperate rage—"

"But he didn't have a lover."

"He might have had one we don't know about."

"Irene Andersson?"

There was only one thing to do. We went back and asked her.

"Björkbom? Björkbom, Martin, isn't he the one who writes—no, absolutely not."

She threw her hands over her face and at first I thought she was crying. But it was just make-believe crying to express absurdity.

"Do you think I was after him, too?"

"We just wanted to ask," I mumbled.

"The answer is no."

"Can you prove it?"

"Probably not. I've never seen the man in my life. I know he wrote about the theater. A play of his that was quite bad ran for a little while. I didn't see it."

"What do you know about Curt Samuelsson?"

"Nothing. Who's Curt Samuelsson?"

"Come on, Erik, let's go," said Katrin.

Irene had sat up and was gazing at me with narrowing eyes.

"You really can't be serious," she said to me, ignoring Katrin. "If I were crazy for murder, I know who I'd jump on. Good-bye."

She got up with flair and immediately began walking away.

"Listen, stop!" I called after her. "I want to talk to you!"

Katrin pulled on the edge of my sweater.

"Wait," she said. "We have to check out what we have first. I don't think it was her."

"She might have been the woman Totte assaulted at Gröna Lund!"

I ran after Irene and Katrin came after me.

"Irene, when were you last at Gröna Lund?"

She stopped and faced us with her hands on her hips.

"Can't you bridle that lunatic of yours?" she asked Katrin. "Are you going to disgrace me in front of the whole town? Go to Wallin's house, instead, if you want to harass someone! Go to that fat little boy's house. Go to the home of the poor, mourning partner in the big, beautiful house! Go to the home of the dedicated nurse! Go to the home of the colleague who wasn't as handsome and didn't have as many patients!"

Poor Irene, she was indeed unbalanced. I agreed with Katrin that now wasn't the best time to interview her, we had to wait until she'd calmed down.

"Sorry," said Katrin. "We didn't mean any harm."

Irene turned on her heels one more time and left.

"Shall we?" I asked.

"Not now, darling, I have a migraine."

"I mean, should we take her advice and check with Wallin and the boy?"

"And the partner and the nurse and the colleague?"

"No. If there's a common denominator, it can't be within anyone's family."

"It can't be the boy. He has a mother who watches over every move he makes."

"True."

We rang Bengt Wallin's doorbell. It was a hollow-eyed man who answered the door, despite the sun that had prevailed for several weeks. He wasn't completely sober. His upper lip curled in a sneer when he saw us.

"What do you want?"

"Is everybody this happy and hospitable here in town?" I asked sarcastically.

"May we come in for a moment?" wondered Katrin.

"Are you from the social bureau?"

"Oh no, this is strictly private."

Reluctantly, he stepped aside to let us in. The venetian blinds were pulled down; the apartment was dark. It was furnished almost entirely with old things in deep shades of wood, too big for the proportions of the room. He'd moved to the side so we could come in, but he didn't invite us to sit down.

"The weather's beautiful," said Katrin.

He bowed his head.

This was hard, terribly hard. I don't know how they do it in the tough detective novels by McBain and the others, just going in and starting to talk. It's not that easy. Not even when you're a reporter and considered bold.

"How are you?" asked Katrin. "Are you eating all right?"

He snorted.

"So it's the social bureau after all! I'm taking care of myself."

"It's not welfare," I said. "It's the press."

Katrin fought for breath, but I continued in a sweep:

"We're interested in what happened out here. There was a murder not too long ago, right? Quite a well known person in the community, as a matter of fact? We understand that you knew him, Mr. Wallin, and we're interested in everything you might have to say about the deceased. What he was like as a human being. If there's anyone you suspect of committing the crime. Yeah, you know. The police haven't been able to solve it."

"Sit down," said Bengt Wallin.

He took a seat at the oval table across from us and stared into my eyes.

"Did I know Per Gustavsson," he said bitterly. "That bastard tried to creep under my skin. I don't know what his interest was. I'd never asked to meet him. I don't consider myself sick. I've always taken care of myself. Ever since I was young.

148

Wait, let me get you a little nip. My father left my mother early on, you see. It was my sister and me. My sister went out and worked and I went to school until I took the graduation exam. There were some problems for my sister and she had to get married, but later on it turned out OK. Meanwhile—"

He went out into the kitchen and got a bottle of Parador that he put on the table along with three delicate wine glasses.

"I don't drink anything strong," he explained. "Just wine."

When we left four hours later, we knew that Bengt Wallin was a lonely person with few friends, but he believed in the duty of the press to disseminate the truth and point out the social evils. We knew the major patterns of his paltry life. We knew that when Gustavsson died, Wallin had been out on the lake: alone. We didn't believe he was physically capable of rowing his boat to the North Harbor, mooring it, surprising and killing Gustavsson without leaving a trace, rowing back and coming on land with two cod and an almost naturally-dead pike. Nor did we believe he had the sharp planning ability that all of this would have required. We didn't think he had either the strength or the temperament. We believed it even less when he said he'd been on sick leave since last spring and spent the majority of the time with his sister and her family in Gävle, and then showed us the tickets verifying the trip. He'd saved them and pasted them into a scrapbook. He'd been in Gävle when both Björkbom and Samuelsson were murdered.

We rode home.

YNGVE YXBERG, 52
TV Producer

Yxberg was a well known TV personality and the popular host of a monthly program, *Confrontation*, that he had created and produced himself.

He was found murdered in Tessin Park after a TV debate in the series *Confrontation*, during which he brought up the increased violence in society and the many recent knife homicides. He'd been murdered with a knife, probably a stiletto with a double edge. The cause of death was lacerations and bleeding in the stomach, liver and spleen. His clothes were in order and nothing appeared to be stolen.

Yxberg was an aggressive man in his field. Being an unaccommodating and controversial figure, he had many ideological adversaries but was without personal enemies as far as was known. He was generally liked on TV, having a simple and direct approach with expressed sympathy for the left.

He was in his second marriage, to his former production assistant. There were three children from the first marriage and another on the way in the new one. His wife suffered a collapse when she was informed about the murder and had to be taken to the hospital.

Yxberg was seen by acquaintances after the TV debate and the wrap-up conversation that followed. At that time, he said he was going to look for a taxi home. He may have been spotted later walking west on Valhalla Avenue. Suspects:

His wife?

His ex-wife?

Political opponents?

Some unknown person from the street?

† † †

If there was one thing he couldn't stand, it was petty people. Narrow-mindedness. Jealousy. Envy.

He'd said it when the magazine interviewed him after the last *Confrontation*, about the blacks' situation in Great Britain. The magazine had called and asked if he wanted to take part in their "Who's Who" series, and although he hated commercialism and all types of personal publicity, he saw a chance to bring out his message. Besides, if the people wanted him to be interviewed now, wanted to know something about his own, private self (which he never revealed on the programs—there he was just part of the team), then who was he to selfishly refuse? He'd taken a certain pleasure in answering the questions:

Who would you really have liked to be?
   I'm satisfied with being myself
Who do you admire most?
   Martin Luther King
What qualities do you value in a man?
   Honesty, loyalty, courage
In a woman?
   The same
With whom would you most like to live on a deserted island?
   My wife
Your favorite color?
   Red!
Composer?
   The many anonymous black voices in the South who created the blues
Food?
   Plain food; freshly caught perch
How would you like to die?
   Still active and productive

He was a simple man. He hoped that had come through in the answers to the inquiries. Actually it was more difficult than you'd think to fill out a form like that without seeming pretentious or drifting into contemplation of the navel.

"Without my co-workers," he continued on the question-naire, "the program could never take place. They're the ones who really do the job. My only function is to inspire them and come up with ideas; anybody could do that. The job itself is Pyret's and Knutte's and Dietrich's. I take my hat off to them."

He saw himself as a worker first. One of the crew.

What he wanted most of all with his programs was to awaken, to help and to uplift human beings.

If he could walk just a little ways down that path, he would be grateful.

Once a month, Yngve Yxberg aired his popular panel pro-gram with specially invited participants discussing a current is-sue. His powerful piece about the race problem in Great Britain had gone down in history. There had been an overwhelming response. The Swedish public got thoroughly shaken up in their living rooms when they found out how things really are in the former colonial superpower, the Iron Maiden's conservative paradise where lineage, dialect and skin color are still assets for people who want to get somewhere in life. As an introduction, as a counterweight to the nobility's old castles and parks, he showed how the poorest of the poor—the black and brown im-migrants and their children—lived in the ghettos. He let them come and speak for themselves, describing their injustices—represented especially by his good friend, the black ex-guerilla fighter Dave Kelly, who'd found asylum in Sweden.

He truly succeeded in getting the average Svensson to empathize, that could be gathered from the response to the pro-gram. A virtual landslide of letters roared in. Many wanted to know how they could help. People said they were ashamed to complain when they actually had it so good, and immigrants to Sweden were urged to show gratitude for living here and not in England. Protest lists containing hundreds of thousands of sig-natures circulated around the country; in the schools, kids asked to work for a day to help the blacks in England.

Debaters from different camps were invited to the program. Of course they'd wanted to get someone from the British embassy, and the fact that no one from there had been able to participate was a set-back for the host. He decided instead to place an empty chair at the central table with a name-plate hanging down. It would say either "Elizabeth II" or "Margaret Thatcher." That had been a little knotty; he couldn't have two empty chairs, one for each of them—it would have spoiled the effect. The question was which of the ladies was worse, which of them would the public prefer to see as a symbol in the empty chair. He discussed it with his co-workers and his friend Dave, and they agreed that the Iron Maiden was probably a tad more cutting after all. *She* had driven through the new race laws, *she* had been responsible for limiting immigration. Pyret suggested a doll, a rather small, ridiculously dressed-up doll to symbolize Maggie. Dietrich and Knutte thought it would be better to have some kind of animal, maybe a toothless lion, a little mangy and shabby. Finally, after yet one more round of discussion, they succeeded in agreeing upon the empty chair that Yngve had suggested. He pointed out that for the sign to be seen properly, they'd have to have a very small doll, and then all of the impact would be lost. A Maggie-doll was conceivable, but in that case it'd probably have to be life-sized, a kind of Madame Tussaud figurine.

The famous wax museum in London refused categorically to loan out their doll for such a purpose and having one made would quite simply take too long, unless they were content with a very coarse and simplified caricature. The risk was that one or another viewer out in the living rooms would fail to identify her—and then, of course, the whole idea would be ruined. Similarly with having an actress dressed like Mrs. Thatcher and smiling foolishly like her. It might not get across. The empty chair with the clearly printed name-plate was agreed upon.

Naturally, the largest newspapers' London correspondents took part. There was also a woman who'd been married to a black man in England who could tell about discrimination and prejudice against herself and her children. A British professor in international law from the university in Brighton, a very strong card, laid out cold facts, numbers and statistics. Dave Kelly and a couple other black friends of Yngve's, who'd gotten asylum in

Sweden to escape race persecution in England, provided weighty testimony.

The hard part was getting hold of someone to present the other side.

Who the hell wants to appear on TV speaking in favor of race discrimination and higher walls against immigration?

A frightened statistician from the Immigration Department had finally been talked into it. He argued that too much and poorly regulated immigration always and everywhere leads to problems, not just in England. The man was easy to debunk. This wasn't a question of statistics, this was a question of flesh and blood human beings! How would you feel if it were your children! The statistician had a couple of ordinary Englishmen at his side—no one else had been available—middle class types who lived in row houses, exactly the sort of people who are likely to oppose black immigration because the price of the property goes down, etc., etc. Yngve played skillfully on their prejudices and greediness as he described the British background of colonialism and conservative rule that had made people be like that.

Nice.

"I know what would be good next time," said Yngve to Dave after the race debate, which had been such a shining success. "There've been so damned many knife murders here at home this summer. Even here, in good old Sweden! What do you say?"

"I think it's deplorable," answered Dave Kelly with a snort, "to hear you babbling about knife murders in Sweden when the world's the way it it. For heaven's sake, take Lebanon! Iran! Argentina, violated by the British imperialists! Take Ireland! South Africa! Honduras, El Salvador! Take me, for example! Did you know that Säpo, the secret police, has been hounding me since the last program? There's some damned cop who's working as a spy. I know. Säpo tried to place the gorilla at my house."

"Yes of course, Dave, you're right," admitted Yxberg. "But right now during people's vacations, I think it would be quite interesting to consider what might be behind the significant rise in violent crime here at home."

"Violent crime!" snorted Kelly again. "What do you Swedes know about violence?"

"No, that's for sure, I don't mean it like that, Dave. I didn't mean to compare, if that's what you thought. But it's true that there's been a painful development all summer long. Completely unknown maniacs have been attacking people who they didn't have anything at all to do with. Of course we also have the usual drunken parties, and even they seem to have been more numerous than ever this year. Every other weekend there've been two or three cases of parties that ended in blows and bloodshed."

"You Swedes are so damned soft," said Kelly, scowling. "Where I come from, even the tiniest child has to get used to being ready for a struggle of life and death."

"Right!" Yxberg inserted, glad to see an opening. "Here, then, you have circles where knife fighting, so to speak, belongs to the subculture. It's a very narrow criminal stratum in Sweden, among outcasts of a special category. Other people, so-called decent Swedes, simply do not have a weapon within reach, so even if they do lose their tempers, it doesn't result in anything worse than maybe a box on the ears or some fist-fighting. I don't mean," he added hastily, "I don't mean that this makes them any better people! They're simply privileged, of course. Often it's precisely among such bourgeois types that you find the really depraved fascists, the really brutal mentality of violence. I just mean that among what's called decent people, this mentality is more seldom expressed as active violence."

Kelly grunted.

"Boors," he said.

"Yes of course, Dave! That's also what I mean. And now take these other knife homicides we've had this summer. A number of cases of battered wives. We don't know the background there. Prolonged friction, sado-masochism, jealousy? Often battery has gone on for a long time before it results in death. We have a couple murders of prostitutes. We have that computer man who was found on the jogging trail. We have Martin Björkbom, a hell of a reactionary guy, but anyway."

"An Arabic immigrant got murdered by fascists," said Kelly. "Maybe you don't think that's important?"

"Exactly, yes, him yes, it was last winter, wasn't it?"

"It's fascism spreading," said Kelly.

"Maybe. But there are other possible reasons, too. I want to do my next *Confrontation* about that," said Yngve Yxberg.

† † †

"God, how can you do it," said Yvonne.

She pressed her lips together, turning away from him when he came up to her with his arms stretched out imploringly. This time it *was* his fault.

"Well anyway, it's not my fault!" said Yngve. "If I could understand why you start these stupid arguments right when I've got important things going on and have to concentrate! Heaven help me, you're no better than Helena! At least she was loyal!"

Yvonne twirled around, confronting him.

"There it is! I knew it! You and your wonderful Helena! Why don't you just go back to her then, I'm sure she's waiting for you!"

She walked quickly towards the door, intending to leave the room but tripping over the throw rug on the wall-to-wall carpeting in front of the fireplace. She fell down on her knees, catching herself with her hands. Immediately Yngve was there with her.

"Now look what you've done!"

"You clumsy fool!"

"I could have a miscarriage! That's probably just what you want!"

He helped her get up and they stood quietly facing one another, each awaiting the other's next move.

"Yvonne—?" he said, letting his index finger glide along her cheek.

She sighed, turning her face away. He let his hand fall.

"Listen," he said, pushing his lower body against hers. "Let's talk about this later."

She stood up straight with her head leaning against his shoulder.

"Go and rest for a while, honey. You know I have lots to do."

"But why," she said. "Why do you always bring these kinds of things up right when you have so terribly much to do so I never get a chance to defend myself? Why? I have to think you're doing it on purpose, you know."

"I don't have time to discuss it right now," said Yngve. "I have to go. Dietrich and Knutte are waiting for me."

"And Dave Kelly, of course."

"Yes, Dave too."

"Too bad Dave's not a woman, then you could marry him."

"Don't be childish now, darling!"

"This isn't the first time you've started talking about these super-important things right when you're in a big hurry and have to go and want an answer within five minutes, but I just can't think that fast. And then you get mad. It wasn't like this before. Now it's Helena this and Helena that and how good she was and how much you owe her."

"Yes, but I do, dammit."

"Then why'd you divorce her?"

"Because I fell in love with you! Don't bring all of this up again now, for godsakes!"

"I'm not the one who started it." They stood crouched and ready to fight.

"OK," he said. "I've got to go. I'm sorry, baby. Knutte and Dietrich—"

"And Dave!"

"And Dave—"

"And Pyret! Don't forget Pyret!"

"OK, and Pyret are waiting for me and we have an important program to do; I don't damn well have time to stand around fussing with hysterical women!"

"Hysterical women, I see, am I one of those now? Last year at this time it was Helena who was hysterical!"

"I'm free from Helena, now I'm married to you, but when I ask you for one little token, one tiny little bit of generosity in re-

157

turn, for Helena's sake, then you've got go around bickering and objecting about everything."

"Only because I don't want to give her the Östergård estate straight out."

"Give her! Östergård is mine, dammit, not yours! And if I want to let her have it and be done with the hassling over it—what the hell do you want? Helena is over fifty, how's she ever going to get another man?"

"What would she *do* with another man if she's as frigid as you say?"

He hit himself on the forehead. He walked towards the door.

Yvonne ran after him.

"Stop!"

"I don't have time, like I said, they're already the hell at it, getting it organized, and I've got to be there to see that everything goes like it should. You just don't understand what responsibility is all about! Arguing about such a dumbshit thing as Östergård five minutes before an important broadcast!"

"Oh, so now I'm the one who started it? But you're the one who said that—"

"OK, OK, we'll have to discuss it later! I've got to go. Is the cab here yet?"

In the same moment, the telephone rang. Yvonne answered it. She handed the receiver to Yngve.

"Dave."

She made a show of standing by the phone until the conversation was over.

"Yes, at your service Dave, how's it going? What do you mean threatened? Now again? Well, I'll see if we can take it up on the program, I'm not sure. It was more the Swedish situation, you know, that—uh huh. Yes. Yes, of course. OK Dave, we'll see if we get that far. Good. See you."

Yvonne smiled scornfully when he hung up, but she didn't say anything.

"The taxi's here."

"I'm going with you."

"The hell you are! We don't want any hysterical women!"

"I'm going too. They'll let me in. You'll see."

He closed his eyes, taking a deep breath. When he opened them again, he smiled.

"Be a nice girl, now. I'll wave at you on the screen."

"Ha!"

"I'll throw you a kiss."

"Do you think I'm going to watch your shitty old program?"

"Goddammit," he shouted, "now I'm beginning to understand why there are so many knife murders in this country!"

He turned and ran out before she had time to answer. The taxi was waiting outside. He jumped in and ordered the driver to go to the TV station before he'd even gotten the car door closed. After two blocks, he realized he'd forgotten his briefcase, and had to ask the driver to turn around and go back. When he came in through the door, he heard Yvonne's voice and the telephone receiver being abruptly replaced. He went into the library where the phone was. She was standing in front of the bookcase pretending to search among the titles.

"Who were you talking to that you were in such a hurry to hang up?"

"I just called Time."

"So what time is it?"

She snuck a look at her wristwatch and he rushed up and shook her.

"You're lying, you bitch! Who were you talking to?"

"Ow! You're crazy! Are you going to hit me? Let go of me, you bastard!"

Right then, the phone rang. Their hands struggled for the receiver. Yngve's won.

"Yxberg!"

"Pardon me, I must have the wrong number."

Hung up. It'd been a woman.

"Are you sitting around complaining to your girlfriends again?" She didn't answer. She looked past him, out through the window.

He shoved the phone and walked to the door. "If I come home late, it's your fault!"

"If I have a miscarriage, it's your fault!"

This time he made it to the gate before he remembered the briefcase.

The cab was still there and the driver made a meaningful gesture towards his head. Yngve crept back. When he opened the door, he didn't hear a thing. He took the briefcase and rode with furious speed to the TV station.

He still had plenty of time to gather his colleagues for a warm-up session before the beginning of the broadcast.

† † †

Sixty-some guests participated in the program.

The camera did a pan shot in order to introduce them.

Of course the usual talk-show regulars were there: Skå Gustav, Professor Bejerot, Pastor Jönsson and Per Ahlmark. Unfortunately, Nestius had a conflict and couldn't come. The head prosecuting attorney of Stockholm was present along with the police chief, a couple of police detectives and several social workers from the suburbs.

Dave Kelly was participating as a representative for the immigrants, together with a couple of Arabic youths who'd been close to Hassan Abdel Karim, murdered last winter. Next to them sat six Chileans who'd been involved in the knife homicide at Djurgården just before the summer solstice. They had a Spanish interpreter along.

Two or three dissipated men who'd participated in knife fights had come. And Yngve had succeeded in getting others whose lives had been affected by the recent violence:

Tommy Carlsson was there, a contentious young politician from the new, unemployment-ridden Motala, son of a man who'd stood for the old socialists' concepts of security and justice and who'd met his fate by an unknown hand at Sergel's Square. Violet Palmgren, a cleaning woman for the women's restroom in the same square, had seen most everything played out at her workplace and found the corpse of the murdered member of parliament.

There sat Christer Nilsson, an actor on the borderline between recognition and fame on the one hand and total collapse from substance abuse on the other, a beautiful, haunted face. Lila Ljungblom—what was she doing there?—a girl who'd been mentioned in connection with some murder and who'd seen to it to keep herself in the limelight.

Cilla Olsson was sitting there too—Katrin's old friend and a relatively well known journalist who had greater ambitions than writing stories about famous people's mothers and girlfriends—with a glint in her eyes, a keen pen and sharper theories about violence between men and women than most people.

Lena Dahl could be seen together with Inger Samuelsson, both recently left alone after senseless, inexplicable knife murders of their respective men. Both were cool, controlled and also strong and conscious enough to want to know answers to how and why instead of just withdrawing and succumbing to sorrow.

Irene Andersson was there. She was holding hands with a young man. Really! That too!

Near her sat two young boys who looked like droopy-eared hound dogs, with dirty hands and feet, shaking their heads to get the hair out of their eyes and mumbling with coarse and awkward voices: Kent Johansson and Rickard Lindgren from Jordbro. They'd lost a friend in yet one more of these meaningless public knife fights between young men of different persuasions.

Right next to them sat the youth's mother, Iris Larsson. Her face expressed speechless rage.

Katrin and I weren't there. We were watching the program at home.

It began with a film clip:

Two men, two women with unkempt appearances. Bottles and glasses on a table. Loud discussion. One of the men gets up and holds a clenched fist under the nose of the other. Screams from the women. The other man gets up too. The women each pull at their own man. A third man comes into the room, asking what the hell is going on, wondering if anyone wants to get their ass kicked. One of the men sweeps the bottles and glasses onto the floor. Loud voices are all talking at the same time. The new arrival strikes one of the women. She screams and falls. One of the men opens up a knife.

Fighting and blood.

The film-clip fades out.

Yxberg:

"Yes, this is the way it is in many Swedish homes over vacation during the summer. We see it in the newspapers the next day as a frightening statistic about the number of murders and homocides committed for little or no reason. Often between people who really don't have anything against one another. They drank too much, and they got into an argument about some little trifle. Maybe it's out of jealousy. But I believe, and this is why I've invited my friends here to the studio tonight, that often there are deeper reasons. That's what we're going to try to investigate here. We live in difficult times. Political conflict is on the rise. The rifts in our society are widening. Antangonism is even increasing internationally between peoples and nations. A wave of violence is going around the world and fascism is flourishing. Maybe it all started in America, but now it's reached here. We'll see one more example."

Film-clip:

A gang of punkers watch a video film, scared kids who egg each other on towards the terrifying and the unknown; no one daring to hold back or show any fear. They go out, and in the subway they meet up with other gangs who've hyped themselves the same way. A boy in the first gang gets into a fight with one of the other gangs, somebody steps in, there's a melee of everyone against everyone and suddenly one boy is lying dead.

The film fades out.

Yxberg:

"Sorrow and depression are running deep in many Swedish homes this summer. A cherished member of the family is gone. But not in a natural way, through old age or disease, not because of an accident, but because of something even worse. We'll think of them for a moment and talk about them and what happened to them. Some of the people closest to them are here with us this evening. We'll hear them tell what it feels like to lose a beloved partner, a son, or a father at the hand of an assailant. But we must also try to understand what led up to these crimes. Is there something in our society that, so to speak, pours fat on the fire? Is there something which drives certain of us to commit violent crime? Is it perhaps just that weapons have gotten more widespread, so they're easier to come across? What do you think?"

Zoom around the panel. It stops on the prominent people.

Dr. Tallbom speaks about broken homes.

Professor Bejerot talks about drugs that have been allowed to spread during the era of tolerant liberalism. Pastor Jönsson acts defensive and Per Ahlmark says that the liberal ideals have been failed.

The whole thing is on its way off the track to a debate of party politics. In fact, only Palme is missing! But no, here Yngve intervenes:

"Of course there are political explanations, but we also have to admit that political murder is a rarity in Sweden. For example, what does someone who's been very closely involved have to say, someone who's seen a friend fall at the murderer's hand? What do you have to say, Kenny Johansson?"

The light focuses on Kenny, who blinks and flips his hair out of his face. The camera goes on to Kricke:

"We didn't start it," says Kricke. "We didn't do anything. Besides, there were lots more of them. We'll know who they are next time."

"You bet," agrees Kenny.

Torsten's mother breaks in:

"It's the police's fault. What do the police actually do? They can keep tabs on little children. Hunt our boys when they're out being rowdy like all boys are. But when there's a murderer at work, nobody sees a thing. Where were the police, I'd like to know?"

She looks around for the police in the studio and it's the chief of police who gets to have the next word:

"I understand this woman's concern. We all get upset when things like this happen. But we can't really have the police everywhere, after all, I wonder what the general poublic would have to say if we did. There are both policemen and guards at Gröna Lund. Sometimes it can get messy there. We've introduced a ban on liquor at Djurgarden, but even so you can get an outbreak of these kinds of—"

Iris Larsson:

"But at the bus stop? Why weren't there any policemen there?"

The police chief:

"We can't anticipate everything."

Inger Samuelsson:

"It doesn't seem as though the police have been directly on the mark since then, either. It's been two months since my husband died and I've been questioned as though I were a suspect myself, and so have our acquaintances. But the police have yet to catch a guilty party."

Yngve:

"Unfortunately, it's probably true that the police are lacking the necessary resources to carry their investigations out completely."

The police chief interrupts:

"Of course it's a little tricky when it happens during vacation time like this. Many of our people quite simply aren't here. A police officer can need a holiday too."

A deputy officer:

"It's not that easy to have an eighteen-hour workday when everybody else is on vacation. And then get verbal abuse on top of it."

A social worker:

"There can be various reasons for these sorts of crimes, and I don't think we should lose sight of that. It's pretty frightening to hear cries for police and more law and order, in my opinion, when instead we need to help each other change society. We have to start caring more about one another, not just judging. Often, of course, these cases involve people with problems. Many folks can't take a vacation at all because they can't afford it. Then they resort to a bottle on Friday and if they have poor relationships at home and maybe also are worried about being laid off, it can easily happen that—"

Irene Andersson:

"But is that any excuse to murder innocent people? You're talking about problems as though they were synonymous with criminality! Can't a person have problems without becoming a criminal?"

The social worker:

"Of course, but we're not all equally strong."

Yngve:

"We know that social problems, unemployment, outcast populations and fear of the future have increased during the 80s. Then these tendencies are heightened by the violence in entertainment so richly accessible all around us. What is Dave Kelly's opinion, a British union leader and political refugee in Sweden? What do you think about the violence, Dave?"

"It's certainly true that people who are having a hard time will resort to violence. People struggle for their freedom. Then violence is unavoidable. We already have immigrants in Sweden who've been harassed for the color of their skin; we have people who've been forced to hide from the police. The violence is just going to get worse."

The camera moves on to the Arabic boys, to the Chileans. They look embarrassed.

Yngve:

"What does Hamid El Maghribi have to say, for example? Now, you were friends with the boy who was murdered way last winter, and to the best of our knowledge, the police haven't gotten very far in solving the case....What did you say?"

Hamid mumbles.

"Could you please speak a little louder?"

Hamid mumbles and the camera moves on to the Chileans.

Dave Kelly:

"There, you can see for yourselves! People who are sitting right here are afraid."

Yngve:

"There's no doubt that prejudice against foreigners has increased since jobs started getting scarce. We Swedes have to take the responsibility for that."

Kricke:

"What do you mean, we Swedes? We certainly never asked them to come."

It got quiet.

Yngve:

"Now, this isn't meant to be a debate about immigration. In the great majority of cases, of course, it's Swedes who both perpetrate the violence and encounter it. No longer does it just happen to lonely, castaway people on the underside of life. Even in proper social circles, violence is beginning to spread."

Tommy Carlsson:

"It's capitalism setting the trap again. Big finance and the middle class wanting to prevent the necessary democratization of the work-place. Just look at them, closing down their companies and moving out of the country to where labor is cheaper, so people are unemployed here at home. That's why we need control of the profits."

He looked around for support.

Yngve:

"You believe that employee shareholding could give us a better social climate?"

"Absolutely! Economic democracy and the right to be consulted, then—"

Per Ahlmark took the opportunity:

"The Liberal Party wants people to be able to control their own resources. We believe in the individual—"

Yxberg:

"One believes in individualism and the other in social solutions."

Carlsson:

"American fascism is going to come here too if the purchasers of labor get their way. My name is Tommy Carlsson. I'll tell you who I am and who my father was. I'm a common worker and Dad was a man who believed in solidarity with the weak in society. He was struck down by a knife. Right here in Sergel's Square. That was the thanks he got for all of his hard work. The commercial powers have taken over in society, and older men like Dad, who are standing in their way—well, capitalism's lackeys see to it to get them removed."

A social worker:

"But we also have to understand the outcasts of society."

Tommy:

"What the hell, are you saying I don't understand the outcasts? I work with them whenever I have time. I'm talking about international crime, about the drug syndicate that's corrupting our fine Swedish youth and devastating the entire economy."

Professor Bejerot pointed out that if no one bought drugs, then soon they wouldn't exist anymore, or drug pushers either.

The social worker:

"But in many of these cases we're talking about, no one really knows who the murderer was and I doubt anyone knows whether he was drunk or high or whatever. Besides, there's always a reason behind every abuse. There might be problems in the marriage, on the job, and so forth. Or a fundamental lack of self-confidence."

Bejerot:

"That's hogwash. People get drunk and take drugs because alcohol and drugs are available. Stop the supply and people will control themselves and you'll have less trouble right away."

Christer Nilsson:

"I don't do drugs myself, but I think it's tacky and unfair to blame everything on drugs. Lots of times it's drunken fights, you know, or disputes between married people who can't pull together—personal reasons, that is. It isn't just that maniacs out in town go around massacring people. There are also those who have reason to murder."

Lila Ljungblom, who was sitting beside him, came into the picture too. She waved to get the floor:

"Exactly! It might be that someone finds they have good cause to murder somebody. Regarding certain kinds of criminality, we tend to feel sorry for the criminal while ignoring the victim. The victim is considered privileged on the basis of his social standing, while the murderer is asocial; we feel sorry for him. Society has inexhausible resources to invest in young men who have broken the law, vandalized and destroyed. It has almost nothing for creative endeavors like original art. These are considered hobbies to be pursued at one's own expense. Asocial activity, on the other hand, is subsidized by all of us. So what are we saying? Every society has its priorities, and thus criminality is the only legitimate form of art."

She smiled radiantly into the camera.

Lila Ljungblom. Strange girl. She was the one who was an actress and worked as an aide in the home.

Here Lena Dahl came in:

"I think that's cynical reasoning. I don't know who you are, but you look like you're healthy and feeling well, it seems to me. You should know how some people live! Frightened people, insecure people, poor people who can't make it in society as well as people like you can."

"If the ladies—" began Yngve, but Lila broke in again:

"If I left here and went and cut up the seats in the subway, would you still consider me just as healthy and decent?"

"I think we've gotten off on a tangent here," said Yngve. "Maybe the ladies would like to finish outside, afterwards?"

"I have more to say," said Lena.

"She has more to say!" shouted Cilla.

"The woman obviously has something else to say," said Christer Nilsson.

Yngve didn't show a trace of irritation. He directed the picture back to Lena:

"Sorry we interrupted, did you have something else to say?"

"My partner was one of those who got murdered," said Lena, "and I don't know who did it. I don't believe either you"—she indicated Lila with a movement of her head—"or you others, except for those in the same boat as I, realize what it feels like. This is just a juicy bone for you to gnaw on, a way to be seen on TV. But I've lost my partner and my children have lost their father. We're in danger of being forced out of our home. It isn't just Per's life that's been crushed, it's ours too. But I want to say that I don't hate the murderer because of it."

A murmur flowed around the panel. Pastor Jönsson nodded in approval.

"I can't hate, because as I said to you over there just now, I understand it must have been a sick person who did it. Per didn't have a quarrel with anyone. He was a doctor; sometimes he had patients who were difficult."

Of course the camera didn't show Irene's face right then, but I'd really have loved to have seen it. Bengt Wallin wasn't there. He believed in the power of the press, so why not the power of TV too, but maybe he hadn't been invited. Maybe he wasn't quite presentable enough, and maybe he wasn't enough of an outcast, either, to be placed in that category.

"He did what he could to help others," continued Lena. "I

don't blame anyone because I realize the person who did it wasn't well, and the fact that he wasn't is society's fault, because it makes people live unhappy lives. I've seen a lot of it myself. So I want to say to the murderer, if he can hear me, that I forgive him. But I would also like to ask him to turn himself in so he can get the help and care he needs."

There was a tangible silence, then Yngve started up with applause. Tears came to the eyes of those of us who were sitting watching the program. Good Lord, Yngve had shot another perfect mark! He must have planned this in advance! He had directed it into being!

Now Inger Samuelsson spoke up:

"I want to say that I agree completely with Lena," she said, giving Lena a kiss on the cheek.

"I don't know either who took my husband from me, or why," she continued. "Nor can I say that I'm so ready to forgive. But I also want to say come forth, whoever you are. Show yourself. Go to the police. You are dangerous to others and in the end, you'll be dangerous to yourself."

One after the other joined in. Smart, damned clever. We wondered if Yngve had cooked this up together with the police or if it had been his own idea.

"There are many of us who've lost our loved ones just this year," Yngve took up the thread. "Here you see some of those who've been hit the hardest. But there are many others in our country. Wives who are mourning their husbands, mothers their sons, children their fathers. In some instances the person who committed the act was caught right away, other times he's given himself up. But the police still don't know who committed several of the murders. We're all sitting here, Inger and Lena and the rest who've been affected. People who through no fault of their own have gotten mixed up in it, like the boys here did, nice boys who never themselves engaged in violence but who saw a friend struck down. We ask each of you, we ask everyone who knows anything about these crimes, and we most of all sincerely implore you who held the weapons when these unhappy events took place, we ask you to get into contact with us immediately either here at the studio or with the police. You can call our number or the police switchboard in Stockholm or the nearest police station. We beg you to do it right away. You need us. We need you."

It was like a good revival meeting. The program about race relations was nothing compared to this. We had no doubt that reports of real and imagined murderers would come tumbling in all night long.

Now Lila Ljungblom was on again. She wasn't crying, but she was very serious when she asked for the floor:

"I thought about the last words you said there, Yngve—you didn't speak about murders anymore, but about unhappy events. I interpret that to mean you've made the usual switch in emphasis from the victim to the murderer? When this program began, it was the victim, the person it happened to, who was standing in the forefront. Now the murderer's the one who's been oppressed. Am I interpreting you correctly?"

"Naturally, the murderer is a victim," said Yngve. "I've always maintained that."

"And the victim, then, who is the victim? Maybe the victim is the guilty party?"

The momentous atmosphere in the studio was changing. There were three minutes remaining in the program. Even if Yngve hadn't really carried off the earlier sequences, surely Lena's moving appeal was the appropriate conclusion for the whole show? To make the emotions run high and get people to start talking, start questioning, start calling in to the TV and discussing everything they knew!

Then Lila Ljungblom came along with her dumb questions and spoiled it all!

"That's an interesting issue you've raised there but I think we'll have to save it for another time," said Yngve congenially.

"It's a very important question!" yelled Lila, and Cilla, who hadn't contributed to the debate so far, got up and agreed.

"Every time a murder is committed and the murderer is unknown, we get scared of dangerous monsters who are running around murdering innocent people. But if he should step forward now and reveal himself, suddenly he'll be a poor, unhappy person whom we feel sorry for. This is an interesting question. When does the switchover occur? Is it when he gets a name and a face?"

"Exactly!" Lila cut in again. "Does it switch when the murderer shows his face?"

She stood up on the seat and the camera focused on her. She had curly brown hair, a fairly small mouth, and large eyes, gray-green.

"Our time is up now," said Yngve, as the broadcast ended.

† † †

"Come on!" shouted Katrin. "We've got to get there!"

We'd looked forward to analyzing the program together, but now it was a matter of finding a niche as quickly as possible, blending in with the guests. A program like that might have a long wrap-up session. Feelings had come to light that needed to be aired and thoroughly explored before they could be tucked away again. Here was a group of people gathered in one place, all with different perspectives on the different murders, many of them directly involved. Maybe the murderer had even been there?

It took a while to get the car out of the garage and then we had nothing but red lights the whole way. People were already beginning to drift off by the time we arrived. A group of reporters were standing outside of the TV station in the process of photographing Lena and Inger, the stars of the evening. Guess who would be telling it all in *The Evening News* and *The Express* the next day?

"Where's Lila?" asked Katrin. "We've got to get hold of Lila!"

"Why Lila, for godsakes?"

"We've got to have someone, don't you see? *The Express* and *The Evening News* have grabbed Inger and Lena; I even know who grabbed whom. We have to have one too!"

"What for?" I wondered. "We don't have anywhere to publish ourselves yet, do we?"

"No," panted Katrin (we were running back and forth as this conversation was taking place), "but I thought her point of view was interesting. She must have left already, I don't see her. Maybe we can get hold of Christer or Cilla, they were talking along somewhat the same lines."

Christer had also been taken into custody by the press. Even when his face was in half-light, it was very beautiful. We said hi as we ran past, but he probably didn't recognize us. I stopped.

"Do you have a little time, Christer?"

The evening paper's journalist who'd nabbed him turned to me, hissing. It was a former colleague.

"Quit, dammit, Skafte! This thing is mine."

"Sure, of course, but can't I have him after you?"

Katrin hunted on. Iris Larsson was also captured.

Finally, we found Irene. She'd stayed inside the station talking to some social workers, apparently rather heatedly, for we heard angry voices nearby. Irene got quiet when she caught sight of us. The man we'd seen with her on TV was walking beside her. They had their arms around each other and there was a kind of aura surrounding them that the wrangling with the social workers hadn't managed to dissipate.

"Oh, so it's you two," said Irene warmly.

Considering our first meeting, her reaction was unexpectedly positive.

"Have you seen Lila anywhere?" asked Katrin.

"Lila, who's Lila? Oh, that sharp little gal, I wanted to talk to her some more too. In fact, I was looking for her when I ran into these social pros. No, unfortunately. I don't know where she went."

"Yxberg, then?"

Irene and the young man were already heading off. We realized that we hadn't seen Yngve since we came. Had he already gone on his way?

We found Cilla squeezed into a corner deep inside at the reception area. She was standing pressed up against the wall with Dave Kelly leaning over her, supporting himself with an arm on either side of her. Cilla was trapped and forced to listen to his torrent of words. We cut in.

"Hi, Cilla, who's the young man? Introduce us!"

Cilla, who'd been leaning way back against the wall, stood up when Kelly took his arms away and straightened himself up. He turned to us.

"Well, if it isn't Dave Kelly!" I said. "I saw you on Yngve's last program. It was very powerful!"

He lit up and reached out his hand.

"Do you know where Yngve went off to, by the way?" I asked before he got a chance to start.

"He said his wife called," answered Dave. "Lucky him who has a wife."

"Doesn't he have two?" wondered Cilla. "An old one and a new one."

"So you saw the last *Confrontation*," Kelly said to me. "Yeah, that was strong stuff. Here in Sweden, you don't really have any violence worth mentioning."

"Which way did he go?"

"He went out the back door, through his office. You can't go that way." No, that was clear. Katrin took hold of Cilla's arm and we ran together towards the exit.

"I have to go home and scratch some lines together, since I was here, after all," said Cilla when we came outside. "Let's get in touch tomorrow!"

It had begun to thin out at the exit. Christer was still there and my former colleague was generous enough to release him to us.

"Did you see where Yxberg went?" we asked Christer and the friend.

The reporter answered, "No, he wasn't ever here with us as far as I know. He's probably gone out privately, so to speak. If he's going out at all—shouldn't he be sitting at the switchboard talking to the murderers?"

"As a matter of fact, someone said his wife called and was absolutely furious," said Christer.

"Who said that?"

"Some studio person who came up as we were on our way out. I was walking right by them so I overheard. She'd called several times and was probably going to come meet him. Then he got in a big rush and went with that studio guy. He didn't go out the main exit like we did."

Well, there we were. Christer looked as though he could consider coming home with us again, but we didn't really want to put him up for another night.

"What'll we do now?"

We didn't have to wonder for long. The police cars came wailing up, blue lights blinking along Valhalla Avenue.

Yet another knife murder had been committed.

It was only a couple hundred meters from the TV station to Tessin Park.

There were the police cars, parked with rotating blue lights. People were hanging out of their windows in the neighboring buildings. Those who'd been out for their evening stroll had stopped and crowded together in the shadows. Their dogs were whining excitedly at the scent. Everyone wanted to know what was happening but no one dared come forward, for fear of getting involved.

The area had already been blocked off when Katrin and I arrived. We saw a police officer we recognized and went up to him.

"Hello, Valle. What's going on here?"

"Go away," he said, not being friendly at all.

"Come on, Valle. I freelance now, write in-depth articles, no reporting. Tell us what happened."

"And end up the *The Week's Crimes*, huh?" he replied.

We don't respond to such things. We waited until he'd regretted it.

"Oh, OK," he said. "Somebody's been murdered."

"Identified?"

"Yes."

"Well, who?"

"You wouldn't believe me anyhow."

The ambulance men came by carrying a stretcher. It was covered with a cloth, as is customary when the person is dead.

Soon our colleagues would be here from the newspapers, colleagues with ready channels to drive their stories through, with salaries and expense accounts. But the thing was ours and would always be ours.

I strode up and lifted the cover.

Katrin gasped beside me.

He was lying there almost like a child, with an innocent, bewildered expression on his bearded face. We replaced the blanket immediately.

"Come on, Katrin," I said.

We left right as the horde of yelling, curious journalists showed up with their camera flashes. Their cars were howling from far away.

"We might get there before the police," I puffed as we wound around the curves out to Liding Island. "You know, they kind of pussyfoot around when it comes to notifying somebody about a death. They put it off as long as possible."

We didn't know the Yxberg's exact address, so we had to stop at a phone booth and look it up. He lived on the northern part of Liding Island.

"What'll we do there?" asked Katrin as we rumbled over the bridge.

"Interview her!" I shouted.

"The brand new widow? Isn't that a bit tactless?"

"We won't let on that she's a widow. We'll say we're looking for Yngve because of the program, then we'll see how she reacts. Don't forget, she called and talked to him. She got him to leave the station, where he was supposed to have been sitting half the night receiving the storm of viewers. She might have been on her way to pick him up. Then they met and had their showdown in Tessin Park."

"Then what?" asked Katrin.

"Then what, that's what we're going to find out!" I answered.

"You mean Yngve was murdered by his wife? You don't really believe she murdered all of the others, too?"

"Someone did it, why couldn't it be her?"

"I just think," said Katrin, "that it'd be difficult for a married woman to sneak out at night and murder men."

"No more difficult than it is for married women to sneak out at night and meet their lovers," I answered. "Besides, Yngve was gone lots of evenings. She might have gotten bored, quite simply, and one thing led to another."

Katrin didn't answer and anyway we'd arrived.

It was dark in the house; the blinds were pulled down. It

wasn't midnight yet, but in August the nights are already dark. The moon was shining, big and golden, casting sharp shadows among the trees.

I went up and rang the doorbell.

No one answered. The house had two floors, probably with the bedrooms on the upper level. I went out in the yard and scanned upwards, trying to figure out where Yvonne Yxberg slept. Katrin waited in the car and seemed mad.

Soon I heard the phone ringing in there. It rang several times, then a lamp was turned on in one of the rooms on the upper floor. I hurled myself forward and rang the doorbell again. If it were the police informing her over the telephone, the boiled pork would be fried. After that she would hardly be in the mood for an interview with Erik Skafte.

But I knew the police never conveyed such messages over the phone.

On the other hand, they could come driving up to the house any minute.

I threw myself with renewed vigor on the doorbell. Katrin came up and stood beside me.

It had stopped ringing in there. A head stuck out a window.

"Hello!" I called tentatively.

"Is that you, Yngve?"

"My name is Skafte," I hollered. "May I come in for a minute? I'm not a rapist," I added reassuringly. "I have my wife along."

"Hi, Mrs. Yxberg!" Katrin corroborated. "My name is Katrin Skafte and we'd like to get some lines about the program tonight. It was really a tremendous success."

"I know. But Yngve isn't home yet."

"Didn't he just call?" I took the opportunity.

"No, that was Dave Kelly wondering if he was home yet. Well, I guess you can come in and wait for Yngve. But you can't stay for very long."

She came down and opened the door, and we stepped up to show our cards. Yvonne Yxberg was a stunning beauty about twenty-five years old. Striking red hair, green eyes, fine figure and a roundish stomach indicating pregnancy. She led us into a tastefully decorated living room with furniture in light shades of wood, a thundercloud-blue fur couch and blue wall-to-wall carpeting with white linen patches that looked like they'd been thrown carelessly on top. I couldn't hold back an appreciative whistle and Yvonne smiled happily.

"Yes, we're quite satisfied," she said. "Yngve's first wife didn't have particularly good taste, you know, but we both think I've succeeded pretty well in designing our home."

"Did you see the program tonight?" I asked.

"Yes, oh yes. It certainly was good."

"Fantastic."

"Did you get a chance to talk some with Yngve afterwards?" asked Katrin.

"I called right away, of course, to congratulate him," she said. "And to tell him how proud I was. Yngve is terribly dependent on my support."

"You weren't angry with him or anything?"

"No, why?"

"Well, I don't know. I just wondered. Since he hasn't come home."

Suddenly Yvonne looked younger and more insecure. She sat down on the fur sofa and started peeling nail polish off her fingernail.

"Do you know where he is?"

I sat down beside her and she looked anxiously from me to Katrin.

"What is it? What do you want? Did something happen?"

"Don't be frightened, Yvonne, it'll work out. What did Yngve say when he talked to you? Did he say he was going to meet someone? Did he mention any other person?"

"No."

Her shoulders collapsed and her little round belly poked out. She put her hands on it protectively and continued:

"Actually, I was a little angry with Yngve when I called. He'd promised to do something for me on the program and then he forgot. I know it wasn't very important, but anyway. When people are in love, they have little things together, little signals. And he forgot. So it made me sad. And I called and said so. Then he remembered and was sorry and said he'd hurry home as fast as he could. I asked if I should come in and pick

177

him up. No, he didn't think so, he wanted me to take it easy. Actually, he'd promised to stay and receive calls, he said. He'd be coming a little later. But then I really did get mad and started crying. First he forgets what he promised me and then he's not even going to come home, he wants to stay there half the night sitting by the phone! I really lost my temper. I told him to come home immediately, otherwise I'd definitely ride in and get him, so he said OK, he might as well come directly home."

"He wasn't going to meet anyone else on the way?"

"He wouldn't dare!"

"What time was this?"

"Right after the program. Ten o'clock."

It was just past midnight now.

"And you haven't been out since then?"

"Of course not, what do you think?"

We believed her. We all stood up.

"But where do you suppose he is?" she asked, taking hold of my arm. "Why hasn't he come back? It's been two hours since we talked."

Seeking comfort, Yvonne pressed herself against my breast and it felt quite nice standing there being her protector. But I realized that if we let her know what we knew, we'd have to stay all night.

"He'll probably be coming soon, you'll see," I said, putting her back down on the couch. "Maybe you can go to bed in the meantime. I imagine he met someone on the way who he absolutely had to talk to."

Yvonne clung to me tightly. Katrin tried quietly to get her loose.

"You know, we don't have time to wait anymore. We've got to get going."

When we'd managed to get me free from Yvonne, we ran quickly.

It was a good thing, because we hadn't gotten further than around the corner before the police car came driving up, stoppingoutside of Yvonne's and Yngve's gate.

178

THE MURDERER

"It can't be Yvonne," said Katrin firmly. "Even if they had a stormy marriage, she'd never murder him in ambush. Possibly hit him over the head with a frying pan or shove him down the stairs. In anger, during an argument. But never in ambush."

I agreed. Our thoughts looped around each other's, half rising and half falling, as in a Bach fugue:

"It must have been somebody from the program tonight."

"Not necessarily. It could've been a demented stranger, but the probability is small. There were a great many people on the site who had something to do with the earlier crimes."

"It can't have been Cilla, anyway, because Kelly monopolized her and we left from there together."

"Not Inger or Lena, either. *The Express* and *The Evening News* had them."

"The tough young boys, then? We didn't see them at all."

"Can you imagine them sneaking up behind Yngve and attacking him? He'd given them publicity, you know. I don't think they had a grudge against him—on the contrary."

"I suppose if they were going to fight, it'd sooner be against each other, between gangs."

"Besides, it wasn't gangs committing the previous murders. It can't have been."

"If so, it'd have to have been skillfully organized rings with well-trained members. No gang of boys."

"I know. And we also talked to Christer Nilsson on the way out."

"He wouldn't hurt a fly."

"Not even your favorite candidate, Irene."

"Did you see that fellow she was with? He could be an accomplice. They left before we did."

"Yes, but if you remember what Irene said in the debate, she was *against* personal problems being an excuse for criminal behavior."

"Her personal problems seem to be solved now."

"Sooner or later the summer will be over and her sick leave will be over and she'll have to go back to work; maybe the love-affair will be over too. Then I wouldn't want to be Irene."

"My, but you're pessimistic! She'll probably work something out now that she's gotten a grip on life."

"If it was her, then the fellow is either an accomplice or else she dumped him in the subway and then went and snuck up on Yxberg—"

"Yes, but why would she do it?"

There wasn't any doubt, after all, about where we should be going. The whole conversation was just preliminary because we didn't know what to say about the person we were really looking for. We didn't want to say to each other: this is the one. Didn't want to hear the other's protests.

For what motives were there, what reasons, why had so many murders been committed by one and the same hand?

I couldn't understand it and I didn't want to discuss it with Katrin.

I wanted to see the murderer face to face and hear it directly.

If only we managed to get there first.

But it isn't very far from Liding Island to south Stockholm, and there isn't a whole lot of traffic at one o'clock in the morning.

We drove directly there. We'd put the address down in the black book that I always carry on me. It was one of the old houses in Mariaberget. Naturally the door was locked, but there was a doorbell for each apartment.

She answered the door, drowsy and disheveled.

"What do you want?"

I stepped in with Katrin quietly at my side. I let the door

fall closed behind me and leaned up against it.

Lila put one hand on her hip and set her head at an angle.

"An interview? About my contribution on TV?"

"About criminality as a fine art, the only one allowed? There's something to that, Lila."

"All creative activity is thwarted except for criminality. My little theater group was denied eight thousand kronor that would have taken care of our budget for another half a year. I went out and smashed street lights all night long. The money was there, of course—it was just a matter of priorities."

"But doing that didn't help your theater group."

"Not one bit."

She smiled.

"Lila, let's go over to our house for a while. I think the police will be here pretty soon."

"Why?"

"They've found Yngve Yxberg."

Her movements stopped. She looked into my eyes, then into Katrin's. Her mouth formed an O.

Lila walked in front of us into her apartment, as different from Yxberg's dream chateau as you could imagine. A rib-backed sofa with a crocheted cover, an old-fashioned kitchen table and two hard chairs, a rag rug. Lila sat down on the couch with her hands resting loosely in her lap. I sat straddling one of the wooden chairs and Katrin sat down on the other.

"Is there anything you want to bring with you, Lila?"

A wordless no.

"What happened after the program?"

She shook her head as if to make herself wake up.

"What'll we do at your house?"

"We're going to talk about these crimes, Lila. About Yxberg and the others."

"What others?"

"That's what you're going to tell us."

Her smile found its way out again. She got up and went into an inner room. I followed her to make sure she didn't try to pull anything. But she just went and got a shawl that was hanging over a chair. She was dressed in something long and loose made of cotton—probably a nightgown. She lay her shawl over her

shoulders. The room was small; there was only a narrow bed
and a bureau. In the corner was a tiled, wood-burning stove.
She turned to me.

"Ready."

If you regard Yxberg's and Lila's homes as two extremes,
ours lies somewhere in between. We were all cultural workers—
Yxberg at the top, with a secure job on TV, fame, and unlimited
resources. We ourselves freelanced but had reasonable agree-
ments with a number of newspapers who let us contribute according to somewhat unconventional terms, for the benefit of
everyone concerned. At the bottom was Lila, ambitious in
theater, a thoughtful girl who supported herself by giving care
(she said) and who took out her frustrated cultural ambitions
in—

I looked at her out of the corner of my eye. Pretty girl.
Curly brown hair, a small, turned-up nose. Slender and delicate.
What had happened to make her go so completely astray?

In my imagination, I began playing with titles for my articles. She was so good-looking that it'd be difficult to go with
the underprivileged bit, about how exploited and ill-treated
she'd been. Better some kind of pampered-dame package:
"Used to getting what she wants"? "When Lila, 28, points at
something she usually gets it"? "A good man is a dead man, says
Lila, 28"? Net stockings and a split skirt. Or perhaps a child-
like, innocent Lolita-style. Pouting mouth...

We parked the car in the garage and took the elevator up.
Lila hadn't said a word the whole time. I indicated where she
could sit. It was going to be in the living room, where we have a
couch, comfortable chairs, a large table and stereo equipment. I
brought a tape recorder in from my study and got it ready.
Meanwhile, Katrin was in the kitchen brewing coffee. Lila collapsed in the deep leather armchair—our only one—and
cuddled up. She leaned her head on the armrest and appeared
to be sleeping. I kept my eye on her while I made my prepara-
tions. I didn't really think she would try to run away—I'd
locked the door with the key and put the key in my pocket. It's
four floors down to the ground.

I turned on the tape recorder and poked Lila on the shoulder to wake her up.

"Let's get started now."

"It all began," said Lila, "when an acquaintance of mine who was a prostitute got murdered by a customer. It struck me as grotesque. It's always men who do that to women, women who've never threatened or harmed them in any way. It'd be more natural, wouldn't it, if it were the other way around—if prostitutes murdered their customers. That you could understand. But that only happens in exceptional cases and then only in self-defense. Men murder women because—well, why?"

She threw out her hands. She looked questioningly from me to Katrin and back again.

"Yes, why?" I said to Lila. "Why do you murder, for example?"

"There you are," she said seriously. "Why do I murder, for example? Yes, well, maybe it's for the same reason."

"What reason? You asked just now about—"

"Let Lila continue, Erik," said Katrin.

"I looked at murdered women and of course I saw that they were victims. Everywhere I saw women being victims and at first I was a little surprised, then I was annoyed and finally I was absolutely furious. What's going on here? What's wrong with women? Are they inferior, or what? Why do they let themselves be bullied and tyrannized century after century?"

She turned angrily to Katrin and Katrin was angry too.

"I don't let myself be bullied!" she said.

"Oh no, not her!" I agreed, nudging her playfully on the arm. "Ask who the hen-pecked husband is in this house!"

Lila rolled her eyes upwards.

"Anyway, I vowed I wasn't going to be made into a victim," she said. "Never! From then on, I decided. I would never find myself...no never, not ever."

"And when was this?"

"Last winter. That's when it all started. Every time a man was just about to patronize me or exploit me or make me into a victim, I struck first."

"Yes, but that's crazy!" I burst out. "Lila, do you realize what you're saying? Did any of these men we're talking about actually *do* anything to you? Did any of them hurt or mistreat you? Oppress you? Attack you? Rape you? Some probably made passes at you, but you could just as easily take that as a compliment. I know you're good-looking if you want to be. There must be more than I who think so. And how did you plan to pull it off? Get away with it in the long run? Didn't you realize you'd get caught if you kept on like that?"

"Oh yes. I certainly did."

"Maybe you even wanted to get caught?"

"Maybe. They say that's often the case with compulsive mass murderers."

She smiled sweetly and rested her chin on her hand. A shudder went up and down my spine.

"You see, it's like this," said Lila. "The man I mentioned who murdered my girlfriend and the other gentlemen too, who beat their wives, etc., they always seem to have an explanation. That's what I wanted to bring up on the *Confrontation* program, though it didn't come off very well. I think there were a couple of people who understood what I was saying, but Yxberg didn't like that turn in the conversation, so he stopped me. That's what we continued talking about afterwards, he and I."

"Maybe I didn't really understand what you meant there," said Katrin. "About when it switches? When the murderer gets transformed from monster to victim?"

"Exactly!" said Lila. "It's a very important point. An undetected murderer is a monster, terrifying and dangerous, leaping out of the shadows. Dracula. Frankenstein. Jack the Ripper. But the exposed murderer, safely under lock and key, is a pathetic figure, if not to say tragic. It isn't his fault that things have gone the way they have, he himself is a victim. It's his mother's fault; she didn't give him enough love. Or some other woman's fault who burned and betrayed him. It could be the fault of the masculine role, or it could be society's fault, liquor's fault and it could even be the victim's—the murdered one's—own fault, for provoking or threatening him. A woman doesn't have those kinds of excuses. It's her own fault that she's the way she is. She can't blame the harsh world of women and she can't blame Dad or the treachery of men. If she's evil, then that's just how she is. Like me, for example."

She opened her rosebud mouth and stretched her arms above her head.

"I wonder if any pardoning flowers will be plucked up on my account or if I'll be condemned as a witch. It'll be interesting to find out."

She sank back in the chair, curling up. Katrin and I sighed. "We might as well start from the beginning, Lila," I said. "One at a time."

"I'm tired."

"So are we. But this has got to be finished by morning, when we're going to take you to the police. We've worked on this case just as long as you have and now it's our turn to step into the limelight, Lila, at your side. We're going to have sole rights to the whole confession."

"OK," said Lila, "but if there are any royalties, we'll divide them. You don't stay locked up forever anymore, you know. I'll be out in a couple of years and then I want my bread."

I was dumbfounded. Katrin laughed.

"You two work it out," she said. "I'm going to go fix some sandwiches."

HASSAN

"We met on the train, the commuter train from Södertälje. I was sitting by myself when he got on at Huddinge."

"Why were you sitting alone?"

"Do you call that a relevant question? Does it make any difference why I was sitting alone? Maybe I'd come from a meeting, maybe I'd been out to a party. It's nobody's business. I made a bet with myself when I saw him get on. There are some people who you just know are going to be *after* you no matter what. If you're sitting by yourself on a bench at the Central Station, you're the one he's going to come up to, you're the one he's going to pant over, and you're the one he'll ask where you're going when you move aside or get up in order to avoid him. He takes that right over you for himself."

"Maybe Hassan came from a culture," I inserted, "where it's more common for people to get in touch with one another. Maybe there people don't sit alone on their seats surrounded by emptiness, staring at ads rather than look another human being in the eyes."

"Oh yes, that may be true," answered Lila. "But I don't believe men in those cultures expect strange women to open their doors for them in the middle of the night out of pure kindness, *that's* something he must have learned here. He came into the car through the door furthest away from me. So it wasn't a question of plopping down in the first, most available seat and happening to exchange a few words. He stepped on, stopped in the middle of the entrance and took a good look around. I knew he'd seen me and he'd sit down with me even though he had at least a hundred other places to choose from. Where do you suppose he sat down?"

"Probably next to you."

"Wrong! He sat down opposite me. He told me Sweden was a shitty country and Swedish women were witches who destroyed men. He was sober, so he must have meant it. Maybe he had good reasons for his opinion. But what did that have to do with me? We'd never even seen each other before. I have the right to be left alone if I want and be spared being jumped on. So I was forced to determine that he'd gone too far, once he did that. Then there's only one way out."

"One way?"

"The exit."

Katrin took a cigarette and gave one to Lila. Lila caught her glance.

"Now you're thinking: there's a mad criminal sitting right here, how is all of this going to end? That's what you're thinking, isn't it? Maybe you're afraid I'm going to jump up and get a stranglehold on you or something."

Katrin shrunk back. But only for a second.

"Actually, you're exaggerating," she said. "I don't believe you want to get me."

"Why not?"

"I know I'm not on your list."

Lila laughed.

"I don't have a list, are you crazy? Where would it end?"

"Let me put it this way, then—your system is evidently not applicable to me."

I made them get back to the subject.

"So you and Hassan came to the South Station," I said. "Then what?"

"He followed me, stood beside me in the door, tried to prevent me from getting off. He said he wanted to go home with me and sleep at my house."

"He was desperate. Don't you have any compassion?"

"I have compassion, but I can't deliver it on command. Compassion means sharing feelings, not obeying orders. Did he ask me who I was, where I came from, if I had any requests?"

Now the murderer's eyes were ice-cold.

"He forced himself on me, demanding my sympathy. It wasn't a question of making an appeal and seeing if I had anything to offer. He wanted to take, and I was supposed to give."

Katrin was silent. She blew smoke rings.

"So I left the South Station. He came after me. There was no guard around. I felt very uncomfortable."

"Hassan was quite a small man."

"Hassan wasn't any bigger than me, but he was aggressive. Not so much against me, but against society, against Swedish women, against a Sweden where he wasn't making it, a Sweden that looked down on him and whose norms were different from what he was used to."

"But he was just searching for human contact!"

"I steer clear of contacts on deserted streets in the middle of the night. At the doorway of the station, I said, in a completely friendly manner, that he should please go away. Until then, I'd acted what you call normally, you realize. Humbly. Evasively. Hadn't told him to get lost. But now I said I was tired, I was going home, he might as well go back to his girlfriend or wherever, but not to my house right then. I wasn't negotiating. *Leisa ladayki mahall.*"

"What?" I asked. Katrin put out her cigarette.

"It's an Arabic expression. I wasn't prepared to surrender a place in bed to a person I'd known for ten minutes and who'd approached me aggressively. He had to be able to understand that. He must, quite simply, respect that. I couldn't see that he had any legitimate claim over me."

"But common compassion!"

"Precisely. Common compassion has driven me to the point where I am now, because I was always expected to be the provider. I told him to leave me alone immediately. I always give them a warning first. I continued walking up towards Bergsgruvan and he kept following me."

"So he didn't heed the warning."

The girl was nuts. *She* dealt out warnings, and people had to obey!

"On the contrary. When I'd turned off the street and up into the park, he was still at my side. He hadn't touched me. But then he grabbed hold of my arm and said now I should listen to him, maybe I thought I was the ruler of the world but now he was going to teach me. About like that."

"But of course it wasn't really you he was after!" I interrupted. "Don't you understand, he wasn't attacking you personally at all, it was his own girlfriend he was mad at. Margareta Åström."

"I'm sorry," said Lila, "but it wasn't him personally I shoved away from me either. I didn't have anything against Hassan Abdel Karim. But that man who took out his injustices on me, he's the one I kept from crossing the boundary. Naturally, I could have kept on running away. I could have tried reasoning with him out in the cold all night long. How many times have you yourself wheedled or run away, Katrin? Run home and rushed in and sat down on the edge of your bed, panting with your heart pounding and feeling in your arms all the way up to your head how you just wanted to strike back, just wanted to hit! And you weren't even out doing anything special, just some everyday thing, but somebody had forced himself on you or insulted you or assaulted you or harassed you. And how many times have you refrained from doing anything about it so as not to hurt anyone or irritate or make matters worse, or, as your husband says, in order to show compassion and sympathy? There's a limit, Katrin, there's a limit when you have to say no."

"But through murder?"

"What other way is there?" asked the murderer.

STHEN

"The old man, yes," said Lila. She smiled to herself.

"The member of Parliament," I corrected her. "So what did he do to hurt you?"

"He didn't touch me," answered Lila. "But he felt he had the right to change my life according to his own assumptions. It didn't interest him what my assumptions were."

"Where did you meet him?"

"At a pizzeria not far from Sergel's Square. I'd worked all evening and wanted to unwind and relax a little before I went home. The old man looked nice and peaceable, so I sat down by him in order to be left alone by the others. But then I got stuck with him instead. He'd hardly seen me before he started talking."

"And therefore you stuck a knife in him," I said sarcastically.

"No, that's not how it was. We simply began chatting over the pizza. The old man was there alone and said he was a very busy fellow, he'd worked hard, etc., and now he was taking a break. He started asking me what I did and I said a little here, a little there, different things. Unfortunately, he misunderstood completely. He took it to mean I was a prostitute."

"But aren't you, really?" I asked.

It was something I'd sensed already the first time we met Lila. There was something about her way of ordering the most expensive dish at Tim's and plunging into it, completely sure we'd pick up the tab. That's how women act who are used to being treated. She'd told us about her odd jobs as an aide in the home and her little roles, but I still didn't feel it jived. Can you really live on that? She said so. I suspected she also had other sources of income.

"Come on, Lila," I said. "Admit it. Surely you catch a fish or two occasionally?"

Katrin tightened her mouth, but if Lila was bothered by my choice of words, she didn't show it. She smiled broadly.

"Sure," she said. "If you're healthy and clean and have money to give away, why not?"

"So he was right," I said brutally. "Then I don't understand why you had to get so offended."

"I didn't," said Lila. "That wasn't the reason at all. I explained to him calmly that he could save his money and energy, I wasn't the least bit interested. I choose my associations myself."

"Have you really been a prostitute?" asked Katrin.

"Ugh," answered Lila. "Who hasn't? Don't all human beings sell themselves? Men in general get better paid. Take all the Volvo guys and IBM guys and General Electric guys, for example, haven't they sold themselves? They sell themselves every day. They sell their very essence. I don't sell any more than I can spare, never my own soul."

"High class hooker!" I said.

Lila was quiet. Her face got white.

"See, look, you definitely got offended," I said.

"Erik," Katrin began, but Lila had already found herself again.

"Then what are you, a pimp?" she asked. "Aren't we sitting here right now so you can sell me tomorrow to the highest bidder?"

"Ha!" shouted Katrin, and I don't know to whom, whether she was exhulting over Lila or over me. In any event, Lila appeared to relax again.

"It's not exactly the same thing," I said.

"No, absolutely not, of course it's much more moral," said Lila. She smiled her strange, inward smile and continued:

"He assured me that he wasn't looking for anything in that area at all. On the contrary, he felt like a father to me. He wanted to lead me onto the right path and make a decent woman out of me. I was so pretty, after all. I'd probably be able to get something better, in his opinion. There were other kinds of jobs, you know, decent jobs. Like his secretary, for example, he held her up as a model of a good and successful woman. She'd also gotten into trouble in her youth, he said, she'd had a son without a father. But she wasn't the type to let herself be sucked down in the muck because of it. She was an independent, self-supporting woman who stood for everything that was right and correct, a jewel for society and for her sex. I asked what she did. She types, he said. Then what did she write? She wrote up what he said to her and what other gentlemen said to her. She made changes when they told her to, and revisions when they weren't satisfied. She put commas where they thought they should be. Her documents conveyed their opinions and their wording and were all in their names. Terribly independent, I said to him."

I heard a snort from Katrin before she put her hand over her mouth. Lila gave me a wicked look.

"Terribly independent and good," she continued, egged on by Katrin's appreciation. "And what did she earn for that? I wondered. He named a figure. Each time? I asked. Or was it for a certain project? No, said the old man, that was her monthly salary."

Katrin snorted again.

"Go drink some water!" I yelled at her.

Katrin got up and went out. Lila stayed behind looking triumphantly at me across the table. We were quiet until Katrin came back.

"I was totally dismayed," continued Lila. "I earn less than that as a caregiver, but at least I'm helping people who need it, comforting them and cheering them up. But that poor woman, I could cry for her and her sisters! Those bosses occupy her very soul, they leave her no escape! They buy her life for a trifle and pat her on the shoulder—if not on the behind, a little carefully, taking their time a little, you know, hoping she'll think they're just being friendly—and call her independent. They hold her up as an example to others! There he sat, radiating his naive goodness, and I could have strangled him with my bare hands."

She was worked up now, her cheeks were flushed and she turned from me directly to Katrin:

"You could feel sorry for little Hassan. He didn't know what he was doing or what was happening to him. But this old man, Katrin! Patronizing and morally irreproachable! How many women has he killed with his so-called goodness?"

"Very likely none at all," I said, determined to answer in kind. "He would've been able to find you a decent job where you could have gotten stimulation and confidence and maybe even a little self-respect. But you were probably too lazy to take a chance like that."

Lila laughed.

"Yes, that's exactly how he sounded. As if it were any of his business. Why do you all worry yourselves? I'm not complaining. I have my jobs, the old people I go and clean for. I've had a number of roles. And at times, I've gotten money from rich men," she said, looking me square in the eyes. "Why do you have such a problem with that? Who in the world *doesn't* get their money from rich men? Name somebody!"

It was useless to argue with someone like Lila.

"OK," I said. "Go on."

"And please lower your tone a little," said Lila, ready to fight. "Neither you nor the gentleman in question have ever had to risk offering your self-respect and the salvation of your soul for the kind of job he was trying to trick me into. Thank your creator for that and keep quiet while I'm speaking."

"Yes, be quiet, Erik," agreed Katrin.

"Then I really did get the urge to kill him," continued Lila. "Not just for my own sake, but just as much for his Mona's sake, and for all of the other women like her. Forced to obey in order to be recognized as independent!"

"Oh, kiss me," I said.

Lila smiled broadly and her eyes met Katrin's. God help me, I shouldn't have said that!

"I was just kidding," I said.

It didn't stop Katrin from giggling several times. I started to feel sick, really sick.

"You have to give him credit for meaning well, anyway," I said to Lila. "He wanted to help you and give you an honest job. Did you really have to take his life for that?"

"Of course not," answered Lila. "I thought it was time to

193

end our conversation. So I got up and said I had to go. That's when he started arguing with me."

"What do you mean?"

"Stopping me. Trying to keep me there. Ha ha, you little old man, I thought, so that's what you really wanted after all, just had to lay it on a little first. But actually he wasn't a dirty old man. He was an awfully nice fellow from the country who believed some simple words on his part could get me to give up the relative freedom and economic independence that I do have, in spite of everything, just to wait on him and his peers. Give me a break!"

"And so then," Katrin prodded.

"I thanked him for his attention and explained that I wasn't interested. Then, of course, I left the table. And the restaurant. But he ran after me, calling. I wanted to get rid of him. I walked up Klarabergs Street and downstairs to Sergel's Square. He followed me the whole time, telling me to wait so he could talk to me. I thought, well, he won't follow me into the women's restroom, anyway. But he was fast for his age—didn't smoke or drink, he'd told me. So I snuck into the women's bathroom. I wasn't really going to use the toilet, I was just going to stand between the doors and catch my breath until he'd gone. But he came in after me. Suddenly he was standing right in front of me in the outer part of the restroom."

"What time was it?"

"It must have been close to eleven. It'd been about ten when I went into the pizzeria, and I talked to the old guy for a little over half an hour or so."

"To Mr. Carlsson," I said.

"To *Mister* Carlsson," agreed Lila. "He invited me to go with him. I asked how much. He said no, no, he was like a father, he just wanted to help me. I drew my knife and warned him, 'Leave me alone and don't mess with my life! I don't make my choices on your terms, *Mister* Carlsson!' He got scared. He backed away. But then he smiled again and started coming closer—he didn't believe I'd really dare to use it."

"That's amazing," I said. "So you just took the knife and stabbed the old fellow."

"That's what I did," said Lila. "Stabbed him."

I felt the blood rushing to my face. It was annoying.

"But he didn't do anything to you!" I yelled.

"He forced himself on me even though I told him to stop," said Lila.

"Is that a reason to kill people?"

"How many times should you have to put your foot down? What do you think? Eight? Fourteen?"

She turned to Katrin, then to me. Katrin bit her lip. She didn't answer.

"So I stabbed him," continued Lila, looking me straight in the eyes. "I figured he wanted it himself. Since he didn't leave me alone when I told him that if he didn't leave now, I was going to stab him. I didn't force him to stay there. I stabbed him but he acted like he wanted it."

I moaned and couldn't bear to look at her, I had to cover my face with my hands. I felt ill, felt like cutting our interview off. Katrin didn't say a word. It was completely quiet and only the tape recorder buzzed along softly.

MARTIN

"Well, Lila?"

She'd pulled up her knees and put her arms around them. Her head was hanging like a fading flower over her kneecaps. She didn't answer me.

Katrin got up and stretched. The night was young—we'd have the whole truth about all of the murders out of Lila tonight, because tomorrow I planned to deliver the articles before we drove her to the police.

I poked Lila on the shoulder.

"Come on, let's get going again."

Katrin had gone out and come back with some knitting.

Lila woke up and bent over the table to look. Katrin described the project to her. It was some kind of sweater with a pattern of borders in several colors.

"I'm using a circular needle, of course," said Katrin. "It's much easier when you're changing colors. You avoid all those loose ends."

I turned on the tape recorder and knocked on the table.

"Ladies! If we could get back to business!"

Lila collapsed in a heap in the easy chair and sulked some more. Katrin knitted silently.

"Björkbom?" I said to Lila.

Lila let out a sound I couldn't interpret.

"What did you say?"

"I said Björkbom."

"Tell us about him. You killed him, right?"

"I sure did."

"You didn't go with him after the premiere. But you called

196

him up later?"

She nodded.

"When did you call?"

"I called on my way home. I don't have a phone, but I was really looking forward to meeting him and he'd said I could. I thought I might as well strike while the iron was hot."

"What time was that?"

"It must have been about twelve-thirty when he answered."

"What did he say?"

Now she sat up, stretching her arms over her head and focusing her eyes on me. The sleepiness was gone.

"He seemed to have been expecting to hear from me. He asked if I could come over right away. But I got the impression he wanted something I didn't. Besides, I prefer to sleep after midnight," she continued, with a glance at the clock.

"So?"

"I asked if I could come in the morning instead. It was Sunday, you know, so neither of us would be working. Yes, of course, he said. I got up at six o'clock, ate breakfast and walked through town to Östermalm. It was quite cloudy and windy—you might almost think another touch of winter was on the way. The water in Strömmen was very rough and gray. He had a bathrobe on when he answered the door. He was eating breakfast. He asked if I had an important errand. No, I answered, not that important. If he wanted, we could just as easily meet another day. Or not at all. Actually he was the one who'd invited me to call, and who'd asked me over when I did. I never forced myself on him. I didn't come uninvited."

"But it was your idea to get together," I put in. "Not his."

She bent her head a little.

"You mean I'm the one who took the initiative."

"Right."

She nodded quietly.

"Then what happened?" interjected Katrin, raising her head from the knitting.

"He asked me to wait until he finished eating. I was feeling uneasy and wanted to go. But he thought since I'd bothered him anyway, he had the right to find out what it was all about. He came up and asked, well, what did I want? At that point I started to get confused. I'd almost forgotten what I wanted. It didn't seem as interesting, as worthwhile anymore as it had when I'd first thought about it."

"I know," muttered Katrin over her knitting. Lila, quick to catch any expression of sympathy, turned in her direction and continued:

"I sat there editing, in a way, what I was going to say. I explained I was interested in his opinion of the play the night before and how he felt about that performance compared with the performance of his own play, which I understood had been done on the same theme, though I found his perspective much more interesting. He asked if that's what I'd come to discuss on a Sunday morning—yes! He asked if I really thought I comprehended anything about all of this—yes! Then he laughed, or rather—"

"Snorted?" suggested Katrin.

"Snorted, maybe you could say. He asked how long I'd been studying the history of theater. I started to wonder why he'd let me come."

She was sitting on her knees in the easychair, folding her legs underneath, and the glimmer in her eyes began to return.

"Maybe he really wanted something else altogether?" I suggested.

"Exactly," she said. "I thought of that, too."

"It's not so surprising, after all," I went on. "You have to admit it's pretty naive to go to a man's home by yourself at that hour of the morning and just expect to sit and discuss theater history."

"So I answered his question," continued Lila as though she hadn't heard me. "I told him I was working with both the students' theater and an independent theater group. I said I felt just the way he did about the problems in the institutionalized theater. He asked what I planned to do about it then."

"Yes," I said. "What did you plan to do?"

"Then I realized he was trying to trick me. You have to admit it's pretty naive to invite a woman to your home at that hour of the morning and expect she'll go along with something besides her own errand."

"You could have left."

Now Lila lifted up her head and I saw the tip of her tongue sticking out of her mouth like a snake's.

"Yes, I could have begged his pardon for troubling him and gone on my way. He thought I should certainly keep on being an actress if that amused me, but I probably ought to leave the serious theater history for those who were better endowed. Such studies required a certain logical ability and breadth of intellect which he hardly believed I possessed. He sat down behind me on the arm of the chair and *didn't* touch me. But he was very close to me, breathing down my neck.

"Then he started talking to me like a father," Lila went on. "He asked if I really believed I had anything to offer in the field of theater history. Sure, you could continue with the amateur parts, he thought, do it. But when it comes to the creative art forms, he had to point out that women in general just don't have a whole lot to offer. All you have to do is take a look around, so that's what he advised me to do."

"The female Shakespeare," muttered Katrin.

"Right! That's almost precisely what he said. That maybe it was just as well if I tucked my thoughts away in a drawer and applied myself to something which suited me better. He'd seldom found female critics to measure up, as he put it."

"Is that so."

Katrin pulled off a piece of yarn, holding her work up in front of her. Lila started to get interested in it again, commenting about the pattern of the knitting. I almost had to bring her back physically to the work at hand.

"He was probably furious that you'd come and disturbed him so early in the morning," I said. "And for such bullshit on top of it."

"Yes, that's what it seemed like," she answered. "He kept on sort of rubbing it in. He said how sincerely tired he was of all kinds of women who imagined they were artists just because they put a pen to paper or stood up on a stage. He asked whether there was anything else I was interested in. And then came his hand. I asked him to take it away. That wasn't the reason I'd come. He talked about how pretty I was and how he'd noticed me the night before at the premiere. He'd felt already then that the two of us would have a great deal to discuss with one another. I asked him to take his hand away, I tried to get up. He held me there and said I was cute when I talked about theater history, but he was sure there were times when I was even more beautiful, like when I was angry. At that point I decided to let him run out the course."

"*You* decided?" I asked.

"Yes. I pretended to change my mind. I said I could be very pretty when I got mad, but also very, very dangerous. He liked that. Then he started getting excited. I took out the knife and he laughed and was really pleased. He told me to put it away, or was the kitty showing her claws? He tried to take the knife away from me, but of course he couldn't. I was the one who was armed, not him. When he grabbed for it I struck at his hands. Then at his eyes."

I closed my eyes.

"Did you stab him there?" asked Katrin.

"You know I didn't if you read the obituary report. Besides, I wasn't really trying to. I just wanted to warn him. But he still didn't realize what he'd gotten himself into. I noticed he was getting turned on by the struggle."

"What do you mean?" shouted Katrin.

"Well, it isn't that strange, is it?" Lila snapped at her. "He was that type, of course. Some men like that kind of thing. He wanted me to come after him. I was supposed to chase him and cut him with the knife."

"No," yelled Katrin, and I supported her:

"Think about what you're saying, Lila. We're talking about a dead man who can't defend himself."

"He didn't want to defend himself!" shouted Lila. "Defending himself was the last thing on his mind. He just wanted more and more. He started to get specific about his instructions. I asked him if he really meant it. Yes, yes, he said. I said in that case, I want some money. He took out five hundred kronor and gave it to me. I said I wanted more. He hunted around a little and came up with another three hundred, and said that was all he had at home. I was satisfied. The whole time he was very excited. He even liked getting out the money. I put it in my pocket."

"He paid to get murdered!"

"That's right. I asked again if he really wanted to keep going. Yes, yes, he said. As you wish, then, I answered. And it happened. I drew the knife out of him and looked at him again, laughing. It seemed as though it didn't even hurt. Maybe not—the edge is so narrow, so thin, almost like that knitting needle. Hardly any blood. But then some drops came oozing out around the edges of the wound. And he started screaming. So I gave him more and more. I had to stab him quite a few times to get him to be quiet."

Katrin had thrown her hands over her face. I was so upset I was shaking; the sweat was pouring from my armpits.

"Why, that was rape, dammit!" I shouted. "You acted like a fucking rapist to that poor guy!"

Lila shrugged her shoulders.

"He asked for it," she said. "He even paid for it and that's pretty unusual for a rape victim, I should think. While he was lying there moaning, a cat darted in. Maybe it'd been in the bedroom. It came in when it heard him. It was a beautiful cat, a Siamese. It arched its back when it saw me and ran back into the bedroom. I followed it."

"Were you going to kill it, too?" I asked, feeling sick to my stomach.

"Of course not. It probably would've been best to take it home with me. But the cat hid and I couldn't find it. I had to leave before anyone else came. The phone rang and he got up to answer it, but as soon as he got up, he fell forward halfway under the table and was dead. I still couldn't find the cat. I opened a window so it would be able to get away from there. Then I left."

"There must have been lots of fingerprints," I said. "Did you wipe them off?"

"Naturally, with a damp cloth," said Lila, giggling.

"How did you handle fingerprints, Lila? You didn't wear gloves in there, did you? You must have touched things, I imagine? The doorknob, the window, the chair..."

"It was a cold morning, like I said. Cloudy and gray. And four days later, when I went to the police to tell them I'd spoken

201

with him at the premiere, it was even colder. I kept my hands in my pockets the whole time except when I had them folded together."

"So you just walked away, perfectly calm?" I asked.

"Perfectly calm is an exaggeration. The money couldn't compensate for the loss of what I'd hoped would be a stimulating intellectual friendship. When I came home, I went straight to bed and slept. It was very, very cold. I didn't get out of bed all day."

CURT

"Oh, Curt!" said Lila, and a smile crossed her face, making her radiantly beautiful. "His name was Curt. He stood there like an angel in the morning light."

"Outside of the porn club," Katrin inserted pointedly.

Lila was startled and looked at her from the side.

"Yes, outside of the porn club. But that had absolutely nothing to do with it."

"Tell it like it is, Lila," I said. "You two met in there."

"What do you mean in there?" asked Lila.

She was beginning to be difficult again!

"Drop the bullshit, Lila. We're going to get through this tonight once and for all and you aren't going to get around Curt any easier than anyone else. So he came into the strip club with the three Japanese and they got together with Ewa, Git and Tanja. And you."

"I don't know what you're talking about," said Lila.

He face was like a steel mask and she refused to look me in the eyes. She wouldn't meet Katrin's gaze, either. Her hands were squeezed together in her lap and she was looking past both of us to some distant place, or maybe just at the painting on the wall. *Elks*, by Bruno Liljefors. I know it's funky, but I guess that's the reason we like it.

"Then we'll just have to start over," I said. "Where did you two meet?"

"We met in the park at Adolf Fredrik's church."

"How did you get acquainted?"

"I was walking from Döbelns Street down towards Svea Avenue. I went by the porn club you mentioned. Right outside of the club, I met a man who'd been walking towards it from the opposite direction—that is, from Svea Avenue."

"You met outside?"

"That's what I said."

"Then what?"

"He said something when I went past. He'd seen me coming around the corner and maybe he thought I had something to do with the club."

"What did he say?"

"Something stupid. Hi cutie, or something."

"Did you answer?"

"No. I looked at him and kept on going."

"You went to Adolf Fredrik's churchyard?"

"Right."

"What were you going to do there?"

"I didn't have anything in particular to do. It was a lovely morning and I'd just gotten up."

Here Katrin interrupted:

"You'd just gotten *up*?"

"Sure. I sleep very little in the summertime. I get up with the sun. It was a gorgeous morning, I wanted to go for a walk. When I got to the cemetery, it looked so fresh and beautiful that I sat down for a minute to listen to the birds."

I looked at Katrin, and she at me. The girl was crazy, no doubt about it. After the psychological examination, she'd be in custody for a long time. Then she could sit in the park at the hospital all night long listening to the birds.

"The clock in Adolf Fredrik struck three," she said. "I only sat for a couple of minutes, was just about to go. But he'd turned around and followed me and now he sat down beside me on the bench. He started talking."

"What did he say?" asked Katrin.

I noticed the hint of a smile in the corner of Lila's mouth. She faced Katrin directly and it was as if I were excluded from the conversation. Girltalk! It was time to change the tape anyway. I raised my hand to get them to stop and they were quiet while I took care of the adjustments, Lila with an ever-broader smile on her face.

"OK, go on," I said.

"Thank you kindly, sir," said Lila and was quiet again.

"Now what is it?"

Lila said nothing.

"It's you!" Katrin said to me. "Can't you quit bothering us?"

It was as though they shut me out, as though I weren't even there except as an extension of the tape recorder. Katrin turned back to Lila.

"What did he say to you?"

"He sat down beside me. He wasn't drunk. He was nicely dressed. I kept sitting there and he started talking about how nice it was in the morning with the birds singing and stuff like that. I answered, agreeing with him. He asked what I was doing out so late and I said what do you mean late, on the contrary, it's very early. I told him I was out walking. Charming, he said. He couldn't allow himself the luxury of doing what he felt like. He worked very hard and had a family to support so he always felt compelled to accommodate himself to others. He wished he had my freedom to go wherever he pleased. I answered that freedom is just something to take for oneself, after all; he need only give up his commitments and his family and then he'd have it. I sang a little bit from Janis Joplin's *Bobby McGee* and he thought that was charming. He suggested I didn't know the realities of life as well as he. He also implied that I probably had some guy slaving away for me somewhere whom I'd left behind in the wee hours of the morning to have a little fun myself. He was actually quite aggressive under his cool, polished exterior, if you know what I mean. He wasn't angry or anything. It was just that he stung me in the heel, so to speak, whenever he got the chance."

"And you went with him anyway!" I said.

"Then why in heaven's name did you go with him?" asked Katrin.

Lila covered her face with her hands and I thought, finally she's breaking down, it's happening! It felt as if I'd seen a person clinging tightly up on a building for several hours who'd finally given in and let herself fall to the net below. But apparently she'd just rubbed the sleep out of her eyes, because pretty soon she looked up at us again with the same clear but distant expression.

"I'm beginning to get tired," she said.

"I'm sure you are. But you aren't getting away from us until you've told the whole story. It's our scoop and tomorrow you're going to go to the police with us. But not until our series of articles is all typed out."

She stroked her face a couple of times.

"OK, where were we?"

"You and Curt were on the bench at Adolf Fredrik's cemetery."

"Oh yes."

She laughed, all of a sudden, and it was a happy laugh, not the least bit cynical, as I'd come to expect.

"When I thought I'd heard enough out of him, I got up and said bye, I've got to be running along now. He didn't like that. He wanted me to stay. I asked why he didn't go home too. He was so lonely, he said. In spite of all of his hard work, he didn't have a real friend. The guys on the job just thought about passing him by in their careers and his wife was completely preoccupied with her own concerns—they didn't have anything in common anymore, they never got a chance to talk to each other. Then I bent forward, patting him, and he grabbed hold of me, begging me to keep him company on the way home. He just wanted to talk a little more. I was like a fairy who'd stepped into his life."

She smiled again and I leaned up to examine her face, looking for the self-satisfied smirk that had appeared before on several occasions, but actually she just looked young and happy.

"He told me he lived in Täby and there was a jogging trail near his house. He asked if I wouldn't just as soon walk there with him as trot along on the city sidewalk. I said yes."

I snorted.

"Yes, of course," said Lila, turning directly to me for a change. "Pretty dumb, right? To go with a strange man in his car. Three o'clock in the morning. What did I expect?"

"Exactly," I agreed.

"Don't stick your nose into everything," Katrin said to me with a thin voice.

Was she going to start making trouble now, too!

"I thought we were working together on this," I hissed at Katrin.

"Please quit interrupting with unnecessary comments," she answered.

And I hadn't even said a thing; Lila was the one who'd said it! I got up and shut off the tape recorder.

"If this is how it's going to be, we might as well stop."

I heard a muffled sound from Lila and there it was again, that cynical, self-satisfied, malicious grin I'd missed seeing on her face a moment ago! The little bitch! This was just what she wanted! I sat down again, abruptly.

"We're absolutely exhausted, all three of us. Should we rest for a while?"

"Why don't you get some rest," said Katrin. "Go lie down and I'll continue with Lila."

The subject herself nodded encouragingly to me and her smile reached all the way out to her ears.

"The little tyke's tired," she said. "He'd better go night-night."

I banged my fist on the table and as it pounded and I felt the pain shooting up my arm, I saw again, as though written in black letters in front of my eyes:

This is just what she wants. This is how she provokes them.

"Wait a second," I said.

After going to the bathroom and then out to get a couple of beers from the refrigerator, I turned the tape recorder on again. Katrin and Lila were sitting quietly, half asleep. Katrin had let her knitting fall down in her lap.

"Ladies!" I said, and they both sat up, straightening themselves out.

"Should I go on?" said Lila.

I nodded.

"He suggested that you two walk on the jogging trail out by his house."

"Yes. So we did. He had his car parked right at the curb and it wasn't far to drive, of course, so we were there in about fifteen minutes."

"And you had no idea at all that you'd gotten yourself into

something stupid?"

"Please," said Katrin, "the fellow was sober and decent, and the sun was high in the sky. Hey, what can a girl do if she can't even accept a ride?"

"Right. So then we arrived," Lila went on.

Now she sat up straight in the easychair, looking at me with clear eyes, as though the next part of the story were intended especially for me. She held her glass out and I filled it up for her. She drank a deep draught, watching me intently over the lip of the glass.

"We got out of the car," she continued after she'd put down her glass, "and we started walking. It was a glorious morning out there in the forest. If you were quiet, you could hear lots of different birds. We saw the lake between the tree trunks and the flowers—oh, it was that magical week of spring, you know, when all the flowers burst open and their fragrance is everywhere!"

I cleared my throat.

"Well, we were walking along and he took my hand. It isn't that easy to walk on a path in the forest hand in hand if you want to go at a good clip. I pulled my hand away. He grabbed it again. I asked him to let go. He started talking about how cute I was and what he'd thought when he first saw me and said I shouldn't pretend, I wanted to do it just as much as he did. And all that. I asked him to lay off and then he stationed himself right in front of me on the trail. We were out in Täby, you know, where he lived, so I told him to go home, his wife must be lying there waiting and wondering where he was. He said I was prettier than her, I had such nice breasts. I told him to leave me alone. He laughed and asked why I'd come with him in that case."

"Exactly," I agreed.

"Shut up," said Katrin.

"I told him to let me be and then he grabbed hold of me quite hard. So I drew out the knife. It all went pretty quickly. I dried the knife off in the grass afterwards, put it back in its sheath and left. I took a morning bus into town. But first I went down to the lake and washed up and rested for a while. It was very beautiful. The sun had been up for a long time and was shining warmly over the water. I watched some little insects who were struggling and working hard. Little ants and beetles. I've always wanted to see a roe deer out in the wild; they live in the archipelago, you know, but close to town the people have probably scared them away. I've never seen anything bigger than a hare, isn't that unbelievable? Not even an elk. And yet supposedly they're just swarming around out there."

She was quiet. I turned off the tape recorder, thinking about the ants that had been lured by the blood and begun gorging themselves on Curt's corpse.

TORSTEN

Lila tightened up her mouth, sulking.

"Relax, Lila! I know you're tired. But we aren't quitting until everything's done. You killed Torsten, didn't you?"

Lila still had her mouth pursed but now her eyes were closed too. Was she sleeping?

"Are you asleep?" asked Katrin. Lila didn't respond.

I considered whether we should take a break. My head was feeling the strain and Katrin looked absolutely exhausted. Maybe we'd get better results if we stopped and rested for a while. But I didn't dare let Lila out of my sight; I didn't trust her for an instant. We wouldn't be able to sleep until we had her whole story recorded on tape.

"You're awake, Lila."

"Of course."

"OK. Did you kill poor Torsten? We know the refugee boys didn't do it."

"How do you know that?"

"They didn't have a weapon. Or a motive."

"Well, did I?"

"I think so."

"Was I there then?"

"I think you were. Lots of people were there, Lila, creeping up on each other under the trees and through the gate at the bus stop—you know the one, it isn't used for a gate anymore. Naturally, you're going to be confronted by Kenny and Kricke and the Chilean boys as soon as the police take over the investigation. If I'm wrong, I'll apologize. But I think you were there, Lila. Am I right?"

She looked at Katrin as though she were waiting for her opinion.

"Were you there, Lila?" asked Katrin.

"May I hear your theory?" Lila asked me.

"I believe you were there," I said, "and it went about like this: Torsten had come after you inside at Gröna Lund. He behaved badly, I'll go along with that. He was acting tough the way boys sometimes do with girls in order to impress the other boys. You couldn't do anything to him there, but when you got to the bus stop, you recognized him."

"Who's Torsten?" asked Lila, dreamily.

"Torsten was a rather simple-minded fellow," I continued, "who was out with his buddies to have a cool evening at Gröna Lund. Other girls would have ignored what he did. Things like that happen all the time, and a normal girl doesn't hold a grudge. Either she takes it as a compliment, though a bit foolishly conveyed, or else she gets mad and hisses and tells the boy to go to hell. But Lila doesn't react like ordinary people. She gets it into her head that she wants the boy dead. That's why I suspect you, Lila. It's a typical Lila-thing we have here."

Lila sucked thoughtfully on her lower lip. She still looked as though she was waiting for a comment from Katrin, but none came.

"How do you feel I got involved in the first place?" she asked."

"I think you were the girl Torsten accosted at Gröna Lund. Instead of laughing and having a sense of humor, this particular lady goes around brooding about revenge. She remembers what the boy looks like and his hat and that he has two friends walking diagonally behind him, one on either side, just like in a western. This Lila remembers; she's a clever girl who registers everything."

Lila nodded in agreement.

"I think this crazy broad, Lila, follows the three boys out of Gröna Lund. They've soon forgotten her, but she hasn't forgotten them. She stays close by. And that's what makes this next murder particularly horrible, in my opinion—it's premeditated. It's not committed on the spur of the moment because the guy happened to offend the sensitive lady. Lila gets mad when he accosts her. This one can accept. But to go for a long time afterwards dwelling on it and harboring revenge, this I find unacceptable."

"That is unacceptable, Lila," said Katrin.

She was lying on her stomach on the sofa, resting her chin in her hands.

Lila lowered her head.

"Then what?"

"So you came sneaking after them, or else maybe you got there ahead of time to watch for the boys when they left the park. It's the same either way. When the big one in the middle—that's Torsten—jumps on the foreign boys, you're sure of your thing. You recognize him. You're probably standing in the corner right by the latticed gate. A fight breaks out between Torsten and his friends on one side and the Chileans on the other. When Juan Felipe makes a move at Torsten, Torsten backs off and Kricke goes right up to Juan Felipe instead. They have a fist fight and a friend of Juan Felipe's also starts tearing in against Kricke. Strangely enough, Torsten disappears out of the picture until suddenly he's lying in front of the bus as it pulls up. Now this wasn't a long period of time we're talking about, more like twenty or thirty seconds. The bus was probably at the corner when everything was being played out. The person who struck Torsten down and then pushed him out towards the street could have gone back through the gate, returning to Gröna Lund. She could have taken the Djurgård ferry—the last one goes at 1:00 am. Maybe she blended in with the bus passengers who were getting off and standing there looking! Or she could have turned around the gate and gone on into town. It only takes a couple of minutes to get past the Biology Museum and over the Djurgård bridge. Someone walking quickly could be a hundred meters away in the time it took for the bus to stop and the driver to get off and everyone to scream and get worked up and start blaming each other. You might almost think one girl who screamed louder than the rest was some kind of accomplice, attracting attention to herself."

"You and your conspiracy theories," said Katrin irritably. "The female mafia, huh! It's really quite obvious that Lila is an independent woman working on her own. Right?"

"Right," said Lila.

It was smart of Katrin. It took me half a second to realize what Lila's answer meant.

"Right, Lila," I said. "Now you've admitted it, isn't that pretty much the way it happened?"

"What difference does it make?" asked Lila. "The town is literally crawling with men who accost women in the same tough way to impress the peanut gallery. Sometimes a girl strikes back. The boys had just better learn to quit provoking us."

"But this is ridiculous," I said. "These were underprivileged boys who felt a need to assert themselves. Boys who might be on their way to becoming outcasts."

"Boys who felt a need to assert themselves," mimicked Lila. "And you thought I should accommodate them? Maybe I even owed it to them?"

"So as not to provoke," said Katrin sarcastically. "Remember, Lila. If you're the one who does the provoking, then you can just blame yourself if something happens."

I started getting furious, not for the first time tonight.

"Yes, but murder!" I said. "That's still got to be a totally different issue! There are poor, insecure boys who act like that, you can't just up and—"

"Then what do you suppose insecure girls do?" asked Lila.

"Well, I imagine there are many ways to—"

"Stab them," said Lila contentedly. "Insecure girls stick knives into boys."

"You don't seem to have an insecurity problem," I countered.

"No, but that's the role I'm playing," said Lila.

She opened her eyes up wide.

"I'm a poor, sensitive girl who's put on a tough, hard attitude. I need understanding. I need care. It's society that's made me the way I am."

"I know," said Katrin. "What Lila really needs is help, not punishment."

"Will you keep your mouth shut!" I yelled to Katrin, hitting my fist on the table. "Dammit, Katrin, whose side are you on?"

213

"On the smaller and weaker ones' side," said Katrin, and Lila howled with laughter.

Red lightning flashed in my eyes and I couldn't restrain my rage.

"Shut up, goddammit!" I shrieked. "Keep your mouths shut, both of you, or else!"

I shoved the table so hard the tape recorder fell off. The tape loosened up and the machine started buzzing. The girls got quiet right away. Katrin put her hand over her mouth and Lila turned away from me toward the wall, so I couldn't see her face. I picked the tape recorder up from the floor. It'd probably be repairable. But I'd have to take the tape out and put in a new one. What if the recording were ruined now, too!

"Now look what you've done!" I shouted to Lila. "It's all your fault! You ought to get a beating, you damned bitch!"

The girls were as quiet as death and neither one of them dared look me in the eyes.

PER

I had to go into the bathroom for a while. I really wanted to take a cold shower, but I had to be satisfied with putting my head under the faucet. It cooled me down. When I got back, Lila and Katrin were still sitting quietly. They weren't looking at each other. Katrin's knitting needles were clinking together and her lips were moving silently as she counted. Lila was hanging over the armrest with one hand under her ear, half-asleep.

"Well, we can continue now," I said. "If the ladies will permit."

Katrin kept counting stitches and Lila yawned.

There wasn't much wrong with the tape recorder. It'd take a minute to untangle the tape that had fallen out, but we could certainly keep Lila at our house as long as necessary. I put a new tape in and checked to make sure it was working.

"Well, let's take the next one. Maybe there aren't so many more, huh Lila? Per Gustavsson?"

Lila moved in the chair.

"That asshole," she said bitterly. "He got what he deserved."

"A man who devoted his life to helping others. Besides, as you may know, he left behind a wife and two small children."

"A live-in partner and a child," said Lila sleepily. "She had one of the kids with another man. She owns half of the house in Vaxholm and has a good job. She should do OK."

"Damn, but you're cold, Lila!"

"I thought we knew that from the beginning," she said, opening her eyes up to me.

Katrin had put down her knitting and was lying on the

215

couch. She had her eyes closed.

"How did you and Per get acquainted? Did you know him before? You weren't listed as a patient."

"Me, a patient?" said Lila. "I'm perfectly healthy, just evil. I don't want to be cured. I don't want to be adjusted. I don't want to accept the same rules of society that were about to crush Irene Andersson."

"When were you last in Vaxholm, Lila?"

"The same day Irene made her suicide attempt," answered Lila harshly.

"Do you know Irene?"

"If I did, I would have gone over to her house before she took the pills."

"Did you know Per?"

"Not until that day. Do you want me to describe my day?"

If Lila had seemed tired and out-of-it when we talked about Torsten Grahn, she was all the more animated now. I couldn't help pointing this out.

"Yes, maybe you're right," she admitted. "It was such a splendid day. I took the morning boat. Sat outside on the way there; it got cold but it was nice, really nice anyway. I can't get enough sun, don't want to miss a single minute of it. In Vaxholm I walked around town, put a krona in the charity kettle—"

"A krona in the charity kettle! You!"

"It said whoever did it would be remembered on Judgement Day. I was down by Hembygdsgården and went over to the bluffs on the other side. Lay sunning myself in the grass, went into the water a few times. I walked around looking at the beautiful houses in Vaxholm. I saw a pretty blue house with white trim. A woman was sitting in the garden doing her embroidery. A little girl was playing at her feet and a baby was lying on a blanket beside them. It was Per Gustavsson's family, though I didn't know it then."

"The one you made fatherless," I said.

Lila continued, "I went out to eat but the potatoes and vegetables were preserves from a jar. I watched the boats coming and going. The last one leaves for town at eight-thirty in the evening and that's the one I took. But first I went for a little stroll, going to the north side of the bluff. There are boats moored all around the whole island, but that's an especially nice spot right there. I dived in and went swimming, then got out and saw a wooden stairway on the bluff where I dried myself off. Pretty soon this man came walking up to his boat. He didn't see me at first because I was up above him. He was quite a handsome fellow, nice-looking."

"Did you accost him?"

"Me, are you crazy? I've never accosted anyone!"

"You took the offensive with Torsten," I said, having trouble getting the words out. "And you're not too good to jump on poor guys like Björkbom and Gustavsson."

"And paw them in dark corners. Did I really accost Martin and Per?" she turned to Katrin.

Katrin sat up and stretched. She extended her arms over her head, yawning.

"Obviously you accosted them," she said. "How can you ask such a dumb question? You talked to them, right?"

She lay back down in the same position as before.

"And then you sat there calling to him," I said to Lila.

"No, actually he was the one who spoke first. He went on board his boat, a big plastic sailboat with a cabin. He went down inside and rummaged around a little. Then he came out and started messing with the sail."

"Evidently you don't know much about boats," I couldn't help remarking.

"No, but I know what I like," said Lila, giggling quietly. "So he came up out of the cabin and that's when he caught sight of me because I was sitting almost directly above him."

"Were you dressed?"

"What a question!"

"So you were wearing something?"

"I had both a dress and a sweater on. It gets quite chilly when the sun goes down and the wind picks up over the water. He saw me when he came up from the little cabin, and we both said hi. I was about to go because of the coolness coming with the evening breeze. I stopped at his boat to exchange a few words. I said it was a nice boat and he asked me if I wanted to see it."

"You definitely accosted him!" said Katrin.

"He helped me on board. I expressed polite admiration and then had planned to go. He asked what I did and whether I was on vacation. I told him I worked as an aide in the home and I was on a day-trip from the city. So what did he do himself, I wondered. Well, yes, he was a psychologist but he was on vacation now and it'd be fantastic to get away from all of the complaining people. He thought it was inspiring to meet me—obviously so healthy and well balanced."

She licked her lips and I shuddered.

"I told him that during my free time I went around murdering people with a knife, what did he think about that? He almost died laughing. Terribly amusing, he thought, what a sense of humor! I was really a comic. Spirited and spontaneous and full of fun. He wished more people had my robust attitude instead of turning their aggression inward and punishing themselves."

"Then your fingers started to itch?"

"I wondered how he'd like to experience a little healthy aggression straight from me. But of course there wasn't any hurry. It was just past seven. He confided to me that human beings all choose how we create our own lives. Everyone who complains about a lousy job or unhappiness in love really wants it to be like that, because otherwise she'd do something about the situation. I objected that complete responsibility assumes total power and did he really feel that people in general have complete and total power over their lives? He laughed and said it was probably just as well we changed the subject because it was clear I didn't know very much about psychology. Why don't you tell me more about yourself, he said. What kinds of exciting types have you murdered lately with a knife? He laughed and I laughed too: there was one who forced himself on me, one who patronized me, two who accosted me and one who actually asked for it. Maybe next time I'd take one who was stuck-up.

"You see, he was just so perfectly sure of himself," she went on. "He'd read the right books, gone to the right schools, owned the right possessions and held the right opinions. From that pinnacle he looked down, judging the rest of humanity. He was his own starting point and everything else was just as distant whether it was on the other side of the earth or a meter away.

He wasn't evil at all. He just couldn't see that everything might not be exactly as he said. Other people were little pebbles on the path. Other people were the film on top of the hot chocolate. Other people were the button on the shirt. They were—"

"The mosquito on your back," suggested Katrin.

"The mosquito on your back," agreed Lila. "Other people were the weeds in the flower bed."

"OK, that's enough now!" I said.

"I just wanted to test him a little, for fun. He'd swallowed the first bit whole. Now it was time to furnish the bait with a hook, and of course I do have my knife. Have I described it to you?"

Lila looked up expectantly, her tongue playing among her teeth.

"It's really a hunting knife, extremely sharp. Has a double edge like a little sword. It's probably Malayan, with a leather sheath and a chain to hang it up. I get goose bumps on my back just thinking about letting my finger glide gently along it. When I actually do stroke my finger along the edge, it tickles, it draws blood. Of course I have a sharpening stone at home in a drawer. A girl has to protect herself nowadays. So while Per Gustavsson was explaining the secrets of life to me, I thought I'd like to see the knife sliding into him, would really like to let him taste it. How would a man like him react to real violence? He who lived in his nice theories about each and every one of us holding our destinies in our own hands, and everything that happens being what we ourselves want, how would he like this?"

She laughed with satisfaction.

"I thought I'd like to see the knife sliding into him. All the way in. I got it out and drew it out of its sheath and while he was watching—while he was watching!—I drove it into his stomach. Over and over again. Like into butter. No resistance. Is that the way a man experiences it?"

She looked at me and her eyes were shining.

I just couldn't respond to her anymore. This time I went out and threw up.

219

YNGVE &

It had been morning for a long time.

It's August now, and the mornings are later, just as the evenings are earlier and the nights have gotten dark. It was a strange summer this year. So hot after so many cold days that it was almost as if you couldn't remember—can it really be like this? Is there really warmth, even here? Can it be something besides gray, sad and dull?

It had been a hot summer. There were knives in the parks, knives in the homes; it was a summer full of blood and violence. Love too. Love for some.

I was standing at the window looking out at the city. Yet another broiling, fermenting, steaming summer day. How long could this go on? The exhaust was rising up from the cars on their way back into town and work again now that vacation was over. Ahead of us after the summer were nine months of darkness and cold.

But the heat was still hanging in the air.

I turned in toward the room.

Katrin and Lila were both asleep. Lila looked remarkably innocent. When she was sleeping, she seemed younger than when she was awake. The naturally curly brown hair, the long eyelashes sweeping down over her cheeks, the rosebud mouth...

I still hadn't decided how I was going to present her in the articles. She wasn't really sexy, she was too fragile. With all due respect to Lolita, that wasn't really Lila either. The pathetic Piat-style, a little depraved, the whore with a heart of gold? A tipped beret with a cigarette in the corner of her mouth? I would hardly be able to paste the hard-boiled label onto Lila.

She hadn't gained anything from her murders. They were committed right out of thin air. But she'd definitely get more publicity now, a bigger chance to be seen and heard, than she ever would have gotten as an actress.

I was contributing to it myself. I didn't give a damn about Lila the actress. Lila with her sharp knife I could introduce and sell.

Katrin was snoring on the sofa, facing the wall. Lila was sitting curled up in the easy chair like a kitten. Her eyelashes quivered when I sank down on the armrest.

She was awake, she knew I was sitting there.

I felt my body begin to respond.

No, I had to be careful. Though it'd certainly be something to write about—my sex encounter with the murderess of the century. What a story: "Just as hot in bed as with a knife." "She kissed and she killed with the same passionate soul." "The mass murderess was putty in my hands."

I was still sitting on the armrest watching her. Lila blinked, felt my proximity and closed her eyes again. From her breathing, I could tell she was awake. I put my hand on her shoulder and felt her warm skin through the thin cotton nightgown. She was a monster, but she was also a woman, a woman through and through. I began to massage her shoulder with my hand.

"Lila," I whispered.

Suddenly she opened her eyes, looking right at me. As I mentioned before, her eyes were gray-green and her lashes were unusually long, curling upwards. She was no striking beauty, hardly a girl you'd turn around for on the street. She wasn't even particularly fresh—there were gray hairs among the brown and little wrinkles around her eyes, as if she'd needed glasses but been too vain to wear them.

How many men had she killed?

How many had she loved?

I tried smiling at her and she caught it up, returning it. Hell, just one number, a short one, for the sake of the article! Katrin would understand. What dynamite! Of course, dear Katrin, of course it isn't absolutely necessary to do something in order to write about it. I'd probably be able to throw together quite a fine piece about Lila in bed anyway, without actually trying it out. But it's undeniable that the real thing gives an extra touch.

Lila and I were still smiling at each other. We couldn't keep this up much longer, the corners of our mouths were beginning to freeze. My hand dug into her collar bone.

Lila stretched and yawned, indifferent as a cat. Her glance searched out Katrin.

"She's asleep," I whispered.

Lila nodded and I swear she looked at me expectantly.

"Let's go in there," I whispered, nodding to the bedroom. I turned around in the doorway, reaching my hand out to her. I closed the door behind us and she went over to the window, opening it and leaning out.

It was already hot. The air coming up from the street was nauseating. The sun was shining through a milky-white haze. The trees in the park opposite us had already begun to lose their leaves.

Lila lifted her face, taking several deep breaths.

I went up behind her, putting both hands on her shoulders. She had small, delicate shoulders. Katrin is built quite sturdily. Katrin is a terrific girl—nice, friendly, fun, up on everything. But she's a little rough, a little loud. There was something feminine, tempting about Lila who—Lila, who'd murdered at least seven men! Still, I felt the urge to take care of her, protect her.

Maybe that's what the problem was. They'd all just been after her, no one had really taken care of her.

There it was! The angle on the story! Lila vulnerable and defenseless in the world of men. The Marilyn Monroe-type, not fully equipped. Continually searching for tenderness and protection.

I had the concept and it made me bold. I pressed closer to her soft, flexible back until I met resistance. I hardened against her.

"Lila," I whispered in her ear.

This was where she was supposed to turn, throw her arms around me, squeeze herself against me and answer "Erik!" in a husky whisper.

Lila turned, threw her arms around me and said: "Yxberg, now?" in a husky whisper.

"Yxberg, shit!"

I let her go.

"OK," I said. "Let's sit in here."

"And the tape recorder?"

The tape recorder was still out there. Turned off, as far as I remembered.

"Wait here," I whispered to Lila.

Katrin was asleep. I think. I didn't check too carefully, so she wouldn't get a chance to ask me anything. But it sounded like she was snoring. It only took a few seconds to unplug the tape recorder and bring it into the bedroom.

If things had gone the way I'd imagined, Lila would have been lying nude in bed with a hungry look on her face when I came in. However, that wasn't what she did. She was still standing at the window, leaning out, watching the cars drive by down below.

"Careful you don't fall out," I said.

"Did you think I was going to jump?"

I honestly didn't think so. Not Lila, she was too tough, too persistent. She was a fighter who wouldn't give up that easily.

"I think we'd better close it," I said nonchalantly, walking up to her. She didn't protest when I pulled down the window.

Our bedroom is sparsely furnished. There's pretty much just the bed and a couple of chairs we put our clothes on. It'd be silly to sit and talk on them. As though I were setting a trap, I arranged the tape recorder on the nightstand and reached my hand out to Lila.

"Come sit down."

She plopped down on the foot of the bed, quite a ways away from me. Her hands lay modestly in her lap.

"OK, begin."

"With what?"

"Yxberg. Didn't you just say his name?"

She bowed her head.

"He got murdered last night."

"Yes."

"Are you the one who did it?"

"If you say so."

If you say so, what kind of ingratiating response was that?

223

"Did you murder him or not?"

She didn't answer, she was looking at the wall in front of her.

"Lila, you were there on Yxberg's *Confrontation* program last night. After the show, Yxberg got a call from his wife. The idea had been for him to stay at the TV station afterwards, but his wife was angry and wanted him to come home right away. He didn't dare do anything but obey. Where do you enter the picture?"

She was still staring straight ahead and I nudged her lightly on the side.

"Lila! Wake up!"

She blinked, turning to me.

"What?"

"Where did you meet Yngve?"

She shook herself as though to wake completely up.

"I want a glass of water," she said.

Damn! I went out to the kitchen, fetching a glass. Katrin had rolled over onto her back and was snoring softly through her half-open mouth.

For a second, I missed Katrin's cheerful, friendly company. Lila was a difficult babe to be with. It wasn't too late to wake Katrin up and take her along for the final turn.

Though of course then it wouldn't exactly be the same final turn....

I went back into the bedroom with the water for Lila. She drank greedily and the color returned to her cheeks, her eyes brightened.

"What do you want to know?" she asked when she'd put down the glass.

"Yxberg."

"Sure, him. Well, yes, we left together, as you quite accurately mentioned. I thought he'd been a jerk to break me off, but of course we knew beforehand that the big thing was going to be the young widow's despairing appeal. It'd gone well and Yngve would be getting all of the credit. Besides, I think they had great hopes of catching a murderer that way. There's always some sentimental fool who will be seized by remorse and confess.

"But there were also other aspects to the case," continued Lila, "for example, those I introduced on the program. When we left the studio, I was right behind Yngve. I wanted to continue the conversation—he'd said something about taking it up another time—but he didn't even recognize me. We'd just been talking five minutes before and now he didn't even know who I was! The show was over, and I wasn't a person, a name for him anymore. He was going to stay and receive confessions from knife murderers on the telephone; he didn't have time for some little anonymous and insignificant Lila Ljungblom!"

The glow was back in her eyes, feverish.

"Someone came and said Yngve's wife had called, and he was supposed to hurry home. He went in to call her while I waited outside. Then he came out again, going on his way down another corridor. I followed him. Finally, he stopped and asked what the hell was this all about, what did I want. I started by flattering him, talking about how good I thought the program was, how captivating Inger and Lena had been. He asked if I'd been there too. Oh yes, I said. I'm the one who brought up the issues of crime being the only acceptable form of art and whether the murderer is guilty or a victim. He laughed and patted me on the shoulder and said maybe that could be useful sometime if it were worked on. You couldn't really present it so brazenly—you'd have to find some poor devil, some outcast who actually had produced himself as an artist, and then maybe you could discover him and get people to buy his work. Like the half-retarded farmhands who painted naivism and got to be big sensations at the Doktor Glas gallery. This wasn't what I'd meant at all. I tried explaining that to him. He'd taken my idea, which he'd scorned at first, and gone on to distort and trivialize it."

"What do you mean *your* idea," I asked, annoyed. "Ideas belong to everyone, and Yngve certainly had a right to *his* ideas."

"Yes, but he got it from me. He admitted that himself. At first he thought what I'd said was rude and ridiculous and dangerous, but once he'd gotten a chance to play with it a little and imagine he'd thought it up himself, he liked it. He'd talk to Dave and get his opinion, he said. He patted me on the shoulder again, and said I wasn't so dumb after all. You're welcome to steal my idea, I said, but please pay me for it. I'm a poor actress and have to support myself with cleaning jobs. You have steady employment here at the TV station and every possible resource at your disposal. Go ahead and steal my idea, but give me a little cash—you don't even have to pay for it yourself. What do you mean, he said, what do you mean steal an idea? Why, it was entirely his own idea to pick up a wretched artist from the street and launch him on TV. What did that have to do with my chatter about crime and guilt and victims and the value of the artist? Well go ahead and commit a crime yourself in that case, he said, and we'll see if it can be something for TV."

She was silent. I waited.

"Well?"

"So then there wasn't much more to it. I figured it was best to take him at his word. Ritsch, ratsch."

Her hand described some sweeping movements in the air. Afterwards, she pantomimed wiping the knife off on her nightgown.

"Lady Macbeth," I said.

"Lady Macbeth," she mimicked. "Bullshit! Do you think she had the guts? She sent her old man to do it, you know. Real women take care of themselves."

Her tense expression was gone and she smiled warmly at me. I shut off the tape recorder and we sat quietly beside each other. Somehow my desire for her had ebbed.

"So what shall we do now?" asked Lila, moving closer.

I reached out my hand and put it on her knee, without lust, just to have someplace to put my hand.

There was no sound from Katrin and when I lifted my head and looked into Lila Ljungblom's gray eyes, I became suddenly and almost painfully aware that I was sitting beside her on a bed.

The little hooker. I was sure she'd prostituted herself more than once. Bit parts and cleaning jobs, what were they? You don't get those kinds of wrinkles in your face from that. Maybe she'd abused something too. Not hard drugs, I didn't believe, but quite definitely hash. I was absolutely sure of it.

Her little jobs and her shabby life and her dreams, her long-

226

ing, her struggle to be seen, to be heard, to be taken seriously, to be—

Respected? Loved?

Loved? Lila Ljungblom?

I reached out my hand, touching her. She jumped as though I'd burned her. But she kept sitting there.

"Lila—"

Was it love she was lacking? Was that why she'd become so hard?

"Lila!"

I had to know. I had to feel. She was sitting right beside me and she'd murdered seven men, but why, why, someone like her? She'd asked me whether she would be understood and forgiven, the way the usual murderer is—his living conditions, his background, his problems, his pain—or whether she'd be condemned as a witch.

She was close to me, sitting very still, but then she raised her head, opening her large eyes and looking directly into mine.

Lila!

I couldn't wait, couldn't take it slowly, couldn't go gently. In a single motion, I threw myself over her and she fell backwards on the bed with me on top. She didn't scream.

I was the one who screamed.

Before it was all over, I screamed and Katrin woke up and I saw Katrin in the doorway.

Katrin was standing drowsily in the doorway with her hair sticking straight up and she started screaming.

It was Katrin who screamed, it was I, but it wasn't Lila.

Lila was perfectly quiet and her eyes shone into mine. They were the last thing I saw. Lila's eyes and then I felt how the blood was pulsing out of my stomach—actually it didn't hurt, I guess I wanted to scream but didn't have a voice and it tickled strangely, actually I wanted to laugh more than scream.

I hardly screamed, it was more like I whimpered. And I saw, though my eyes were starting to get hazy, that Katrin had left the doorway and sounded like she was going to vomit.

The one who laughed was Lila, even though she was lying underneath me and my blood was pumping out through the wound in my stomach and the next wound and the next—for she turned the knife down there while her smile deepened—the one who laughed was Lila.

About the Author

Elisabet Peterzen is the author of eleven books and has contributed to a number of anthologies. A resident of Musköten, Sweden, she is interested in writers' and women's rights, nature and animal preservation. *The Last Draw* is the first of her novels to be translated into English.

SELECTED TITLES FROM SEAL PRESS

MYSTERIES

LADIES' NIGHT by Elisabeth Bowers. $8.95, 0-931188-65-2

STUDY IN LILAC by Maria-Antònia Oliver. $8.95, 0-931188-52-0

FIELDWORK by Maureen Moore. $8.95, 0-931188-54-7

MURDER IN THE COLLECTIVE by Barbara Wilson. $8.95, 0-931188-23-7

SISTERS OF THE ROAD by Barbara Wilson. $8.95, 0-931188-45-8

FICTION

ANGEL by Merle Collins. $8.95, 0-931188-64-4

MISS VENEZUELA by Barbara Wilson. $9.95, 0-931188-58-X

BIRD-EYES by Madelyn Arnold. $8.95, 0-931188-62-8

LOVERS' CHOICE by Becky Birtha. $8.95, 0-931188-56-3

GIRLS, VISIONS AND EVERYTHING by Sarah Schulman. $8.95, 0-931188-38-5

AMBITIOUS WOMEN by Barbara Wilson. $8.95, 0-931188-36-9

WOMEN'S STUDIES

THE OBSIDIAN MIRROR: *An Adult Healing from Incest* by Louise M. Wisechild. $10.95, 0-931188-63-6

HARD-HATTED WOMEN: *Stories of Struggle and Success in the Trades,* edited by Molly Martin. $10.95, 0-931188-66-0

LESBIAN COUPLES by D. Merilee Clunis and G. Dorsey Green. $10.95, 0-931188-59-8

GETTING FREE: *A Handbook for Women in Abusive Relationships* by Ginny NiCarthy. $10.95, 0-931188-37-7

Available from your favorite bookseller or from Seal Press, 3131 Western, Suite 410, Seattle, WA 98121.
Include $1.50 for the first book and .50 for each additional book.